Praise for the Rare Book Mystery Series

"Readers of crime fiction will enjoy the ride and look forward to bookstore owner Michael Bevan's next adventure."

—Sally Goldenbaum, bestselling author of the Seaside Knitters series

"It's possible that we've all wanted to own a bookstore at one time or another, and this is a terrific introduction into the work involved in buying, selling, and trying to keep your head above water."

—Reading Reality

"Bevan is a very unique personality, and his past and present are extremely interesting and well written. Let's hope there are many more installments."

—Mystery Playground

LEFT TURN AT PARADISE

Rare Book Mystery
Book 2

THOMAS SHAWVER

**ROUGH
EDGES
PRESS**

Left Turn at Paradise
Paperback Edition
Copyright © 2023 (As Revised) Thomas Shawver

Rough Edges Press
An Imprint of Wolfpack Publishing
9850 S. Maryland Parkway, Suite A-5 #323
Las Vegas, Nevada 89183

roughedgespress.com

Paperback ISBN 978-1-68549-286-1
eBook ISBN 978-1-68549-285-4

To Nancy

"I wish you to ensure that the style and contents might be unexceptionable to the nicest readers. My desire is that nothing indecent may appear in the whole book…"

—Captain James Cook to the Reverend John Douglas, editor of his shipboard narratives

"Sneering in my face, the old procuress said, 'What sort of man are you thus to refuse the embraces of so fine a young Woman,' for the girl certainly did not want for beauty…"

—From the Journal of Captain Cook

"It is impossible to believe that he (Cook) committed nothing at all to paper after his entry for Sunday 17 January 1779."

—Professor J.C. Beaglehole, writing in his Textual Introduction to the Hakluyt Society's edition of Cook's Journal

LEFT TURN AT
PARADISE

Chapter 1

I still see him before drifting off to sleep.

The corpse leaned against the crystallized limestone at the edge of the underground pool, upper body exposed, head tilted up, and eyes open as if admiring the light show. He had Asian features, and the mottled skin had turned a dark cherry color. The gaping mouth, with the luminescent blue insects feeding inside it, shifted intermittently. I suspected he'd been dead a week.

We didn't stay long enough to determine what killed him. It didn't seem to matter at the time; not with the sound of heavy footsteps echoing off the walls of the corridor outside our subterranean chamber. But if we had known, perhaps we would have scrambled to daylight sooner.

Mind you, nothing surprises me anymore; not after that last episode in which a psychotic millionaire tried to turn my daughter and her movie-star boyfriend into human dartboards. As luck and considerable help from

Josie Majansik would have it, they survived, if not unscathed, then at least with their dignity intact.

I'm not sure the same can be said for me.

After years of trying to make a mark in this world and continually seeing my efforts come to naught, my guiding philosophy had come down to two maxims:

1. The best pint of Guinness is in the place where your friends are, and
2. If the minimum wasn't good enough, it wouldn't be the minimum.

It's not that I was opposed to ambition. I simply seemed allergic to any success it brought.

Case in point: At varying times between the ages of twenty-three and thirty I was Notes Editor for Iowa Law Review, served six years as a Marine officer, married a wonderful woman with whom I produced a beautiful (if headstrong) daughter, and started a law firm that while not exactly white-shoe—our major clients were payday loan shysters and strip clubs—was highly lucrative.

Such accomplishments may look good on a resume, but if you were to peep under the covers, you would find that, given sufficient time and temptations, I'd managed to screw up nearly everything that came my way.

I'll not bore you with the details. Suffice it to say that eighteen years ago, I spiraled downhill following the death of my wife in a car accident, packed my then-six-year-old daughter off to London to be raised by her grandparents, and lost, along with my moral compass, the privilege to practice law.

Redemption of sorts followed a decade later when,

like a monk so enamored of the divine that he takes a vow of poverty, I opened a small used bookstore in a leafy urban section of town called Brookside. I had few options after getting disbarred, and there was simply nothing else, with the possible exception of rugby football, and making love—both of which tend to be amateur sports—that I enjoyed more than books.

I named the shop Riverrun. It's the first word in James Joyce's Finnegan's Wake, a strange, painfully obscure allegory of the fall and resurrection of mankind. I never got past page four of the novel—other than Harold Bloom, who has?—but not only did I like its gentle alliteration, the name connoted just the right amount of literary gravitas I hoped would appeal to customers in an urban neighborhood with two universities.

Brooksiders, thrilled to find a bookshop that looked and felt like something out of a Dickens novel, flooded in from day one. I took to the trade like a natural, discovering a knack for screening trade-ins, setting the right prices, and letting books of quality sell themselves. After five years of modest profits, however, dark clouds had gathered over the business.

It was late afternoon in mid-January and Kansas City was experiencing one of those once-in-a-century snowstorms that seem to occur every other year these days. I was preparing to lock up the shop when the mail carrier—understandably, three hours late—showed up to make his delivery. After I told him I'd be sure to reward his efforts next Christmas, he muttered something about little green apples, and I returned to my desk to sort through what he'd brought.

Nothing looked particularly interesting until I saw the catalog for the California International Book Fair.

Alternating between Los Angeles and San Francisco each year, the fair is one of the most prestigious antiquarian gatherings in the world. Josie could watch the shop while I spent a weekend in the City by the Bay fondling old folios and adding quality to Riverrun's inventory.

To pay for the trip, I planned to sell several of my rarer books to exhibitors there. My first American edition of *Siddhartha* by Hermann Hesse should reimburse the airfare. Charles M. Doughty's *Travels in Arabia Deserta* would do for lodging and meals. I'd be taking Sir Richard Burton's *City of the Saints* as well. But the main reason for bringing it and my British first of Ian Fleming's *Dr. No* was to show prestigious dealers from around the world that my little Kansas City bookstore had more to offer than tired copies of books by the likes of Harold Bell Wright.

I spent twenty minutes removing the listing of those books from the Internet and another half hour pricing recent trade-ins. It was nearly seven o'clock by the time I finished.

Earlier I'd made a dinner reservation at Café Provence next door, but the blizzard made even the promise of steak au poivre avec moules marinières uninviting. So, after locking the shop, I scraped ice off the windshield of my Jeep and drove home, passing at least four car accidents on the short journey.

Feklar, the demon cat, greeted me in my hallway. Careful to avoid the snow and ice dripping from my boots, he proudly dropped the head of a mouse in the puddle at my feet. I'd found him as a kitten trapped in a dumpster outside a Taco Bell, and despite five years of domestication, he'd never completely lost his feral instincts. I suppose that's why we got along.

I opened a can of tuna fish for him in the kitchen, then grabbed a Coors from the fridge and fixed a bologna sandwich. I ate it standing over the sink while pondering what to say to Josie when she returned from Wyoming.

Nothing immediately came to mind, so I shifted gears to focus on the upcoming book fair. That's when the thought occurred to me that I would need the large briefcase I'd used as a lawyer to carry my rare book offerings to San Francisco. After finishing my beer, I went upstairs, let down the folding ladder, and climbed into the attic. Once I got the flickering twenty-watt lightbulb to work, I spent the next fifteen minutes crawling among tufts of fiberglass insulation looking for the battered carry-on.

I finally found it. And something else as well—a yellowed cardboard box with markings made two decades earlier when my wife Carol and I were packing to move from Newport, Rhode Island, back to the Midwest.

Lifting the lid, I saw old photographs, a crusty salt-water-stained packet, and other paraphernalia from when I served at the Naval Legal Services Office in that beautiful seaside town. The two years there had followed my harrowing tour of duty in Iraq and it was the happiest time of our lives, highlighted by the birth of our child.

In hindsight, of course, I should have put the lid back on the box, picked up the briefcase, and gone straight to bed instead of letting the memories rush back to me. Like Pandora's misdeed, however, there's no way to put that stuff back once the top comes off.

On the other hand, if you believe in fate, you might as well believe in it for your own good. If I hadn't peered inside that old box, I would never have been attacked by Mongrel Dogs, sampled human flesh (surprisingly tasty when garnished with fennel, pulped apple, and chicory), nor played the Captain's Mistress with the fertility god Lono.

And then what would I have to brag about at rugby reunions?

Chapter 2

In Newport, Carol and I lived off base in a nineteenth-century whaling captain's house that had been converted into three separate apartments. After putting our infant daughter to bed on our last evening there, we began to pack up photos and other items we'd stored in an old rolltop desk. Herndon Taylor, who lived across the hall, had given the desk to us shortly before his death.

Herndon was a retired rear admiral who, as a young officer, had survived Pearl Harbor and the Battle of Leyte Gulf. During the last year of the war, he worked in London as an American military attaché to the Court of Saint James's. I suspect it was because my wife was English that he had cottoned on to us.

Or it could have been because an old photograph of his late wife showed a remarkable resemblance to Carol—the same slim figure, good-humored mouth, and lively eyes inviting you to play any game of your choosing; a mixture of tennis court and bedroom.

Whatever the reason, Herndon liked us enough to

invite us to his apartment one evening for a session of poker. With Annie nestled in a bassinet on the floor, we played Texas Hold'em on a table set in front of a bay window that looked out upon the old Touro Synagogue cemetery.

It was a fine-looking room, the kind you'd expect of a cultivated man who had seen much of the world. In addition to personal items and what looked to be original satirical prints by Hogarth and Rowlandson, there were half a dozen framed antique maps on the walls. But the thing I remember best was the painting of a rugged naval officer wearing a dark blue jacket, a white waistcoat with gold buttons, and white breeches who cradled a folded chart of the southern hemisphere in his long fingers.

The face, with its staring eyes posed to observe a distant point off to his left, exuded determination. The uniform and powdered wig may have defined this man as a British post-captain in the latter half of the eighteenth century, but the rugged demeanor and keen look of intelligence marked him as a man who could just as easily steer his ship among the stars centuries from now.

"That's Captain James Cook," Herndon said, catching my gaze. "For an old salt like me, there is no better role model. He could read the sea like a blind man reads the face of a coin with his fingertips."

"At my primary school in Sussex," Carol said, "our teachers considered him the second coming of Christ. The boys called him 'Cap'n Crook' just to be cheeky. All I remember is that his men found the ladies of Tahiti so nice that a few of them tried to stay."

"That's one way of looking at desertion," Herndon muttered.

I picked up the turn card. "Killed by the natives in Hawaii, wasn't he?"

The old sailor peered over his hand at me.

"In one sense," he said, dealing the river card. "To the British, however, he's immortal."

I nodded politely, not realizing how true Herndon's words would prove to be one day.

He received a diagnosis of pancreatic cancer a few months after that card game. Shortly before he moved to a hospice care facility, Herndon had four cadets from the Maritime Academy transfer the desk across the hall to our place. He died six weeks later.

Rolltops were designed to be easily disassembled so as not to have to lug the whole thing whenever you wished to move it. On our last night in Newport, Carol and I had lifted the top off the twin pedestals when she noticed something wedged against the lower back panel. It was a small, canvas-backed packet of water-stained pages.

It now strikes me as ridiculous that I didn't carefully examine the contents at the time. But, with my sights set firmly on a law career, I had deluded myself into thinking any writing that didn't contain the commercial code, a statute, or a ruling based on stare decisis wasn't worth the effort of studying.

I did, however, glance over Carol's shoulder while she gingerly opened the canvas bindings. The words on the first leaf were in a crabbed style so small as to be nearly illegible. Together, we read aloud: "Sam'l Gibson, Pvt., R.M., 1768-71, En'dor."

The name and dates meant nothing to us. The pages that followed were as difficult to decipher as the first.

"Put it in the box with the other stuff," I said.

"We've more important things to do than spend our last hours on Aquidneck Island trying to read the diary of a long-dead soldier of the sea."

"All right, but promise me we'll have another look when there's time."

Before placing the ugly little packet in the cardboard banker's box, Carol pressed a cornflower she'd picked up that morning while pushing our baby in a stroller on Cliff Walk.

"To remember how wonderful life can be," she said.

Twenty years later, the dried flower still rested between the first and second pages. Carefully picking it up by the stem, I brought the petals to my lips. I don't know what I expected. Perhaps I was trying to conjure the feel of Carol's touch, the sound of her voice, her refreshing optimism.

Nothing came of it. For a long time after the car crash, I thought a lot of the good in me had died with her. Now, looking at where she had pressed the flower between the pages, I noticed that a ghostly palimpsest of the once-colorful petals remained.

I squeezed the desiccated blossom in my hand and watched the fragments drift to the floor.

Still, it took another five minutes before my bookman instincts took over, leading me to realize that an eighteenth-century journal, tattered as it was, might actually be of some historical value. I decided to take it to the shop in the morning to give it a more thorough look.

After all, hadn't I promised Carol I would when time allowed?

Chapter 3

The next day I shoveled a foot of snow off the sidewalk in front of Riverrun, hung my L.L. Bean barn jacket on a hook next to the counter, and without bothering to put money in the cash register, set Samuel Gibson's journal on my desk.

The fact that the words had been penned nearly two and a half centuries ago wasn't particularly significant. I'd handled several diaries and letters at least that old, but the "R.M." after Gibson's name meant that he was a Royal Marine. As a former Leatherneck myself, I wondered what conditions had been like for a shipbound British private prior to the American Revolution.

On my second deployment to the Gulf, I'd spent two weeks aboard a Navy troopship and never got used to the sardine-can sleeping quarters. To be trapped in tight spaces remains my greatest phobia. I couldn't imagine what it would have been like to hammock in the stifling confines of an eighteenth-century bark for two years. Six feet long and strung just fourteen inches from the next, the webbed cocoon would have been the marine's sole refuge.

I used a magnifying glass to help decipher his handwriting:

Sunday, 28 Aug. 1768. It's been a fortnight since our Marine complement of 9 privates and 1 drummer led by Serj' Edge-cumbe came aboard. I am still no friend of the Sea, or it to me, but at least my Guts have settled. Methinks it good to write of this Globe trot should I not return…

I thought of the young man, probably no more than twenty, sailing for the first time to the other side of the world. His fears must have been offset by eager anticipation as to the adventures ahead, particularly the delights awaiting him in Tahiti. The island had been first visited the year before by the HMS Dolphin, captained by Samuel Wallis, and reports of the amorous beauties in that tropical paradise were surely enough to excite any young man's wanderlust.

This night I guard the captain's door and am sore afraid because while they say he is a kindly man he has a most fear-some look. I'd rather be in the cargo deck where I can pen my words in peace. He ordered 12 lashes for Pvt Tom Dunster who would not eat those vinegary weeds and catted a tar for not washing his hands after cleaning the goat stall. A Captain setting off on a long Voyage must set rules from the start. He tells us the kraut will keep the Scurvy away, but I doubt this.

Skipping ahead, I noticed Private Gibson usually chose Sunday to write. Was that because he pulled guard duty in the hold those days, scribbling his recollections as he sat atop a keg of gunpowder? There would have been few other places on that ship with sufficient privacy. Wherever he did it, the handwriting —full of capital letters in all the wrong places—was uneven, sliding down the page sometimes as if the hand was jerked by a crashing wave or the sudden appearance of a nosy shipmate.

After half an hour, my eye strain was leading to a migraine. I went to get coffee next door.

It was just past nine a.m., and despite the previous night's blizzard, Café Provence was bustling with neighborhood regulars and students from the nearby college.

Professor Charles Walsh, the former curator for incunabula at the Linda Hall Library of Science and Technology, sat in the front looking like an envelope without an address on it. Elbows on table and palms on forehead, he slumped over an untouched plate of sausage and eggs sunny-side up.

When I pulled up a chair across from him, he slowly raised his melancholy face.

"Never again, Mike," he began in a voice that sounded like an eagle being goosed. "Never again will I succumb to Agnes's insatiable physical entreaties."

Agnes was his wife of sixty-plus years.

"Been overdoing the fandango, have we?"

"A January tradition, I'm afraid. It seemed like a good idea several decades ago."

Deirdre Lescalle approached our table and gave me a concerned smile while placing her hand lightly on my shoulder. She was a local girl who, with her French husband as chef, had opened the bistro six months earlier, replacing the bakery.

"*Ça va*, Michael?"

"*Oui, ça va bien*, Deirdre."

"Jean Paul and I were worried about you when you didn't show for dinner last night."

"Sorry. With the snow and all…"

"No problem. You want the usual?"

"Please."

"When does Josie get back?"

"Tomorrow, if she doesn't fall off the Grand Teton."

Her eyes were filled with concern.

"Are you guys okay?"

"One hundred percent," I lied.

"How's your flute-player friend?"

Sandra Epstein, the musician in question, performed in the wind section of the Kansas City Symphony. She also played a mean tin whistle at Fitzpatrick's Galway Pub where I occasionally joined in the *seisúns*. The previous weekend, while Josie was scampering among the Tetons, I had sung to Sandra's accompaniment until final call.

Hiding one's infidelity in the Brookside area of Kansas City is like trying to cover an elephant with a dish towel. Given the number of friends the three of us had in the community, it didn't take long for one of them to text Josie that I'd left the pub clinging to Sandra. No matter that I was too drunk to drive or do anything else. Good Samaritan that the flutist was, Sandra drove me home without so much as tucking me into bed.

Having already explained the situation to Josie, I didn't feel like protesting my innocence to every woman in the neighborhood.

When I told Deirdre this, she smiled sweetly and sashayed off to get my double espresso.

I turned back to Walsh.

"What do you know about the British Navy during the eighteenth century?"

"Their magnificent ships of the line ruled the

world," he said, relieved he didn't have to listen to any more of my ongoing soap opera.

"Ever hear of the *HMS Endor*?"

He shook his head. Then he reconsidered. "There's The Witch of Endor, but it's a fictional cutter portrayed in *Flying Colours* by C.S. Forester. Why do you ask?"

"I have a journal written by a Royal Marine who claimed to serve aboard the *Endor*. The first entry is dated 28 August 1768."

Charlie put down his fork.

"That doesn't make sense. I know the name of any English warship of that era large enough to warrant marines on board. Perhaps your man was a would-be novelist creating a below-deck version of Horatio Hornblower? Where can I find this masterpiece?"

Ten minutes later, he finished his breakfast and joined me at my counter, watching with amused interest as I handed him the journal. It wouldn't be the first time I'd asked Charlie to confirm what I thought to be an important find only to have him declare it of scant monetary or historical value.

Upon reading the first paragraph, however, his dubious demeanor suddenly transformed into that of a bird dog on point. Charlie adjusted his glasses, slid his tongue slowly across his upper lip, and, like a sluice miner who had detected a speck of gold dust, thumbed greedily through the stiff browned pages.

After five minutes of this, I asked his opinion.

Instead of answering, he moved to my computer to type "Samuel Gibson, Royal Marines" on the search engine.

The first heading to come up stated CCSU—the Royal Marines on Cook's Voyages. Listed under the heading was Gibson, Samuel, Pvt, followed by Dunster, Thomas, and ten others, including Molesworth Phillips, the last surviving member of the illustrious...

"En'dor is an abbreviation of *Endeavor*," Walsh proclaimed in a voice an octave higher than usual. "THE *Endeavor*. Captain James Cook's ship on the first of his three historic voyages."

I pretended to look impressed, but the scribbled diary of an eighteenth-century lobsterback didn't seem to rate up there with Marco Polo.

"Don't you get it, Bevan? Only a select number of officers and gentlemen passengers were allowed to keep journals. And anything that might prove embarrassing to the Navy was edited by the admiralty before it could be published. If caught, the man would have been lashed for penning this. Or even hung."

The professor returned to the computer and after studying the screen for a minute or two, looked up.

"It says here that Gibson served on all three of the expeditions, advancing in rank from private to sergeant. As a marine, he would likely have been at Cook's side on that fateful February in 1779 when the Hawaiians attacked them. This being his first journal, he might well have kept records of the other two voyages. Imagine finding them, too! It could provide what all the other journals, Cook's included, never have done."

"And what's that?"

"Reveal something of the great man himself, of course! While we have intricate detail of where he went, what he saw, and whom he met, we still know very little about Cook, the inner person. His official reports were bought and read by thousands of an adoring public, but there is nothing in his writings or that of his officers to suggest his weaknesses and idiosyncrasies until that fatal third voyage. How delightful it would be to read, unencumbered by official Admiralty oversight, the secrets of that elusive personality!"

Walsh took off his glasses to rub his eyes. "You have something that is not only unique, Michael, but perhaps extremely significant. What do you intend to do with it?"

"I'm going to the California Book Fair in a few weeks to get a feel for the market."

"Excellent idea. I suggest you put Holt House first on your list of exhibitors to show it to. It's the premier merchant for all matters relating to Pacific exploration. How much do you know about Cook's accomplishments?"

"Not much, I'm afraid. It's not something American schools bother to teach."

"And more's the pity. We aren't a people prone to celebrate history's great men and women if they weren't born here. But there are still those in Great Britain and its former colonies who would literally kill to defend the honor of Captain Cook."

"You must be joking."

"Not at all. Last year a Royal Navy veteran bashed in the head of a publican in Portsmouth. The barkeeper's only crime was to insist Cook was a despot worse than Bligh and no better a navigator. Only slightly less bloody has been the interminable feud between a pair of cultural anthropologists named Middleditch and Oyestebek as to whether the Hawaiians actually believed Cook to be divine. Care to hear more?"

For the next hour, interrupted only by a few of Café Provence's customers poking their heads in to inquire if Riverrun was open, Charlie provided a fascinating primer on the Yorkshire farmer's son who outdiscovered Columbus, Magellan, and Da Gama combined. The gist of it was this:

In 1745, James Cook, age seventeen, began his maritime life as a lowly apprentice seaman on a merchant collier in the North Sea coal trade. In the following decade, he rapidly rose in the ranks to first mate, becoming an expert at navigating the treacherous English coastal and stormy Baltic waters. But James Cook felt destined for greater things. With the onset of the Seven Years' War in 1755, he transferred to the Royal Navy to fight the French off Canada's shores. Following the peace, he spent years charting coasts on both sides of the North Atlantic while fine-tuning his knowledge of mathematics and astronomy —skills that would prove essential for his future success. But, for all practical purposes, his career had stalled.

Then, in a most unlikely conjunction of politics and rare common sense by the Admiralty, Cook, a noncommissioned officer with no social connections, was chosen to lead three expeditions to the Pacific Ocean.

The first, on the *Endeavor*, lasted from 1768 to 1771; the second, from 1772 to 1775, in which he commanded the *Resolution*, with its sister ship, the *Adventure*; and the last, from 1776 until his death in 1779, as captain of the *Resolution* accompanied by the *Discovery*.

In that eleven-year period, with no more than brief breaks between voyages, Cook's obsessive work ethic, curious nature, and determination led him to lands as foreign to Europeans as planets outside our galaxy would be to us today. By the time of his sudden death on February 14, 1779, he had explored one-third of the unknown world, circumnavigating and charting New Zealand, surveying the east coast of Australia, touching the fringes of Antarctica and the Arctic, and chronicling exotic Polynesian customs.

The mission of the third voyage was to sail up the north coast of America in search of a northwest passage linking the Pacific to the Atlantic. Stymied by impenetrable ice in the Bering Sea, he returned in late 1778 to the Hawaiian Islands, which he had discovered earlier that year. It was an opportunity to repair disintegrating ships and replenish supplies as well as sea-worn bodies. But for reasons known only to Cook, he decided to circumnavigate the Big Island for seven weeks before dropping anchor at Kealakekua Bay on January seventeenth.

But by then, James Cook had been at sea too long. Fifty years old, worn out by a decade of unceasing stress that would have destroyed a lesser man long ago, he was fighting time, weather, and an increasingly unsettled mind.

Physically, he remained impressive. In an age when the average height of a British male was five feet five inches, the captain stood six feet two. He dressed the part, too.

"The Hawaiians had never seen a white man before," Charlie told me. "Just imagine what they must have thought as he gazed down upon their canoes from the forecastle of his ship—a craft in size and design like something in a dream. Bedecked in a wide bicorne hat, brilliant blue coat with gold-laced buttons, and Wilkinson cutlass, Captain Cook had all the earmarks of a superior being."

Fittingly, Kealakekua meant "pathway to the gods." Ancient Hawaiian prophecies had long predicted the return there of a pale god on floating islands during the annual New Year/Harvest festival called Makahiki. This period traditionally began in late November—the very time that the *Resolution* and the *Discovery* first appeared over the horizon. Given these remarkable coincidences, it's no wonder that the natives believed this impressive creature was Lono, their white god of fertility and peace who had come to greet them in the flesh.

The ships were overhauled, pork and vegetables provided for the galley, and thanks to the comely and accommodating women, crew morale improved. But after a few days, the obsequious veneration directed at Cook by the Hawaiian priests went to his head; so much so that his officers feared their leader suffered from dementia.

The local chiefs weren't particularly pleased, either. There was only so much food to be taken, and these strange voyagers were voracious. Who would have thought gods and demigods could be so hungry?

According to the legend, the reign of Lono stopped with the end of the Makahiki festival in early February. The deity was then obliged to sail his canoe back to his mystical island over the horizon. Although unaware of the significance of the timing, the British ships happened to depart Kealakekua Bay with Cook at the helm on February 4, 1779.

Then, tragically, things changed. The ships were caught in a violent storm off Maui and were forced to return to the bay six days later to repair a broken foremast. From the Hawaiian standpoint, this was blasphemous. Now it was the time of Ku, the god of war and human sacrifice, as represented by its human avatar, King Kalani'opu'u.

Cook and his men were oblivious to the Hawaiians' resentment. On the last day of his life, the captain made foolish and provocative decisions that led to his death at the hands of the very people who had worshipped him.

Back in Europe, the news of Cook's tragic demise elevated him from being merely famous to becoming the martyred saint of the Enlightenment.

"Smallpox, syphilis, missionaries, and imperial exploitation followed in the wake of Cook's ships," Charlie told me as he concluded his lesson. "Justifiably or not, Cook is the symbol of everything that destroyed the native way of life throughout the Pacific."

Chapter 4

Three weeks later, I stepped out of a cab at the corner of Eighth and Brannon in rain-drenched San Francisco to join a line that stretched in front of the Concourse Exhibition Center.

It was a half hour before the doors of the center were to open, but there must have been five hundred people ahead of me shivering like stragglers on a retreat from Moscow. Not having brought an umbrella, I pulled the wool cap farther down my brow, flipped up the collar of my barn coat, and sat on a low brick wall to wait. I passed the time listening to a goateed gent describe the Siege of Mafeking to a stylish, silver-haired matron who looked as if she longed to drop a hand grenade down his throat.

Finally, unable to stand any more of the logorrheic assault, she said, "I understand this was during the Second Anglo-Boer War. Am I correct?"

"Why, yes, it was," the man said. "If Baden-Powell hadn't—"

"Are you familiar with what Arthur Conan Doyle had to say about the siege?" she interrupted.

"No, but—"

"Jannie Geldenhuys?"

Silence.

"Or Major Dennis? Fransjohan Pretorious perhaps?"

"Afraid not."

"Then I suggest you go to a library and brush up on your ignorance."

At last, the doors opened and the alligator line began shuffling into a building that resembled an airplane hangar circa 1960 East Berlin.

It doesn't matter if you're at an estate sale in Fargo or the Olympia Book Fair in London. When the bell rings, the idle chatter stops and the race is on. Then you'd best be ready to find the tables specializing in your subject matter and decide whether or not to buy. Once you walk away, odds are if you have second thoughts and go back for it, it will be gone.

I shook the rain off my coat at the entrance, gave the attendant my ticket, and walked into a vast hall already bustling with dealers, buyers, and assorted bibliophiles. Most of the latter weren't there to buy but to merely see and touch beautiful books, like fans who wait for hours to catch a glimpse of a famous actor or athlete.

I ambled down the aisles, gazing left to right at the fabulous wares being offered, picking up catalogs (some, like Phillip J. Pirages's Catalogue 56, can be works of art and bibliographical masterpieces) and stopping to touch the feathery softness of Moroccan leather and vellum.

It was all there, everything that I loved about my

adopted trade. In an atmosphere redolent with the aroma of old paper and leather were the most beautiful and desirable books, maps, and manuscripts to be found anywhere.

Within the buzzing hive of the conference center, I felt alive and free from all the cares of the outside world. If ever I needed confirmation as to what my niche in life should be, this was it.

Still, I noticed that many hopeful sellers, particularly those who had shepherded their treasures across oceans, seemed anxious. This may have been due mostly to the rain pounding against the green Plexiglass roof thirty feet above their stalls, threatening inventories worth millions. But there was also an atmosphere of dread relating to a change in the paradigm of bookselling itself.

What had worked for centuries was no longer a given in the new technological era. Now a touch on the computer makes anyone an expert. Adding insult to injury, the easy access to other dealers' listings had forced the prices on relatively common but attractive books—the bread and butter that paid the rent for open shops—down to ridiculously cheap levels.

When not fretting about potential leaks, the booksellers eyed the scene with expressions alternating between hopeful and bemused as browsers lovingly picked up desirable books and then, after noting the four- or even five-figure prices, regretfully and very carefully returned them to shelves.

But not every dealer's inventory was up to the standards offered by the likes of Peter Stern, Bernard Shapero, and Helen Kahn. When I paused at one table to check the condition of a copy of Brendan Behan's *Borstal Boy*, a paper jobber jumped from behind a bookcase like a prairie dog coming out its hole, only to return to his game of solitaire when I moved on. Given the quality of his stock, he'd be lucky to cover his booth fees. It was an unpleasant reminder of my own situation.

I passed through this section of less-established, mostly local dealers and walked up a ramp to a more exclusive area where I found the exhibitor Charlie Walsh recommended as most likely to appreciate Private Gibson's journal.

The exhibit space for Holt House Rare Books at #517 included three wide oak tables upon which were displayed first editions by such legendary sea captains as João de Barros, Sir John Barrow, Nicolas Baudin, and Count Benyowsky.

Behind the tables stood a glass case, its top shelf containing a complete set of the official accounts of Cook's three voyages—eight volumes, plus the atlas folio with two hundred and three engraved plates and charts. They were uniformly bound in half morocco and all were in beautiful condition except for some slight rubbing at the corners.

On a second shelf, next to the actual Royal Society Medal issued to Cook, was the first appearance in print of his epoch-making account of the successful measures to control scurvy. Accompanying these items were William Wales's astronomical observations made during the second voyage and Lieutenant James King's official account of the last voyage—the first to chronicle the murder of Cook.

There must have been a dozen other memoirs—including those of Rickman, the Forsters, and Sparrman—that were related directly to the three great expeditions between 1768 and 1779.

I stared through the locked glass door, wondering how Gibson's water-stained composition would stand up to them when a lean, well-dressed man with a Surfers Paradise tan and a mane of silver hair asked if I needed assistance.

"Perhaps we can help each other." I handed him my card with the Brancusi caricature of James Joyce on it. "I'm Michael Bevan."

"Clive Sexton," he answered in an upper-class Aussie accent. "I assume by your card that your area of focus is Irish literature. Might you have any firsts by Oliver St. John Gogarty? I've a customer who can't get enough of him."

"Sorry," I said. "No firsts by Yeats, Padraic Colum, or John Synge, for that matter. I'm limited to whatever comes in the door and, being situated in the middle of the US, it isn't easy focusing on Celtic studies."

"I should think it's no more difficult than anywhere else. After all, one of the great collectors of books by and about Friedrich Nietzsche lived in Omaha, Nebraska."

Sexton pointed to the shelves that held an inventory worth at least three million dollars. "People think that because Holt House is based in Sydney, these treasures were found in our neighbors' attics. They tend to overlook that the works were published and sold in England, and few Australians in the succeeding two centuries could have afforded them even if made available. Not a problem now, of course. Our firm has gone to great effort and expense to bring them back to where the adventures occurred. Thankfully, people around the world now know where to find us. Care to inspect our wares more closely?"

"I'd be honored."

He opened the case with a key and handed me a beautifully leather-bound edition titled *Account of the Voyages to the South Pacific Made Between 1764-1771*. The authors were an all-star cast of eighteenth-century seamen: Byron, Wallis, Carteret, and Cook.

"That's the Hawkesworth edition. He edited Cook's journals after the captain left on his second voyage, rewriting and misrepresenting the original text in an effort to spice it up."

"I take it the captain wasn't pleased."

"Cook was furious, but the result was a best seller for its time."

Sexton handed me another volume, one of four under the simple title *Cook's Voyages*.

"Here," he said. "This is a much more accurate account of the first and second voyage because this time Cook didn't let Hawkesworth meddle with it. Sadly, he never saw it published. He'd departed on his final voyage before it went to the printer."

I placed the book on the table and gently opened it at the center so as not to crack the binding. Selecting a page at random, I silently began to read:

Saturday, 20 November 1770. Winds Southerly, fair and pleasant weather. Employ'd Wooding Watering &c and in the AM sent part of the powder a shore to be air'd. Some of the Natives brought alongside in one of their Canoes four of the heads of the men they had lately kill'd, both the Hairy scalps and some of the faces were on: Mr. Banks bought one of the four…

For the next ten minutes, while Sexton attended to another browser, the matter-of-fact words of Britain's greatest explorer, who was unrivaled as a commander and navigator, transported me to the *Endeavor* as it circumnavigated New Zealand and barely escaped disaster on Australia's Great Barrier Reef.

"Well," Sexton said after the other customer moved on. "Meet your expectations?"

"And more. His account provides incredible details of the lands and people he met. Cook must have had charisma oozing from every pore."

"Really? The image I take from his writings is different. I see a sensible manager who handled singular challenges in wildly unpredictable settings. Therein lies his greatness. If Cook oozed anything, it was competence—that is, until the very end."

Sexton closed the book and placed it back on the shelf among its brothers. He turned, all business now. "You can have the Hawkesworth set for forty thousand dollars. Regrettably, the Voyages will cost considerably more."

I smiled the smile of a poor bookseller. "What makes you think I could afford to own any of your books, much as I would like?"

"Cut of your jib," Sexton said with a dismissive lift of an eyebrow. "My mistake."

Stung by his attitude, I debated briefly whether to tell him I possessed something rarer, if not more important, than any of his editions. I opened my brief-case to present Sam Gibson's journal.

"Crikey!" he exclaimed, dropping any pretense of a Cambridge education after reading the first page. "Where did you come by this?"

"In Rhode Island, about twenty years ago. But I only recently determined what it was."

"May I examine it?"

"Sure."

Sexton put on a pair of white gloves before letting me hand it to him. The journal, unlike his beautifully bound volumes, may have resembled a battered shoe, but he wasn't going to treat it like one. He turned the pages as if they were feathers.

"Small, maybe four by five inches," he said to himself. "Heavily water-stained, handwriting in pencil is shaky and hard to read. Bound in canvas, extremely worn, likely contemporary with the journal."

Sexton, friendly again, gave it back to me.

"I want my assistant to see this."

Turning, he called to a slight figure typing on a laptop computer at the opposite end of the booth. "Hullo, Bartow! Come here."

The flaccid-faced youth who looked up from his work with undisguised annoyance wore a shirt that might have been white once. His Adam's apple bobbed above a frayed collar and an absurdly narrow bow tie. The tie was blue. The images of toy rubber ducks on it were yellow. He had the peeved look of an adolescent who had just been awakened by his mother to take out the garbage.

"In a fackin' minute."

Clive Sexton's cheek twitched and his tan took on a purplish hue, but he didn't challenge the impertinence. Instead, he turned back to me.

"Billy Bartow, as you may have noticed, is an absolute shit. But I've seen him pull a first-edition Beatrix Potter from a widow's dumpster in Adelaide. He sniffs out rare books like a rat for cheese. He's a genius when it comes to authenticating documents. One tends to overlook his less flattering qualities."

Bartow continued to gaze at the computer screen like a parakeet in search of a cuttlebone. Eventually, after gnawing fingernails on each hand, he stood and shuffled toward us.

My second impression was no better than the first. Billy Bartow was no teenager but a twenty-something suffering from arrested development. A small, bony man with a snub nose and decayed teeth that protruded beneath a wispy mustache, his distrustful gray eyes seemed to have flecks of gold in them. His lank hair was the color of an overboiled carrot.

Sexton introduced us, and I had the pleasure of briefly gripping a hand as limp as a raw breast of chicken.

"Take a look at this, Billy," Sexton urged.

Bartow ignored him. Instead, he spoke to me.

"I don't appraise books for nothin', mister."

"Excuse us for a moment," Sexton muttered, seizing his assistant by the elbow and ushering him, not too gently, behind the tall case.

Upon their return, Bartow appeared, if not apologetic, then almost civil.

"Right," he said, without bothering to put on gloves. "Hand it over."

I gave him the journal. With Sexton hovering over him, he began to read, seeming to have no difficulty deciphering the writing.

"Get to Point Venus," Sexton urged after a few minutes.

Bartow flipped through the journal. "There." He pointed at the pages with a scabbed index finger. "The date is the sixth of June 1771. He's helping set up the transit."

"To do what?" I asked.

"To watch Venus pass across the sun," Sexton informed me. "That was the primary purpose of

Cook's voyage—to observe the transit of the planet that would determine the distance from the earth to the sun."

"And here," Bartow said excitedly. "Gibson writes about meeting the girl Metauie before deserting the ship to be with her. What a horny bastard!"

Bartow continued to read, silently moving his lips until his freckled face turned crimson at some salacious detail.

Sexton, after perusing the text over his assistant's shoulder, looked up. "Private Gibson certainly knew what to do once he had a woman in his grasp."

"And here's him meeting Tupaia, the Raiataen," Bartow exclaimed as if watching a movie. "Look! First contact with the Great Barrier Reef. Oh, they'll soon be sorry…"

By the time he'd finished, the little man's demeanor had brightened considerably. The transformation from gnome-like misanthrope to noble interpreter and guardian of history was astounding. The golden flecks in his eyes were actually shining.

"Right," Sexton said to me, taking back the journal. "What might you be asking for this old thing, Mr. Bevan?"

I pinched my chin as if in deep thought, when, in fact, my bowels were rumbling to the tune of the William Tell Overture.

Seeing my hesitation, Sexton added hastily, "Or perhaps you'd prefer a trade for something of comparable value on our shelves…"

Fortunately—or perhaps not, considering the horror it eventually led to—the lawyer half of my brain kicked in before violating the law of effective negotiation by making the first offer.

As tempting as the invitation to begin bartering was, particularly given my financial circumstances, I thought the most I could expect to get from Holt's stable would be two or three reasonably important books. Along with the half dozen I'd acquired after seven years in the business, it still wouldn't be enough to make my mark in the rare book trade.

"I appreciate the offer, Clive, but I think I'll look around a bit more. See what the market will bear for something this unique. Certainly, you'll have the right of first refusal."

Bartow started to say something, but Sexton silenced him with a flickering glance.

"Of course," he said, looking back to me. "I'll mention this to my partners in Sydney. What's your number should I wish to contact you?"

"The email address is on the card I gave you."

"Fine. Be sure to check for messages."

As Billy Bartow slunk back to his computer, Sexton touched my elbow. He motioned for me to follow him to a nearby coffee cart.

We ordered coffee, then stared at each other for a few seconds.

"Cut of the jib?" I said. "What the hell was that about?"

"Sorry, Bevan. Don't get off your bike. Snide remarks tend to flow from me when realizing I've lost what I thought would be a sizable commission. You do seem the type to be cashed up, however."

"It comes from having once been around those who have it. I wasn't to the manor born."

"Good on ya," he said, dropping his posh accent. "My mum's been a waitress at the Melbourne Australian Club nigh on forty years."

The Aussie sipped his coffee before coming to the purpose for our little confab.

"You're not the only one with a Sam Gibson journal," he said.

I must have looked gob-smacked, for he added, "It's of Cook's second voyage. Very few know about it. Now that yours has appeared, this should shake things up considerably."

"Who has it?"

"The proprietors of The Book and Bell, an antiquarian shop in Cecil Court, just off the Charing Cross Road, London."

"Wait a minute," I said, whipping out the book fair brochure. "The Book and Bell is exhibiting here!"

Sexton put down his cup and stood up. "They most certainly are."

Chapter 5

I followed Sexton to exhibit space #525, but no one was behind the counter.

"She's down the hall, Mr. Sexton," the dealer in the next booth said. "I'm guarding the stock 'til she gets back. Feel free to browse."

Displayed behind the closed glass cases were treasures of a different kind from what I'd seen at Holt's. Signed and inscribed British first editions by Somerset Maugham, Evelyn Waugh, and Virginia Woolf stood next to similarly autographed American works by Faulkner and Hemingway. A bamboo stand held a complete set of Marc Chagall color etchings illustrating a work by Louis Aragon. One of only two hundred and twenty-five originally published copies, it leaned against a brown and orange presentation box of Découpages et Photographies de Pablo Picasso. A color linocut of a seated woman signed by Picasso had an asking price of twenty-four thousand dollars. I'm not an authority on celebrity signatures, but the number seemed reasonable.

Once again, I felt simultaneously inspired and defeated. All around me were examples of what success looked like, yet I remained at a loss as to how to make it as an antiquarian book dealer.

This melancholy thought was soon interrupted when a rustling figure swept past me, cradling several thick catalogs in the crook of her arm. She was a shade under six feet, with wide shoulders and narrow, boyish hips. Her raven hair tumbled in unruly waves halfway down her back.

"Thank you, Mr. O'Connell," she said crisply to the man in the next booth who had guarded her books. The voice was British with a trace of a Scottish burr.

"Anything for you, Ms. Wilkes."

Even with her back to me, I sensed that she was a rare edition, but it wasn't until O'Connell departed to his booth and she turned her head slightly that the literary rarities I'd been admiring suddenly seemed as mundane as week-old magazines.

Her profile displayed a long aquiline nose with flaring nostrils, a strong chin, and full red lips that curved slightly downward. Her voice may have reflected a touch of the Highlands, but her complexion wasn't of the peaches-and-cream variety; more like a dusky Tuscan rose kissed by the Mediterranean sun. I guessed she was thirty (I learned later she was five years older than that) and in the full ripeness of sultry, knowing womanhood.

She wore a navy-blue jacket, a yellow cashmere sweater, and a gray pleated skirt. A silk scarf sprinkled with copper-colored hexagons was tied in the French style around her long neck.

I was still ogling her when Sexton appeared at my side. She turned full face to us then, and I must have instinctively recoiled. Her dark, almond-shaped eyes surveyed me with a touch of resigned amusement and a ton of resentment.

"Michael Bevan," Sexton said. "This is Penelope Wilkes, part owner of The Book and Bell."

"Please call me Pillow," she said, adjusting the scarf to cover a bit more of the bone-white scar that stretched from below her right ear and down the right side of her neck like an elongated spider's web. "I so hate 'Pen.' Or, God forbid, 'Penny.'"

What else do you hate? I thought as I clasped her hand. Her grip was firm and businesslike, without invitation to know her better. The nails were carefully manicured and she wore no rings.

"Is Adrian about?" Sexton asked.

"He's with Ken Lopez somewhere in the hall bartering for a Kerouac."

"When he returns, please have him drop by my booth. Michael has something interesting to show him."

Pillow Wilkes shot Sexton a look that could have splintered an iron rail.

"And might I be interested in it as well, Clive? Or is Mr. Bevan's treasure too precious for the likes of me?"

"God, no," Sexton answered quickly. "Nothing of the sort. It's just that…"

By then, I had already pulled the journal from my briefcase and handed it to her.

She accepted it with a muted "Thanks" and began to study the pages.

After a few minutes, she looked up at me.

"I never believed it would happen. How did you come by this?"

I told her.

"My partner discovered it years ago at a shop in the Cotswolds," she said, speed-dialing on her cell phone. "It was as much a steal as I gather your find was. A little bit of knowledge goes a long way in this business."

While she waited for the connection, I couldn't help but wonder what was under all that silk and cashmere. The scar, as shocking as discovering a crack in an otherwise perfect Etruscan vase, didn't seem so important when considering the rest of her. Pillow Wilkes was the real thing all right; a smart, refined beauty whose proud carriage indicated she was nobody's fool.

No lover's easy conquest either, I figured, unless the game was played according to her rules.

"Bloody hell, he's turned the damn thing off again."

"I've got to get back to my booth," Sexton said after Pillow had left her message.

"I appreciate your bringing this to our attention, Clive," she said. "I hope you'll agree that it's best we keep this knowledge to as few people as possible."

"Of course. Aside from Bartow, I've not mentioned the existence of Adrian's journal to anyone."

Pillow's cell phone beeped, and she excused herself to answer it behind one of the high cases.

After a minute, she returned and handed the phone to me.

"Hello, Mr. Bevan. Adrian Hart here. I understand we share something in common. I'm stuck for another hour negotiating a purchase. What say we meet where you are staying to compare notes? I'd prefer not to do this at the center; too many inquiring eyes."

"Sure. I'll be at the Marines' Memorial Club, Sixth and Sutter. Three o'clock sound okay?"

"Right. See you there."

When I gave the cell phone back to Pillow, she was staring intently at something down the aisle. I followed her gaze. Billy Bartow was heading toward a delivery exit. He looked furtively over his shoulder before opening the door and disappearing into the steady rain.

38

Chapter 6

Adrian Hart looked every inch the English public school product gone a bit soft in early middle age—medium height, compact build, a snub nose, blond hair spilling across an unlined forehead, the beginning of a double chin below thin Protestant lips. He sported a black velvet blazer, a silk tattersall weskit in alternating sky and navy plaid with matching bow tie. The shirt was pale pink, the pleated trousers gray. Hart's eyes matched the color of his pants. He held a leather-bound copy of Montaigne's Essays in the stubby fingers of his left hand.

I normally like the English. After all, I married one. But I didn't cotton to Hart at first. Maybe it's because his soft leather shoes and the weskit cost more than my first car, or that he spoke with a highly affected accent, emphasizing the end of certain pronouncements with the arch of an eyebrow and a condescending sniff from the nostrils.

He also said "indeed" a lot, the British equivalent

of the tiresome "ya know?" that has infiltrated American speech.

For all his snobbish airs, Hart didn't seem the type to spend hours behind a counter debating with customers as to whether fore-edge paintings were nothing more than a "cottage style" adornment. There was a fey hardness to his look. No doubt a knowledgeable bookman, I suspected that once Adrian Hart set eyes on a volume so scarce as to be nearly unprocurable, he'd resort to any means to get it in his bag.

We settled into leather chairs before a marble fireplace in the eleventh-floor library of the Marines' Memorial Club. The blue-green waters of San Francisco Bay shimmered beyond the high windows of the classic Beaux Arts hotel.

"Nice place," Hart remarked, studying the crystal chandelier above us. "Reminds me of the East India Club in London."

"A brief career in the Marines has had some benefits."

"Indeed. I served Mars as well. Royal Navy."

"Aboard a ship?"

"My skills along military lines were rather more plebeian; did seven years with Special Boat Service."

That got my attention. The SBS is a commando regiment equivalent to our Navy SEALs and Marine Recon.

"You're surprised," he said.

"Sorry, you…"

"Don't seem the type? I'm one of those odd ducks who may prize Vogue fashion photographs from the 1930s but also find time for the occasional hike up Mount Elbrus. I might say the same of you. Who'd ever suspect such a big strapping fellow to be a bookman?"

"What would you have me be? A golf pro?"

"No," he said, rubbing his chin and narrowing his eyes at me. "Something rather more sinister—a Jesuit defrocked for all the wrong reasons, perhaps?"

I glanced at my watch. Hart took the sledgehammer hint.

"Now, Mr. Bevan, how came you by the journal?"

"It was in an old desk given to me by a retired admiral in Newport, Rhode Island. He was an avid collector of naval artifacts and may have acquired this while serving at Allied Command in London during the war."

I pulled the packet from my briefcase and handed it to Hart. He took his time studying the middle pages, at one point turning the rough canvas at different angles to observe the childlike figure of a Tahitian canoe Gibson had drawn in one of the margins.

"It's our marine, all right," he concluded in a businesslike voice. "The handwriting, the phrasing, the remarkable insight into the foibles of his betters as well as his shipmates—it all points to a remarkable young man. Coming from a rural Hampstead background, yet able to write like this, I'll wager his father was a village vicar."

He set the journal on the coffee table next to the Montaigne.

"Mine is considerably more detailed," he continued, "and the penmanship is less crabbed. Gibson was a seasoned hand by the second voyage; promoted to corporal and into the good graces of Captain Cook despite his attempted desertion on the first voyage. But yours contains that ripping tale of how, besotted by a

Tahitian beauty, he absented himself, only to be dragged back to the ship in chains. It says a great deal about the captain that he didn't hang the spirited young fellow from the yardarm."

"Cook's leniency paid off. No other marine served on all three voyages."

"Nor, I suspect, as loyally. Did you know Gibson learned to speak the native lingo? He was always at his captain's side during negotiations with the island chiefs."

When I said I hadn't known that, Hart eyed me carefully. Then, as if making a decision, he bent forward and spoke in a confidential tone although we were alone.

"How long have you been in the trade?"

"Seven years this spring. Used books mostly. Nothing particularly special."

"Open shop?"

"Yes, although a lot of sales are through the Internet now."

"What were you before?"

"A trial lawyer."

"Ah, a barrister. Why give that up?"

"Does it matter?"

"One doesn't abandon a hard-earned and respectable profession merely because you love the smell of old parchment."

"And why not? There's nothing I enjoy more than finding a rare edition, particularly one I'll be able to turn for a nice profit. But I'm preaching to the choir, aren't I?"

Hart smiled with his eyes. When he did that, I began to like him. More importantly, I began to trust him.

He nodded. "Of course you are. I've yet to meet a bookseller who was a paragon of commerce. Both of us could be doing something more lucrative with our time. I suspect, however, that if you had been more successful as a barrister, you would have become a collector of fine volumes, not a tradesman. Sorry to be blunt, but time is limited."

"I was a good lawyer once. Certain things happened."

"Run off with the church funds?"

"Something like that."

I didn't mention my wife's death, the subsequent drug use, and emotional breakdown. I guessed Hart knew anyway. In the hour before our meeting, he would have typed my name on his computer, and the Internet would have produced the newspaper account of my disbarment. There was no hiding place on the World Wide Web.

"Would you return to the law if you could?"

"I've thought about it. More so lately, what with technology all but taking over and making us nothing more than data processors. How did you manage to get where you are?"

Hart eyed me warily, distrust mixed with the desire to know more about me. I gathered he was more comfortable asking personal questions than answering them.

The seconds passed slowly. I picked up the Montaigne and opened to a page that began,

The gladiator, prone on the sand, clings to hope although the thumb points down on every threatening hand...

"I was headed for silk," Hart answered, following a

long stare at the floor. "But the Lloyd's insurance debacle wiped out my father's estate and, with it, my chance for a law career. I joined the military for free room, board, and a bit of challenge, then attended university, followed by an apprenticeship with Maggs Brothers. My reputation seemed made when I discovered a box of Boswell's letters to Samuel Johnson behind a pantry at Lord Auchinleck's estate. The firm's management denied me promotion, however. They claimed my methods in gaining access to the country house were unethical. Of course, that didn't stop them from keeping the acquisition. I resigned and opened The Book and Bell."

"With Pillow Wilkes as your partner?"

Hart nodded. "She lacks literary acumen, and her bartering skills, so necessary in this trade, are little better than a Moroccan rug dealer's. She has gobs of money, however, and finds it great fun to support a quality shop in Cecil Court. It's been a profitable match for both of us."

"In other ways as well?"

"Dear Bevan," he said, smirking. "My interest lies on the other side of the fence; or bed, as it were. As for Pillow, I've not detected much interest of that sort with either sex since her marriage to that dreadful baronet, Alistair Wilkes-ffolkes, ended."

"A pity. She's beautiful."

"Do you think so?" Hart sniffed. "A book with broken bindings never appealed to me, no matter the provenance or rarity."

"She can't help…"

"The burns?" he said, reaching into his satchel and pulling out a folder. "She could look like a lizard and it wouldn't matter to me. It's what's broken inside. Let's get down to business, shall we? I found this while researching old police records at the British National Library. It should explain some things."

He handed me the folder. Inside was a photocopy of an eighteenth-century news sheet titled The Quarterly Pursuit that reported an affidavit of Robert Anderson, Royal Navy. It had been given in the presence of Sir John Fielding, a London magistrate, on 18 September 1780.

"Who is Anderson?"

"A friend and shipmate of Gibson's on all three voyages," Hart said. "Go ahead, read it."

I, Robert Anderson, Gunner's Mate, Royal Navy, declare the following to be true to the best of my knowledge. On the second day of August in the Year of our Lord one thousand seven hundred and eighty, and in the seventeenth Year of the Reign of his Majesty King George the Third over Great Britain, France, and Ireland, etc, I did journey to London with Samuel Gibson, Serjeant of Marines, formerly of His Majesty's Sloop the Resolution. Our intent being to visit John Hawkesworth, L.L.D., for to sell certain personal records penned by Serjeant Gibson during his last voyage with the late Capt James Cook.

The publisher's offices being closed due to the late hour of our arrival, we stopped for supper and other sustenance at the Lucky Bull Tavern, Cheapside Dock. Serjeant Gibson quaffed more gin than proper sense demands and did boast to all within, rogues and good men alike, of the riches his book would most assuredly bring him. At the calling of curfew, we departed the Bull in search of lodging not very sober. It was near a butcher's stall in the shadow of the Tower that a linkboy led us to a pack of thieves and murderers who set upon us with clubs and knives. I awoke to find poor Gibson

dead and all our possessions taken. I recognized one of them
from the Bull but know not his name. He is a large brute,
fourteen stone or more…

I know a thing or two about ill fortune, most of it caused by my own doing, but Gibson took the prize when it came to snatching defeat out of the jaws of victory.

"Obviously, he wasn't killed for his money pouch," I said to Hart.

"Indeed. Thames watermen, a disreputable bunch under any circumstances, would have appreciated the importance of a firsthand account of Cook's last adventure. We can assume the thieves hocked it to a bookseller or printer, but criminal investigations being what they were, the trail grew cold. It has remained so for two hundred fifty years."

"Have you determined the previous owners of your journal? Or mine, for that matter?"

Hart gave me one of those tilted-head looks, like a robin sizing up a worm.

"You really are most fortunate to have found me, Bevan. I should expect some consideration for the time and effort I have placed over the years in tracing their provenance."

I didn't like the tone of his voice any better than the implicit threat behind the words.

"What provenance? You haven't told me anything yet, Hart. Do you want to work with me or not?"

He flexed the fingers of his left hand as if clutching a knife.

"Well?"

After a long moment, his smarmy smile returned

and he pulled from his satchel a July 1978 edition of the Antiquarian Book Monthly Review.

"An article in here by George Lewisohn, since deceased, reports that the first two journals were sold in the spring of 1780 to a Penrith book dealer near England's Lake District. The author presumes the seller was Gibson's wife because the transaction took place before her husband's return from the third and last voyage."

"Gibson must have been enraged when he returned to find what his wife had done without his consent."

"Indeed," Hart said. "But news of Cook's murder and that of four marines was received in England in January 1780, ten months before the ships returned to London. I'll wager Mrs. Gibson assumed he was one of the dead and sought to ease her sorrow by selling his scribblings, which meant nothing to her. She received one guinea for them; enough to buy new bedsprings and then some."

"Quite a coup for the Penrith bookman."

"It would have been, but, according to Lewisohn's research, the Admiralty soon caught wind of the unauthorized writings. They confiscated them, storing both within the basement archives of the Royal Navy near Whitehall. There they remained until the Second World War when a direct hit from a German V-2 rocket destroyed much of the structure along with thousands of rare documents. Luckily, the tin box containing our two journals protected them from the resulting fire. They were taken to a location for sorting out, where the archivist decided that a bookseller friend—and not the Crown, which had ignored the diaries for two hundred fifty years—should profit by them. They ended up in a bookshop on Fulham Road, London."

"What did they sell for?"

"Not as much as you'd think. Postwar England was devastated economically, and rare books and documents were going for absurdly low prices. No one appears to have been interested in the hard-to-decipher writings of an enlisted Royal Marine when you could get first editions of Keats and Shelley for a pittance. The book dealer was old, he'd lost two sons in the war, and the provenance of the journals was shaky, given that the archivist wasn't going to admit he'd stolen them from the Navy."

"Admiral Taylor probably bought the first journal from him," I said. "He remained in London for a year after the war."

"That fits. But he wasn't offered or couldn't afford both. The second ended up with a bookseller named Potter whose shop was in the Cotswold village of Burford. It's where I bought it a decade ago. When I inquired of this gent if he knew of any other journals by Gibson, he thought the first had been sold to an American—undoubtedly, your friend Taylor—but he was vague concerning the existence of a third."

There was more silence as Hart pondered whether to divulge the next bit of information. His eyes widened. Mine didn't. I was getting tired of the dramatics. I threatened to begin reading the Montaigne again.

"However," Hart finally said. "Mrs. Potter was rather more forthcoming. There are times, after all, when I'll do anything for the cause."

I imagined the two of them in the back room of a rural shop thrashing about on creaking wood floors while Mr. Potter, oblivious to being cuckolded, recalculated his dwindling accounts for the twentieth time.

"She gave me the name of a former clerk at the pensioners' hospital in Greenwich rumored to possess the diary of one of Cook's below-deck men. I located the old man in Bath, but dementia had clouded his wits. His daughter, however, thought that he'd sold it through an ad in Antiquarian Bookman magazine. She remembered wrapping it for shipping to an address in Hawaii, but the customer's name and any records of the transaction had been consigned to the trash bin long ago."

"Does your trail end there?"

Without bothering to answer, Hart folded his arms across his chest and changed the subject with a question of his own.

"I take it you hope Private Gibson's first journal will enable you to become a 'legitimate' antiquarian dealer?"

"I prefer the term 'respected.'"

"Very well. Individually, each of our journals is a treasure, providing valuable and previously undisclosed insight into Cook the man. Given its primacy, yours is equally as important as mine. If I may say so, however, the second journal appears to be far more detailed and interesting. By then, Corporal Gibson had come to realize the significance and uniqueness of his point of observation. He knew he was witnessing history. In the first voyage, he was merely a spirited youth focused on his own exploits."

"But together," I said, "their value increases exponentially."

Hart leaned forward. "Precisely. For that reason, I am prepared to offer you considerably more than anyone else. I should think one hundred thousand dollars would allow you a considerable upgrade of your stock."

"Interesting," I managed to mutter, avoiding Hart's eyes by focusing on a portrait of 'Chesty' Puller on the wall behind him. The crusty general's hawklike eyes glared back as if warning me to beware of Brits wearing silk weskits.

I was still pondering how I might say "Yes, and could that cashier's check be deposited in my bank account by tomorrow," when he said something that brought me back to earth, and not a little angrily.

"Or, if you prefer, I will sell you mine for the same amount."

First Sexton, then this guy. Why did everyone think I was rich?

"I can't come up with that kind of money."

Hart raised a quizzical eyebrow.

"I see." He returned the magazine and the copy of Anderson's affidavit to his satchel. "Sorry, chum, but leverage does have its advantages."

I looked at my watch again.

"What if the third journal were to be found?"

"That is a rather large 'if,'" he said after drawing a deep breath. "I have no more inkling where it may be than you. My inquiries in Hawaii proved fruitless."

"Undoubtedly, being firsthand observations, Gibson's journals represent something interesting. But just how important were they coming from a grunt marine?"

"He was far more than that," Hart declared. "By the third voyage, Gibson knew enough of the native lingo to be Cook's translator as well as personal body-guard. I doubt that any of the people, with the possible

50

exception of Lieutenant Gore, knew the captain better. As a result, Gibson would have been a witness to the deterioration of Cook's mental as well as physical health."

"How bad had it become?"

"During his last eighteen days on earth, Cook produced neither log nor diary entry. I suspect it was because the normally meticulous observer never intended to return from the Pacific."

"You can't be serious."

"I most certainly am. The beginning of the rot can be seen in Gibson's second journal. I am certain that, if found, the third will provide the truth."

"The greatest English seaman shown to be a deserter? That won't sit well with the Royal Navy."

"All the better, then. The truth will be out. It would be one of the biggest scoops in maritime history and may well answer why in Cook's last moments he waved off any attempt to save him. The marines and sailors in the boats just off the rock closest to him surely wouldn't have abandoned him in his greatest hour of need. Did Cook intend to protect his Hawaiian attackers? And why didn't the officers of the ship seek to recover his body immediately after the natives retreated? Consider the value of having that information in your hands."

I sat back, struggling to imagine the firestorm in Britain if Hart's conjectures were proven.

"Do you really think a third journal exists?"

Hart smiled, but his lips were pressed tightly together and his eyes had turned hard. The palms of his hands slowly skidded back and forth on the smooth leather arms of the chair.

"No more than I knew you had the first. Come,

Bevan," he coaxed genially. "If you wish to bet a hundred thousand dollars on your finding the third someday, I will sell mine to you. Otherwise, I'm prepared to buy yours this very afternoon."

"I suggest we each keep ours for a while," I said after a long hesitation. "If the third journal appears on the market, then we can discuss partnering to obtain it. How we share the proceeds can wait until we have something tangible."

Hart's smile dissolved.

"Should that be the case, I might agree to share some of the pot, but certainly not fifty-fifty. If I find it, I will offer you fifteen percent of the combined value of the three. I have the resources and the contacts. You don't. Really, Bevan, take the hundred thousand dollars today. Bird in the hand and all that. Talk to Clive Sexton about this. He's a reputable enough chap —for an Australian."

"You're probably right," I said, standing up. "But I'd like to sleep on it."

"Very well, do that; but I suggest not too lightly."

Chapter 7

I returned to my room on the sixth floor of the Club where I placed the journal in a drawer, tucked between a sweater and a stack of underwear. After a quick shower and change of clothes, I rode the trolley over Russian Hill to The Buena Vista, a café bar at Hyde and Beach famous for its Irish coffee.

It was late afternoon and still raining, but the place was packed with tourists and a smattering of young professionals from the financial district. I found a table in the corner next to the plate glass window looking out to Alcatraz and the Golden Gate. While sipping an Irish coffee, I recalled Herndon Taylor mentioning an eerie coincidence associated with Cook's ships and Newport, the town where Carol and I discovered Gibson's journal.

After the completion of its historic voyage, the British put the *Endeavor* to use during the Revolutionary War as a prison ship. In 1778 they scuttled it in Newport Harbor in an attempt to blockade the port from attacking American and French forces. Fifteen years later, the *Resolution*, by then converted to a French whaler, had a similarly ignoble fate when it ran aground in the same Rhode Island harbor and was abandoned.

At the time, the two ships coming to rest in the same waters meant nothing more to me than a quaint snippet of local history. But so many years later, as I sat in the café watching the fog creep across San Francisco Bay, his story took on a personal significance.

Was it more than chance that Gibson's journal had found its way to me so near the graves of both ships? Had fate linked me to the ghost of James Cook?

I ended the evening at a bar on Ninth and Dash where, at some point after my fourth or fifth whiskey, I decided to accept Hart's offer.

Staggering back to the Marines' Memorial Club, I used the room key card to open my door and awoke six hours later with a hangover that would have made John Barrymore jealous.

Shortly after seven a.m. I stood over the bathroom sink chomping on a couple of cherry-flavored Tums when my cell phone played its piano riff ringtone.

"Bevan here."

"Tell me you have it."

It was Adrian Hart's voice, but it was not at all plummy.

"Have what?"

"My journal, damn you! Gibson's second voyage."

"I thought you'd left it in London."

"Well, I didn't. There were people whom I intended to show it to at the fair before I heard about you."

"Sorry, Adrian, but I—"

Suddenly, I felt sicker than even my hangover warranted.

"Wait a minute," I said, dashing to the armoire and opening the drawer.

At least the thief hadn't taken my Fruit of the Loom undies.

An hour later, Hart and I and an equally distraught Clive Sexton sat next to each other in a windowless room of SFPD's Property Crimes Division learning how the thief hacked open my door by plugging a programmed gadget into the power port near the key card lock.

"Every tech-literate school kid between here and San Jose knows the trick." Lieutenant Fishbank sounded somewhat surprised that we didn't. "Now, Mr. Sexton, when did you first notice that William Bartow was missing? And please, speak directly into the microphone."

I'd never bothered to insure my book holdings. Nonetheless, I filed a claim on my general homeowner's coverage and received a very polite, very prompt, and very expected rejection. It didn't help to know that Hart's exclusive antiquarian insurer had offered him a mere ten thousand pounds for his loss, "pending certification of its authenticity."

Despite Clive Sexton's pleas, accompanied by his empty threats to quit the company, Holt House Rare Books refused to consider any reimbursement to our shops. According to their lawyers, even if the thefts could be pinned on Bartow, he was an independent contractor whose fraudulent actions could not have been foreseen.

Granted, I'd been foolish to not place the journal in the valuables locker of the Marines' Memorial Club.

It shouldn't have surprised me that even a modern key lock system was vulnerable, but I was at a loss to figure out how Bartow knew my room number until I recalled Sexton's comment that the lad had a nose for finding books. He'd probably added quite a few to his portfolio in the past by just such larceny, sneaking from book fairs in mid-afternoon and heading for hotel rooms where dealers often leave purchases from the previous day.

The biggest mystery, however, was how Bartow thought he could profit from the theft of Gibson's journals. What dealer or collector would risk paying for such easily identified stolen goods once word got out?

"They'll show up," Lieutenant Fishbank had said. "Just a matter of time."

Neither Hart nor I found any comfort in his words.

Chapter 8

I returned home the next day to a city still locked in winter's deep freeze. The months stretched into spring, but the search for Bartow and our journals went nowhere.

My daily email exchanges with Adrian Hart trickled to two a week, then nothing. Eventually, the loss settled into a corner of my mind like a faintly disagreeable odor.

Thanks mostly to Josie's coup in selling the signed edition of *The Plays of Eugene O'Neill* and her heroic effort to convince an interior decorator to buy two hundred hardbacks I'd destined for the trash bin, Riverrun Books enjoyed a break-even quarter. Josie even got Eddie Worth IV to drop four hundred dollars for an 1858 bio of the Earl of Kildare. Every morning found me waking up downright cheery.

You'd think I would have learned that such bliss only meant things were about to get worse. Ask any nun.

Despite the decent numbers for the first quarter, I

knew the days for bookshops like mine were ending, and the Gibson journal had been my last chance to make it as an antiquarian dealer. Nearly half of my sales for the past year were due to listings on the dot-coms AbeBooks and Alibris. A year before, they'd comprised only fifteen percent. People were coming in less and less. The gap between store and Internet sales was sure to increase. Most of Riverrun's income went for rent and utilities. Having an open shop, for all its intellectual and psychological benefits, was bleeding my meager savings.

A dismal second quarter made it even more clear how dire things were. By June, every other used-book store owner in the area had closed. One who had specialized in mysteries and thrillers continued to sell her inventory from a home computer. I could have done that, too, but sitting in front of a blue screen typing in title, author, price, and condition of old classics wasn't what I had in mind when I sought to reinvent myself.

At the age of forty-five, I had twenty-three thousand dollars in the bank. My house was debt-free, but I couldn't afford to have the leaky roof fixed or pay a kid to cut the grass. I needed to start making real money again, and the logical option was to return to a profession I had come to intensely dislike.

After a long talk with Josie, I called Tim Winter. My former law partner had loaned me the money to start Riverrun. Now I was contacting him to help me close it. Tim and I had always had a complex relationship. A lot of it had to do with my relationship with his wife before he knew her.

Alice O'Hare and I had been childhood friends and on-again-off-again lovers during our college years.

If I hadn't met Carol, we might have tied the knot. Tim caught Alice on the rebound, and he wasn't the type to forget it. When I was accused of murdering a fellow bookman, he took my case. But I got out of that jam with precious little help from him, and I never got over the feeling that he secretly relished my fall from grace. He wouldn't have cried had I been convicted.

Now Tim seemed happy to help restart my career as long as I—and Alice—understood it was due to his beneficence and subject to his continued control.

"Still think the board will reinstate my license?"

"Sure, Mike. They were ready to do it two years ago if you'd bothered to apply. I've got an office waiting for you here."

Before I could thank him, he added, "You'll be 'of counsel,' however."

"Of counsel?" I asked, stifling the urge to remind him that I'd been the founder of the firm he now headed.

"Afraid so. Otherwise, it wouldn't be fair to our senior associates. Build your client base, do the work I know you're capable of, and a partner's chair will open up eventually."

I envisioned a desk in a windowless room midway between twenty-something associates and a mile from the corner offices of partners who were my age or younger. I'd be handling no-fault divorces and fixing traffic tickets into my fifties.

"I understand," I lied. "Thanks."

"No problem," he said in a voice dripping with condescension. "Honestly, Mike, it's good to hear you've come to your senses. I figured economic reality would trump this conceit of becoming a real anti-quarian dealer, but it's taken longer than I expected."

I greeted his comments with ten seconds of seething silence. Winter, besides being a top lawyer, was one of the Midwest's finest book collectors. Early on, Tim's expertise had been as valuable to my fledging book career as his initial financial backing. Now he was telling me he never believed I would succeed with Riverrun. I considered telling him to take a flying leap over a herd of flatulent sheep.

Instead, I managed to remind him that I had repaid his loan, with interest, two years earlier.

"Of course you did. Don't get me wrong, Mike, this little bookshop was right for you when your options were, shall we say, limited. But now you have a chance to restart a once-flourishing career."

A career built defending strippers, drug dealers, and loan sharks, I said to myself. Some flourish. Some career.

We talked a bit more about how the liquidation of assets would proceed, whether the landlord would let me out of the lease six months early, and other depressing end-of-business affairs that seemed to have a striking similarity to funeral arrangements.

Chapter 9

One week later, Josie opened the bookstore while I spent an extra hour at home studying for the upcoming bar exam. Despite a diligent effort fueled by half a pot of coffee, I found the Rule Against Perpetuities made as little sense to me as it had in law school. To clear my head, I worked out with weights in my basement then headed to the shop.

I had just settled behind the counter to begin listing new acquisitions when Josie emerged from Café Provence holding a steaming cup of cappuccino.

"A lady's been asking for you," she said, pointing a thumb toward the café. "In there."

"Do you know her?"

"No, but apparently you do," she said dryly.

"What does that mean?"

"If you don't know by now, babe, I've got some land in Florida…"

She headed to the philosophy section, shaking her fanny like a table dancer in the Sirloin District.

I walked through the entrance of the bistro, stopped to scan the bustling room, then took twenty seconds to readjust my eyeballs.

Pillow Wilkes sat boldly erect at a table in a far corner, her back against a tall window through which sunlight streamed. A half-eaten croissant lay on a china plate beside a teacup. She wore a soft gray business suit, and despite the heat outside, a black cashmere turtleneck.

Her dusky rose complexion was as I remembered from San Francisco. So were the full red lips and strong chin. Even in the morning brightness, her hair was the color of midnight, absorbing color rather than reflecting it. Three long fingers rested casually above the right side of her jaw so as to cover the top portion of the scar not hidden by the sweater. The incongruous mixture of hardboiled determination with that hint of physical insecurity was striking. She seemed to have no understanding of the effect that her beauty, marred as it was, had on people.

When I approached, she gave me the slightest nod as if we'd seen each other earlier that morning instead of a year and fifteen hundred miles ago.

If that was to be her game, I decided to play it as well. I pulled up a chair across from her, plopped my elbows on the table, and casually cupped my chin in the palms of my hands.

"Small world," I said.

"Adrian has gone to New Zealand. I need your help finding him."

I barked a laugh.

Her deep-set eyes stared evenly into mine.

"Billy Bartow is there as well."

"How do you know?"

"A colleague at Otago University spotted him at a book fair in Christchurch. Adrian erased the email message, but not before I got a glimpse of it. He swore me to secrecy, insisting I not go to the police or alert the insurance people."

"Why doesn't he want them to handle it?"

"Adrian suspects Bartow is close to finding the third journal. If the police get involved, it might drive the little shit further underground. The chance of getting the stolen journals back—let alone finding the third— would be lost forever."

"Hart didn't intend to let either of us know. Why should we help him?"

"To protect our own interests, for one thing. He's not thinking straight. Adrian might have been able to handle the loss of our journal, but he feels terribly responsible for yours."

"That doesn't sound like the self-centered braggart I met, Pillow."

"You don't know him like I do."

"All right, so maybe he's a decent human being who's suffering a first-class case of remorse, but that's not enough to make me think he isn't in full gallop on a wild-goose chase."

"We owe it to him to help."

"The guy's a former commando. They tend to be self-sufficient."

She took a deep breath. To my amazement, a tear formed at the corner of an eye.

"Adrian's been drinking too much," she said, dabbing at the waterworks with her napkin. "Something he never did before. Two months ago, he made a horrible mistake in an appraisal of Lord Wycliffe's incunabula. It caused the Smoot Museum all sorts of problems with the Inland Revenue. If he doesn't find Bartow and recover those journals, I think he'll harm himself."

"Ever think, given his current mental condition, he dreamed up Billy Bartow's reappearance?"

"But the email from New Zealand?"

"How do you know it even came from there? You say he deleted the message."

"Why would he send it to himself?"

I couldn't answer that, but I was looking for any excuse to get out of this appalling development.

Then another tear—this time from the other eye—slid down her comely cheek. It was getting downright embarrassing. Customers at nearby tables were looking askance in my direction. Deirdre Lescalle shook her head accusingly.

Don't get me wrong, I'm as willing as any Sir Galahad to help a beautiful woman in distress. But traipsing halfway across the world to search for her partner, who sounded a trifle pixilated, seemed a bit much.

The look in Pillow's dark eyes, however, wasn't about to retreat.

"Even if Adrian were hallucinating, he needs our help," she said, touching my hand. "More than that, I need it. You're the only person I can depend upon."

She was a crafty one all right. Something began to stir within me and it wasn't my mind. Nonetheless, I shook my head and tried to look profound.

"Look, Pillow. You've made a mistake coming here. I'm a man of modest ambition who has been offered a chance to make real money again in a grown-up profession. I'm finished dealing with characters who wrangle old books for a living."

I'm no stranger to withering looks—Marine drill instructors, mother superiors, and a particularly nasty Cape Town neck-breaker have all frozen me with their peepers—but Ms. Wilkes could hold her own with the best.

She didn't say a thing, content to play some kind of piano concerto with the fingers against her cheek while her other hand squeezed the teacup as if it were my throat.

I looked sideways out the window, then back to her. Summer was arriving in the northern hemisphere, and I didn't intend to miss it gallivanting around the wintry Antipodes.

"I'm not the one to help find your partner," I insisted.

"I thought you were made of sterner stuff, Bevan. Adrian has his faults, but he's shown courage and gumption to go after what was stolen. As I recall, you lost a prize to Billy Bartow as well."

She finished her tea, got to her feet, and handed me a card with her international cell phone number.

"I'll be at the Wellesley Club in Wellington until the twelfth."

With that, she exited the café, dragging every eye in the place with her.

I paid the bill and returned to the shop where Josie greeted me with a sly smile and the first-class airline ticket to New Zealand Pillow had left for me.

"Interesting woman, Mike."

"Yup."

"She told me all about it before you arrived."

"She did, huh?"

"Well?"

"Well what?"

"Is your passport current?"

"D'ya think I'm nuts?"

"Most definitely, if you don't follow her."

I started to tell Josie to mind her own chickens. Instead, I looked out the window and pretended to be interested in a couple of robins doing what robins usually do that time of year.

She reached up to my face, bringing me back to her.

"The days of the quaint bookshop around the corner are long gone, Josie."

"Don't give in yet. How many times have you forgotten to eat while reading The New York Review of Books? You're a bookman, Michael Bevan, right down to your last synapse and corpuscle. Be true to yourself for once. And while you're at it, consider what I mean to you as well."

"I don't follow you."

"I simply don't know how you'd behave if we got in real trouble again, whether you'd be first on the lifeboat or last to leave the sinking ship."

Never one to appreciate lectures, especially when they concern me, I retreated behind the counter. It was a barrier that proved as effective from her assault as the Maginot Line had been for France.

She stormed up and searched my face across that two-foot divide.

I avoided her eyes and rubbed a hand across my forehead. It didn't do much good.

"I don't get you anymore, Mike."

My eyes lifted.

"I can say the same for you. What kind of woman insists that her lover fly off to New Zealand with that long-legged Amazon?"

"Anything to keep you away from Sandra Epstein." Josie smiled, but her smile looked a little tired.

Chapter 10

I didn't get much sleep the night before departing. What should have been a romantic evening tripping the bedsprings fantastic with Josie had been tense and mechanical. Perhaps she felt guilty having urged me to go on this harebrained venture, or maybe it was a subconscious attempt by both of us to make the parting seem not so doleful. The last time we'd been apart, it verged on becoming permanent, and, despite the recent rapprochement, our love affair was still looking frayed.

I blamed the open relationship we'd decided upon a year earlier. The old "Let's give it a try before committing to marriage" had been my idea. I'd suspected that once Josie helped to get the bookstore on sound footing, she'd become bored, and her restless nature would lead her back to the more thrilling life she'd known before—as if selling tattered editions by Sherwood Anderson or mastering the ABCs of bookbinding wasn't rip-roaring excitement enough.

Smart, feisty, disturbingly courageous, and

possessing a body one doesn't often find outside an Olympic training camp, the former FBI agent was more cartoon action figure than flesh-and-blood woman, the very things that had attracted me to her in the first place.

All well and good if you're into adrenaline-charged thrill junkies. But I also had a business to run, and every six months or so, Josie felt compelled to engage in some daredevil escapade. The previous August had seen her running a marathon with Tarahumara Indians in the desolate Copper Canyon of Mexico. Then it was Wyoming on the Outward Bound winter survival course. Now she was pushing me out of my comfortable nest, as if challenging me to be more adventurous. I shuddered to think what she'd expect of me next, given that the natives were restless in Samarkand.

We didn't say much on the drive to the airport. When Josie kissed me goodbye, I had the unshakable feeling that I'd never see her again. I think she did, too.

Twenty hours later, my premonition appeared to be coming true. The sou'easter blowing out of the Antarctic funneled through the Cook Strait and caught the 707 in its crosswinds during the approach to the narrow, hill-bound Miramar Peninsula.

While the aircraft wobbled sickeningly through one air pocket after another, I made the mistake of peeking out the window. We were so close to the roiling waves that saltwater sprayed the bottom of the wings. As if I wasn't already aware of our dire situation, a woman seated behind me screeched, "Jaysus, look there!" and pointed to a pair of tugboats, toylike among the towering swells, racing to rescue a large ferry listing near the jagged shoals of the harbor.

"Windy" Wellington was certainly living up to its reputation as one of the most difficult major airports in the world in which to land.

Several more throat-bobbing seconds followed before the wheels slapped down on the absurdly short runway, the reverse thrust buckets opened, and the plane taxied to a stop with me leading the round of applause for our pilot. I was still shaking when the taxi dropped me off at the Duxton Hotel.

I put a "Do Not Disturb" sign on the outside handle of my room and flopped onto the bed without taking off my clothes. Five hours later, a nightmare featuring an aircraft tumbling through fire-streaked skies was interrupted by a series of ever-insistent knocks. I staggered half asleep to the door.

"Sorry, sir." The assistant concierge handed me a note. "You weren't answering your call button. The lady insisted you get this immediately."

It was from Pillow, telling me to meet her at the Wellesley Club at four o'clock. That gave me less than an hour to shuck off jet lag, get presentable, and find the place, which according to the city map, was ten blocks from my hotel.

I felt halfway human by the time I stepped onto Wakefield Street. The skies were still overcast, but the earlier tempest had calmed. I declined the doorman's offer of a cab, preferring a walk in the fresh salt air after twenty hours cooped up in airplanes. I did, however, accept his loan of an umbrella.

On a corner stoop across from the hotel slumped a mahogany-skinned young man. He was dressed in greasy chinos and an equally grimy leather jerkin. A wooden crutch lay beside him, and next to that, a cap with a few coins scattered in it. His dreadlocks were bound with a neon-yellow bandana, and his tangled beard was spotted with crumbs. He cupped in his hands an arctic tern with a broken wing that must have blown in with the gale.

Gently raising the bird to his face, he attempted to feed it a piece of bread held between his lips. When it became obvious that the tern was having none of it, he snapped the white-feathered neck and dropped the creature into a pocket of his jacket.

I crossed the street, placed a two-dollar coin in the cap without meeting his eyes, and walked on. When I looked back a few seconds later, I saw him stand with the help of the crutch and limp zombielike along the edge of the harbor.

Farther along the quay, I mingled among pasty-faced government office workers and shoppers thronging the city square on mid-morning tea breaks. The Down Under autumn weather was similar to Seattle's, and everyone was dressed in sweaters and anoraks, invariably black or gray. Some sat on metal railings and the steps of government buildings, chatting amiably about sports and politics while keeping wary eyes on the dark clouds scudding above the harbor.

I had just stopped at a vending truck for a cup of coffee when two groups of beefy gang members brandishing steel bars, axes, and hammers swarmed from opposite corners into the center of the plaza. Fifty or more to a side, they faced off like opposing football teams, hurling obscene threats at each other. Those bystanders who could slunk instantly to the safer peripheries of the square. I wasn't one of them. Whether it was jet lag numbing my senses or my general tendency to watch train wrecks from the standpoint of the tracks, I stood there slack-jawed and woolly-eyed, innocent as a new-laid egg and just as bright.

A leader for one of the packs stepped forward, raised his hand, and slowly brought it down again, resulting in silence from both sides. But the resulting calm, eerie in its suddenness, was merely an orchestrated prelude to the astonishing savagery that followed.

This leader waited several more seconds, then with bulging eyes and grotesquely extended tongue, produced a hideous yell:

"A-a-a-! He ringa pakia!"

In response, the men behind him began to clap their hands on their thighs.

Again, the leader's cry: *"A-a-a-a! He waewae takahia!"*

That set off a fierce and frenzied posture dance that included a rapid vibration of hands, wildly exaggerated eye rolls, and protruding tongue flicks.

Anyone who has witnessed New Zealand's national rugby team perform the *tauranga a tohu haka*, the traditional Maori war dance, knows how impressive it can be. Whether presented as a fierce sporting challenge or a ceremonial welcome, it has few equals when it comes to facial distortion and rhythmic movements.

But what these thugs exhibited was a perversion of the traditional Maori ritual, accompanied as it was by tonsil-rattling insults in English that were vile enough to make 2 Live Crew cringe.

Similarly dressed in the universal motorcycle-horde outfit of filthy jeans, ripped T-shirts, and hobnailed boots, the only way to distinguish each gang member from his enemy was by their "colors," à la Crips and Bloods.

The side that initiated the challenge wore leather vests dyed red and black with the cartoon of a British bulldog and the name Mongrel Mob/Raitorua emblazoned on their backs. Some wore Nazi helmets over their long, plaited hair, while others sported wool hats or bandannas.

Their opposites wore predominately dark blue colors and the logo Black Power and appeared to have Tongan and other Pacific Islander features. Whether Maori or Islander, a member of the Mongrel Mob or Black Power, they all had varying degrees of European ancestry; something that—despite the British bulldog logo, the Nazi helmets, the "Sieg Heils"—they clearly despised. Most of the faces were covered with gang-slang tattoos interspersed among swirls of traditional Maori motos.

My first thought was that I was watching some kind of radical street theater, like the mock cowboy gunfights staged in Dodge City on the Fourth of July. After all, this was taking place in the heart of the capital of New Zealand, supposedly one of the most law-abiding countries in the world.

But when the Mongrel Mob's choirmaster charged his blue-clad opposite with a raised hand axe, cleaving the man's clavicle, I suddenly realized this wasn't a weirdly extravagant flash mob performance.

Somebody bawled, *"Taupokina! Taupokina!"* which sounded a lot like "Attack!" The rampage ignited in earnest. Finding myself caught on that hellish stage of swinging axes and clubs, punctuated by the screams of wounded gangbangers and howled profanities, I bolted toward the nearest side street, blubbering gibberish and waving my umbrella like it was a Mameluke saber. My false heroics didn't last long. Facing a pack of bloodthirsty poltroons, I sprawled into a fetal position, suffering only a few stomps to my head as they clambered past.

A minute or two later, I emerged from the melee relatively unscathed but considerably wiser as to Wellington welcoming committees.

When at last a sufficient number of police arrived to halt the carnage, the skies opened up, washing away the blood on the cobblestones and scattering combatants and onlookers alike. I proceeded along the quay, leaning into a horizontal tempest that shredded the umbrella by the time I arrived at the Wellesley Club.

Soaked to the armpits, I reflected how, during my first few hours in New Zealand, I'd experienced a harrowing airplane landing and had a front-row seat at teatime to a gang war. Feverish enough excitement for a used bookman, but I'd known worse when an antiair insurgent missile brought down the CH-53E helicopter ferrying me and a platoon of Marines to Hajaf, Iraq.

I expected to find a uniformed concierge inside the handsome marble building that housed the oldest social club in the city, but no one was behind the service desk. The only light came from flickering teardrop-shaped bulbs encased in wall sconces. At just past four, the place looked abandoned.

The driving rain had turned to sleet, making a sound like the fingers of a skeleton drumming against the beveled windowpanes. I wandered into the empty restaurant where I cozied up to an electric space heater set on top of a bench.

After warming my backside, I walked to the maître d's stand, dropped the remains of the umbrella into a trash basket, and rang a bell. This brought a rustling sound in the kitchen, followed by a waiter wearing a starched white jacket, a black vest, and black trousers who walked as if his feet hurt. His narrow bow tie was striped with the Wellesley's gold and maroon colors. He held a dish towel in one hand and an empty wine carafe in the other. His smile exposed crooked, yellowish teeth.

"We open for dinner in an hour, sir."

"Ms. Wilkes…"

"Oh, yes," he said, nodding toward a shuttered door. "In the bar. She's enjoying a pinot noir from Two Paddocks vineyard. Shall I bring you one as well?"

"Fine."

Pillow sat at a small round table farthest away from a blazing log fire in the walnut-paneled room. Caricatures of Wellingtons sporting, political, and business leaders covered the walls. Except for the pictures, everything in the room was dark. Dark brown walls; dark leather chairs; black table tops; a maroon rug.

She stood when I approached, offered a dry smile that left the rest of her face unmoved and greeted me with a brisk handshake. As before, she wore little makeup. There was a severe elegance in the clothes that covered her from ankle to chin, like a nun's habit designed by Chanel.

Her face was all business, if not a little wistful.

"I knew you would come," she said once we had settled into our chairs. "But thank you anyway."

"Why so certain?"

"You seemed remarkably bored. Or was it frustration?"

"Far from it. I'm quite happy with the way things are."

She took a sip of her wine and stared at me over the edge of her glass. For an instant, I thought I'd detected an inviting gleam in her eyes.

"Wouldn't you be happier to have your journal back?"

"Of course," I replied. "Like you and everyone else on the planet, I could use more money."

"But it's more than that, isn't it?"

"I don't follow."

"I don't mean to offend, but I suspect you aren't particularly satisfied with the way your life has gone. I could see it within fifteen seconds of our meeting in San Francisco. It was even more apparent at your shop."

Her voice had lost some of its hardness.

"It takes more than words to offend me," I said. "Besides, I've heard it plenty enough from someone else."

"Miss Majansik?"

"Lucky guess."

The waiter appeared with the platter. He filled my glass and left the carafe on the table. When he noticed the water dripping from my clothes onto the floor, he asked if we would be more comfortable closer to the fireplace.

"We're fine," Pillow answered sharply.

The light from the sconces on the wall above us glinted in her dark hair. Her staring eyes, those dark drowning pools, bore into my brain. Her right hand, as usual, fiddled with the fabric covering her neck. Her nails were like a sensible child's, clipped and unpolished. I said I liked the wine.

"It's local," she said. "Sam Neill's vineyard."

"The actor?"

"Yes."

Wetting her finger, she drew it along the top of the glass. She gave me a curious look, as if calculating something.

"You asked me here," I said. "Suppose you tell me why."

She stopped with the finger.

"Last week, one of Clive Sexton's Holt associates took the commuter flight from Auckland to Wellington with Adrian. I suspect he intends to contact a professor at Victoria University named Cattley Middleditch."

"The author of *Farewell to Elysium*?"

She nodded. "Have you read it?"

"No, but I've heard of him. The book ignited a debate with another Cook scholar, didn't it?"

"That's an understatement. Middleditch believed that when Cook stumbled on the Hawaiian beach, he was immediately worshipped as a god. A Yale professor named Uley Oyestebek found that view to be ethnocentric, even racist. Anthropology is a discipline filled with endless arguments and this was a big one: a real pissing contest even in a field notorious for clashes rather than conclusions."

"No doubt both would love to read what Gibson had to say," I said. "Particularly if it confirms their thesis. Is Middleditch aware that our journals were stolen?"

"I'm certain of it. Holt's people have appraised books for Victoria University for a long time. They would have alerted the professor to be on the lookout for anyone trying to unload them. I've arranged for us to see him tomorrow."

"Good. Now, tell me more about your relationship with Hart. Who's using who?"

"I don't know what you mean."

I put my glass on the table and leaned back in the chair. "Pillow, you seem to know a lot about me, but I know very little about you."

She answered by untying the scarf. "How's this for starters?"

The scar spread over the entire right side of her neck before disappearing below her blouse. Bright pink ridges rippled across a flat gray surface resembling in texture and color the skin of a shark.

"I'll show you the rest if you wish," she added in a voice as cold as a dead penguin.

"I didn't mean it that way."

She studied me sardonically, relishing my discomfort. "What's the problem, Michael? Disfigurement not your cup of tea?"

"That's unfair. Give me a little credit for admiring your beauty."

"You mean you like my face, my waist, my thighs. You'll take those and shut your eyes to the rest."

She stared at me contemptuously before adding, "You think you know all about women, don't you?"

"Certain women, maybe."

"But just the ones who find you attractive."

"It certainly helps to know if a girl I fancy has good taste."

"Ugh!"

"And what about you, Pillow? How long has it been since anyone had control over you?"

I thought she would ignore the question and storm out the door. Instead, her tone softened.

"Only one," she replied bleakly. "And no one ever will again."

She got to her feet. "Come on. You've followed me this far."

I left money for the waiter. Then I followed Pillow into the hallway and up a broad staircase to her room.

Before opening the door, she hesitated. "We can keep the lights off if it bothers you."

"You still don't understand."

"Yes, I do, Michael. More than you'll ever know."

Chapter 11

The high-ceilinged room was old-fashioned comfortable with William Morris wallpaper and a leather club chair parked next to an oak-framed window. Half-opened venetian blinds allowed a peek of the harbor. An overhead light encased in a copper-tinted dome emitted a warm glow. A rumpled quilt covered the otherwise unmade bed.

"I'll be just a minute," she said, going into the bathroom.

I should have left her a note saying I'd meet her the next morning and slipped away.

But I didn't.

For all my intentions to remain faithful to Josie, I felt compelled to understand this perplexing person who could be so abrupt, so cold. If the only way to break through that frigid exterior was to make love with her, then so be it.

That's how I justified it anyway. I knew I was going to feel empty, disgusted with myself five minutes afterward, but… Oh, hell. It was raining torrents outside, and I'd lost my umbrella.

I waited by the window, watching seagulls dive-bomb a ferry coming alongside a wharf. When that got old, I studied the electric heater on the floor. Across its concave aluminum back ran a thin metal band glowing orange with the heat. It warmed my ankles, but that's the most I can say for it. A few minutes later, I heard the toilet flush, then the running of water in a sink. Another minute passed before the door opened. It was worth the wait.

Pillow stood naked beneath the transom, her feet spread slightly apart. The turtleneck, skirt, and jacket were folded neatly over her left arm. Her right arm hung by her side. She said nothing, hid nothing, just stared straight ahead at a spot somewhere behind me showing no sign of embarrassment.

Had I been a younger man, I might have found the performance intimidating.

Her left breast was firm and perfectly shaped, but a six-inch-wide corrugated sheath of damaged flesh extended from her neck to the beltline on the right side.

I tried to focus on her face, but it was impossible.

"You might at least pretend not to be shocked," she said, still looking past me.

"It doesn't matter."

"You're a liar."

I walked up to her, took the clothes from her arm, and dropped them to the floor. "Remember in Kansas City when you said I was the only one you could depend upon?"

"Vaguely."

"Did you mean it?"

"Yes."

"I'm here to help, Pillow, but you've got to trust me."

"I trust you."

"Then you can start by telling me the truth."

"Not yet," she said.

I drew her into my arms.

She shuddered, but only for an instant before her moist lips opened and a nimble tongue flickered against mine.

We danced that way for a few heartbeats until she said, "I think you'd better get undressed."

She lay on top of the quilt while I did my best not to imitate Jacques Clouseau in the shedding of clothes.

"My, my," she said when I crawled in next to her.

"Okay?"

"Hmmmm. You forgot to turn off the light."

"I like to see what I'm getting into."

"Charming," she said. "Can we get on with it now?"

I'm not exactly an amateur when it comes to the mattress Olympics, but Pillow surprised me with her wild abandon, as awkward as it was insatiable. She was obviously no stranger to lovemaking, but she set about the work as if it was all new to her. When it was over, I didn't feel disgusted. More like abashed, as if I'd deflowered an abbess.

I awoke around three. Even in sleep, she had covered her neck with her hand. I kissed her gently. She opened her eyes, blinking as if surprised to find me still there.

"We need our rest," she purred drowsily, stretching her arms to the top of the bedpost. "Big day tomorrow."

"Where are we meeting the professor?"

"At his rugby club. He's refereeing a junior-side match in the morning and will see us afterward."

"I'm an old boy rugger myself."

"Do tell."

I started to recount my exploits with the Eagles, but before I could describe the torpedo pass that set up my first try for the Eagles, she climbed on top of me. There aren't many ways to shut me up once I get going on rugby, but she managed to find one.

"Are you all right?" she asked with a wicked smile once she'd crawled off my shattered corpse.

"Let's just say I know how a stallion feels when it gets broken in."

"An apt analogy," she said, reaching for a final touch. "Am I a good lover?"

I laughed.

"What's so funny?"

"Yes, Pillow, and tomorrow I'll have the scars to prove it."

Her smile faded.

"That was stupid," I said.

"You meant nothing by it."

I sat up and brushed the hair back from her forehead.

"Still, I'm sorry."

She looked out to the harbor. then muttered something unintelligible before disappearing into the bathroom.

I got into my clothes and waited for her to come out.

"Pillow?"

I heard the hissing noise of the shower being

turned on. I opened the door, listened for a moment. Then I quietly shut it without going in.

The rain had stopped by the time I left the Wellesley Club. It was just before sunrise and the night sky was clear and fresh. I gazed at the Southern Cross and the other unfamiliar stars as I walked along the brick path bordering the harbor. At one point I stopped to read a plaque, one of many along the way that the city council had sponsored. It was by a Wellington poet named James Baxter who wrote in 1919:

> *I saw the Maori Jesus*
> *Walking on Wellington Harbour.*
> *He wore blue dungarees.*
> *His beard and hair were long.*
> *His breath smelled of mussels and paraoa.*
> *When he smiled it looked like the dawn.*

I continued along the wharf, passing the museum and the city hall, and made it to the Duxton without encountering the Maori Jesus, the Mongrel Mob, or the youth who had cradled the broken-winged tern.

When I finally fell asleep, my dreams were haunted by the memory of Pillow's muffled sobbing behind the shower curtain. I felt dirty as hell.

Chapter 12

At noon the next day, Pillow, all business again, drove me down the Hutt Road between steep forested hills and the bay into the town of Lower Hutt.

After parking in the tree-lined lot of the Petone Recreation Ground, she led me toward a two-story concrete grandstand. To get to it, we had to skirt around the sidelines of a pitch on which a junior Petone team and a visiting side were well into the last half of a match. Most of the players on both squads had Maori features. I couldn't help contrasting these fit, wholesome kids with the loathsome brutes I'd encountered the day before in downtown Wellington.

I followed Pillow to the top of the stands to a door that declared "Members Only," and we entered a broad open room similar to traditional rugby pubs I'd seen from Wexford to Johannesburg in my touring days.

Cheaply framed photographs of past heroes and championship teams filled two pine-paneled walls.

Middle-aged men clustered around tall Formica tables sharing war stories and pitchers of beer. In a corner close to a packed trophy case, two elderly gents wearing threadbare sweaters and striped club ties hovered over a backgammon board. A tennis match being shown on a fifty-inch flat television screen above them went unnoticed. Anchoring the north end was a long, marble-topped bar where an immense man pulled pints of lager for three women, two Maori and one *pakeha*, a non-Maori New Zealander. They were dressed in identical windbreakers emblazoned with Petone RFC.

Five gray-haired men of varying girth sat in metal folding chairs in front of three large windows, observing the action on the field below. The badges pinned on their blazers indicated they were selectors, scouts whose decisions could lead to a coveted All Blacks jersey for an exceptionally talented young player.

When we approached the bar, the bearded giant behind it beamed upon recognizing Pillow.

"*Kia ora koe punua ngeru?*"

How are you, Kitten?

"*Ka pai.*"

Great.

I stared bewilderedly as the two leaned over the bar to press their noses together, followed by an animated discussion in the Maori language. It wasn't until then that I realized that Pillow's dusky coloring, striking profile, and statuesque body weren't of the Mediterranean variety. When she lapsed back into English for my benefit, she'd even traded her Scottish accent for the Kiwi version.

"Mike Bevan," she said. "Meet my old mate, Kia

Parker."

Shaking the giant's hand was like surrendering my fingers to an ice crusher.

"What you down here for?" he asked, turning his massive head back to Pillow.

"To see Professor Middleditch. You think we came for your hui burgers?"

Kia grimaced. "You hurt my feelings with that talk. Maybe you want some sea anemone soup. Good for the bowels. I caught a couple of flounders yesterday. Keepin' 'em fresh in a water safe. Get some celery, crushed pineapples, and throw in a couple baked potatoes. Make you a real dinner. You got time?"

"I wish."

"Pah! Let me know when you do. The flounders won't keep forever."

"Maybe later. Where can we find Cattley?"

"Refereeing the match below." Kia pointed at the pitch. "He'll be up soon for his pink gin."

I peered down at the field. A high-shouldered, slender man with a thatch of thinning gray hair stood over a pile of burly youngsters. He blew his whistle, pointed at the two front rows who had caused the scrum to collapse, then motioned for the sides to form up and commence shoving again.

Kia took out a couple of frosted pint glasses and poured us drafts of Moa stout. He pulled one for himself and raised a toast.

"Kia *ora koe*."

Good health to you.

While we clinked glasses, three teenage boys wearing rugby gear sauntered into the club, rolling their heads in rhythm to whatever music was playing through their iPod earphones. They took a table farthest from the window and casually dropped their scruffy kit bags on the floor, much to the annoyance of the older regulars.

"From Otago," Kia said, nodding in their direction. "They got the next match with our under-nine-teens. Surly bunch of hori—trailer trash—if you ask me. That big one with the kuru spiral pendant, he's right bad. Used to be with the Bees. Mebbe still."

"Bees?" I asked, confused.

"Youth gang. Wannabes for the Mongrel Mob who do the running for the older blokes."

"Ahh, come on, Kia," Pillow said. "Odds are he's no better or worse than you were at that age."

"You been gone too long, Kitten. Nowadays they think getting these kids into tikanga programs will fix bad habits. It takes more than some old fella trying to teach traditional values at a Disneyfied excuse for a marae."

"I saw some of that action yesterday at the City Center plaza," I said. "A hundred gangbangers going after each other with chains and axes in broad daylight."

"Not uncommon these days," Kia said. "The 'Dogs' around Wellington never used to stray outside Porirua. Kept to themselves, even in Cannons Creek. No more. And it ain't just the Mongrel Mob and Black Power. Them Samoan King Cobras from Auckland set up shop in Hutt Valley and Miramar last year. The Head Hunters are down here, too."

"Some folks excuse them," Pillow said to me. "They say they aren't as bad as they seem, that they live by a code of honor."

"Yeah," Kia snorted. "That's if you believe gang rape, killings, and drugs fit the code. There's loyalty to each other, but no respect for anything or anyone who don't wear their patch. Anyone of 'em will stomp your ass if you cross them, accidentally or otherwise. Now they got P—crystal meth—to add to their ecstasy. No values, no respect. And they blame their miserable existence on the system."

"But no guns," I pointed out.

The big man shrugged. "They got them, too. Sawed-off shotguns mostly. Just not as much firepower as in the States. Give 'em time."

"How do you two know each other?" I asked, eager to change the depressing subject.

"I met Kia at Arrowtown Primary," Pillow answered. "He was more like a bodyguard, actually. My big mouth used to get me in trouble."

"That and your looks. All the boys wanted to mess with you."

Pillow stared at her friend affectionately but accusingly as well.

"Why you move away, leave me alone like that?"

"You know why," Kia said, looking contrite for not having done more. "My papa took a job in Welly."

"It wouldn't have mattered. No stopping the Craddocks when their blood was up. They still in Rimutaka?"

"They been out four years. For good behavior, if you can believe that."

I looked out of the corner of my eye at Pillow. Her face flushed a little and her tongue played with the inside of her left cheek.

She nodded toward the door. "Ah, here's our man," she said.

A tall figure stood silhouetted against the mid-morning sunlight.

Chapter 13

Kia moved to the far end of the bar, where the three women looked like they needed another pint.

Professor Cattley Middleditch wore an expectant look as he scanned the room. His thick tortoiseshell glasses were perched on a long nose streaked with the broken capillaries of a quart-a-day drinker. Below it was a pencil-thin mustache of the type David Niven once favored.

Pillow waved to get his attention.

Seeing us, he stepped forward, gave her a brief peck on the cheek, and gingerly shook my hand. Although he was tall, Middleditch's fingers were short and thick with the yellowed nails of a smoker.

He sat down, motioned for his pink gin, and leveled his watery eyes at me. "My niece tells me you're here to help locate the Gibson journals."

"Recover the journals, Uncle Cattley."

"Of course, dear. But I rather think they belong to

more than just an individual or two. Don't you, Mr. Bevan?"

I stared blankly between the two of them, trying to adjust to what I had just heard about their relationship.

"Pillow didn't tell me that you were related."

"I'm not surprised. She loves to harbor secrets. Her mother, Esme, is my sister."

He turned to Pillow. "She'd like very much to see you."

"Why should things be any different now?"

"She has changed for the better."

"I'm relieved to hear it."

The uncomfortable silence following Pillow's heavy sarcasm ended with the delivery of his drink.

"Thank you, Kia. Nice and chilled, is it? Excellent."

The professor's lips puckered as he took a sip, quickly followed by another.

"Has Adrian Hart attempted to see you?" I asked when the glass returned to the table.

"Several times. But I've avoided him so far."

Pillow finished her beer and stood up.

"I'll let you two get acquainted while I get some fresh air. When I get back, we can talk business."

The professor sighed after she left.

"I take it mother and daughter don't get along," I remarked.

"I should know not to bring it up, but Esme insisted that I try."

"What happened between them?"

"Pillow pretended throughout her adolescence to forgive the drinking and general lack of maternal affection. It was unhealthy. When she left for university

91

in the UK, she cut all ties. Apparently she has told you little of her family."

"We're not much past the introduction stage."

Middleditch smiled to himself. He knew his niece somewhat better than that. "What do you know about her father?"

"Nothing."

"His name is Ivo Mackin and my sister was his mistress. Ivo was once one of New Zealand's wealthiest men."

"Any relation to Wetere Mackin, the All Black fullback?"

The professor's eyes widened slightly. "One and the same. He played rugger under his Maori moniker, but it made sense to emphasize his three-quarters pakeha blood as a businessman. Made his first fortune with shipping containers. But the real money came when he cornered the tin market in Malaysia. Later, he acquired saltwater conversion plants in the Middle East. Not bad for a lad from Porirua."

"I take it he was married."

Middleditch nodded. "Technically, he still is—to Millicent Praeger-Hyde, the daughter of our former Deputy Prime Minister who gave him his start in business. They have a daughter who was born three days before Penelope's delivery at the same hospital in Auckland. The newspapers had a field day when Ivo arrived with bouquets for both mothers. It's one thing for a powerful multimillionaire to cavort discreetly with call girls, quite another to openly acknowledge his mistress and illegitimate daughter. This isn't France."

He stopped briefly to signal Kia for another gin, then continued.

"Ivo, being Ivo, claimed not to be fazed by the

publicity and soldiered on, overextending his business empire, bullying partners and shareholders alike. He'd become poison to Millicent's family and colleagues in the upper realms of business. Their ostracism cut deep and wide.

"Over time, his Midas touch deserted him. The tin market collapsed and his desalinization plants in the Emirates were nationalized. His personal fortune, once valued at half a billion dollars, dwindled to a third of that. The final nail in the coffin came five years ago when he was indicted in Australia for his role in a price-fixing scheme that cheated customers and suppliers out of one hundred million dollars. Ivo fought the case and lost, costing him treble damages. Forced to sell his companies, he turned half of the proceeds over to his wife and legitimate daughter. Then, for all practical purposes, he turned his back on the world. He headed to Hawaii before he eventually ended up in Paradise."

"I don't follow. Are you saying Mackin is dead?"

"Oh, certainly not," the professor said, downing his drink. "Even if it were true, Ivo's sins wouldn't admit him past heaven's gates. The wily devil set up a traditional Maori compound in Mount Aspiring National Park."

"Wouldn't the government control everything there?"

"There are exceptions. The New Zealand government, through the Waitangi Tribunal, started returning lost ancestral lands to Maori in the 1990s. Ivo used his great-grandfather's position as chief of the mountain Kati Mamoe tribe to regain ownership of an isolated valley known as the Land of Tears."

"Does he have title to it?"

"That's pretty much the case. Or soon will be. The idea was to have transparent, effective tribal governance of these returned areas. But Ivo wasn't about to answer to a tribal council. He still had friends in parliament, particularly with the New Zealand First Party, and was personally granted hereditary rights.

"To retain the land and qualify for tax exemptions from Inland Revenue, he's recreated a community where native customs and values, tikanga Maori, supposedly rule. Ivo brought in gang members, prostitutes, and other questionable types culled from Auckland and other cities for the avowed purpose of rehabilitating them."

"Do you think it's legitimate?"

Middleditch swallowed the last of the second drink. Then he edged closer to me.

"I'd never say this to my niece, but I think what her father is doing is a bunch of claptrap. A ruse to have the taxpayers give him an incredibly valuable property. New Zealand already has a Department of Conservation. It doesn't need a pseudo traditionalist pretending to be guardian of the land. In a few weeks, Ivo's five-year trial will have passed and the federal government will transfer to him full title. Tax-free, no less."

"Assuming the people he's brought up there are merely props, what if someone wants to leave the compound?"

"Apparently, few wish to. If a person is expelled or decides to leave, he or she tends to become a lost soul shortly after returning to their old haunts."

"Are you saying they're brainwashed?"

"I don't know what to call it, Mr. Bevan. But something happens in that Maori Shangri-La to lead a person to will his own destruction once outside it."

I thought of that empty shell of a young man in Wellington with the injured tern.

Pillow's return to the room interrupted his tale.

"Some things never change," she said, sitting down. "I went to primary school with those girls. Arataki's having her eighth child and Betty Mura refuses to file a restraining order against her brutal shit of a husband. I'm glad I left when I did."

She signaled Kia to bring her another beer.

Turning to her uncle, she said, "Well?"

He pretended not to understand. "What's that, dear?"

"Have you brought Michael up-to-date?"

Middleditch hesitated. "I only got to the rise and decline of your father's far-flung enterprises."

"Please. Michael has come a long way to help."

"This is neither the time nor place to discuss the matter."

He shifted his heavy-lidded eyes reluctantly to me. "For now, I'll just say Ivo approached me five years ago. He seemed obsessed with James Cook; wanted me to tell him everything I knew about the captain's last voyage. At one point he casually mentioned having the memoir of a marine who sailed on the *HMS Resolution*."

He signed a chit for his drinks and, getting up to leave, said to me, "I suggest you visit the Turnbull Library this afternoon to conduct research on Maori mysticism and magic. You might also look for an article concerning a deathbed confession by a shipmate of Samuel Gibson. The sailor's name escapes me, but the article was in the *London Gazetteer*, circa 1790 or thereabouts. You'll find it most interesting, perhaps even helpful. Then join Penelope and Hart at my office at ten in the morning when I'll have more to say on the matter."

I glanced at Pillow. The high neck of her blouse had slipped an inch or two. The mottled pink and gray skin that was visible seemed to pulse in time with the beating of her heart.

It suddenly occurred to me that our search might have more to do with finding her father than tracking down Hart and the journals.

But if that was the case, why drag me along? I hadn't traveled eight thousand miles to be involved in a family reunion project—particularly since my personal experience in such matters had been somewhat mixed.

Of course, as things developed, getting kith and kin to reconcile turned out to be the least of my troubles.

Chapter 14

The next morning, I took a cab to the National Library. Designed in the same brutal architectural style that had disfigured much of central London in the 1970s, the four-story cement building covered an entire block on Molesworth Street.

Recent renovations to the interior, however, had produced a charming environment worthy of the remarkable collections within it. The most noteworthy tenant was the Alexander Turnbull Library, a billion-dollar collection that was the definitive source on Pacific exploration and Maori culture.

All I knew about the indigenous people of New Zealand was that, due to their skill as warriors, they were never conquered by the British. In the modern era, that warlike nature naturally evolved into rugby prowess. But I was ignorant of other aspects of their unique culture, especially the hold that the supernatural still had on their daily lives.

I entered the Independent Reading Room, settling

at a search station under a huge mural portraying the Maori creation story. Dour purple, brown, and gray swirls contrasted in a sinuous pattern with bright orange and lemon colors representing the evolution of the universe from a formless void to the world of light. Beneath the image, I turned on the computer and began searching under the general category of "Maoridom."

The name Elsdon Best kept cropping up. Best's bio said he was an ethnologist who was the last of a small number of scholars in the twentieth century who had observed traditional Maori customs and beliefs as they were before the modern era. A treatise he'd presented to the Auckland Institute in 1901 titled "Maori Magic" looked interesting. I went to the front desk to request it and copies of the *London Gazetteer* for 1790 that Middleditch had recommended.

The ginger-haired librarian wore thick, black-rimmed eyeglasses that covered half her face. Her bulky, dark blue cardigan sweater boasted a "Save the Whales" button.

"Can I help you?" she asked indifferently.

I told her what I wanted. She called down to the archival stacks for it to be brought up.

She glanced at the Claddagh ring on my right index finger.

"You Irish?"

"Nope. American with green blood."

This produced a smile and slightly crooked teeth.

"My granddad was a Yank Marine stationed in Welly during the war. Fell in love with my grandmother and in 1946 came back just like he promised."

"Sounds romantic."

"Yeah. Granddad missed the States though. He said that living permanently in New Zealand was like going to a party and dancing all night with your mother. But having grabbed him once, Granny wouldn't tempt fate by letting him return for a visit. The police band played 'Sweet Home Chicago' at his funeral."

She got a little misty.

"My name's Beryl, by the way. Beryl Cowper."

"And I'm Mike Bevan."

We shook hands. Hers was soft and delicate. Before I could learn more about her, a young scholar with a pointy beard demanded help logging on to a site. Beryl excused herself to help him.

While waiting for the treatise to be brought up, I perused the document sign-out sheet. In addition to a dozen Maori names and thirty or more English, Scottish, and Irish ones, there was Mr. Fong from Fuzhou, China; Miss Aja Bek from Zandvoort, the Netherlands; Madame Adriana Hruska of Budapest; and Dr. Ion Paleologue, lately of Bridgetown, Barbados, following reassignment from Ovidius University of Constanta, Romania.

While absentmindedly pondering why Dr. Paleologue was exiled to a Caribbean Isle, I noticed another name that nearly froze my esophagus.

Midway down the column, dated the previous week, was the semi legible signature of William Bartow, town and country not included.

I shoved the ledger under Beryl's nose.

"Do you remember seeing this man? It's important."

"So we can see," the pointy beard huffed.

"Just a moment," Beryl said, adjusting her glasses

to study the ledger. There was a long pause before she looked back to me.

"I vaguely remember him."

Another, shorter, pause. "He seemed a rather odd duck. Quite keen on Captain Cook. He had us bring up several items from the stacks."

"Thanks," I told her. "If you see him again, please don't let on that I was here. We're rivals when it comes to eighteenth-century exploration. You know how it is."

"Sure thing," she said, returning my wink as an assistant appeared carrying a manila folder for her. He had a concerned look on his face.

"Sorry, Beryl," he said. "But all twelve issues of the *London Gazetteer* for 1790 are missing."

Another eyeglass adjustment followed.

"Right. Thank you, James."

Then to me, "I'm sorry, but it seems that particular year has been misfiled. I'll contact you as soon as we locate it. Please sign the checkout ledger and include your local address."

I left my signature and the name of the Duxton Hotel thirty lines below Bartow's scrawl and returned to my chair in the Reading Room with the Elsdon Best document. Glancing at the first page of the loose-leaf treatise, I was surprised to see it hadn't been typed but was handwritten in the author's elegant cursive style.

I began to read.

Deaths from *makutu*, or witchcraft, were numerous in the days of yore and still occur even in these times of the pakeha Europeans. Tapu, roughly meaning a spiritual restriction or implied prohibition, and *makutu* were practically the laws of Maoridom.

The old-time Maori had to carefully guard himself

against magic rites, against infringing the laws of tapu, because a hair of his head, a shred of his clothing, a portion of the earth whereon he had left his footprint would, in the hands of an enemy, be sufficient to bring about his death.

In every walk of life, during every action, whether eating, drinking, sleeping, or taking his walks abroad, whether among friends or foes, death walked side by side with him, awaiting the opportunity to strike him down and dispatch his spirit to the gloomy underworld —the Po, or realm of darkness, of oblivion.

In the early part of the recent century, a belief developed among the Maori of the southern iwi that the spirit of a Hawaiian god which, fleeing its enemies, took refuge in their mountains...

"Looking for this?" a vaguely familiar voice said from behind my chair.

A tattered, canvas-backed journal suddenly appeared next to my right hand on the table.

I jerked my head around to find Adrian Hart looking down at me with a stage conjurer's grin. He'd lost a considerable amount of weight. His eyes, underlined by deep shadows, gleamed unnaturally.

"And this!"

The second Gibson journal joined the first.

I leaped from the chair, shouting so loud that Beryl Cowper, seeming more than a little perplexed at our joyous reunion, hissed for me to quiet down from across the room.

"How on earth did you get them?" I whispered, leading Hart by the arm to a corner near the staircase.

"Elementary, really," he replied with a feigned cheerfulness. "I assumed Bartow would eventually turn up here, but I'd almost given up hope until last week when he emerged, Orpheus-like, from the stacks in the basement. I watched him pick up his briefcase at the front counter. Then I followed him to a parking lot off Molesworth Street, surprising him as he unlocked his car door."

"Bartow didn't put up a fight?" I asked as we sat on a sofa so small that our knees touched.

"What, that febrile jellyfish? He must have realized long ago the futility of profiting from the theft. Indeed, I felt rather sorry for him. Gave him an earful, of course, citing all the trouble he'd caused us while destroying his own reputation. He'll probably go on to pilfer the Magna Carta someday, but I hadn't the heart to turn him into the police."

"You must be joking!"

"Oh, I'll let them know I recovered our property, but what's the point of inflicting further damage on the poor sod? I squeezed the price of my airline ticket out of him, leaving him just enough to do his mischief somewhere else."

"But what about Holt House? And Clive Sexton? They've suffered quite a black eye because of him."

"Their reputations aren't my concern. They hired the bloody thief and, along with their investigators, did damn little to search for him. Soon enough, the insurance company will be demanding the trifle amount it paid for my loss. Before they come calling, I'll continue to use their money to seek the third journal."

I was bothered by Hart's lack of ethics. And surprised, too, that he'd let the man who had caused us such misery get off scot-free. Bartow, unable to secure legitimate employment in the only profession he knew, would certainly continue to wreak havoc on the notoriously naïve community of antiquarian book lovers.

But having Gibson's first journal in my hands again made it easy to forgive Hart's puzzling decision. After all, he'd caught the fish; maybe it was his right to toss him back after recovering the goods.

"We must tell Pillow," I said. "She's been terribly worried about you."

"Not to worry. I just came from seeing her at the Wellesley. How do you think I found you here?"

As we stood to leave, I said, "Thank you, Adrian. I had my doubts about you."

He seemed touched by this. A bit of color returned to his face, and his smile seemed genuine.

"Indeed, Bevan. You aren't the first to mark me as a cad. I've sharp corners, but I'm a good mate when it comes to trouble."

He extended his hand, and I took it.

Now that we were bosom buddies, he suggested that a walk in the fresh air was what we needed to get better acquainted. His hotel was on the way to mine.

"Sure," I said.

"We were born too late, you and I," Hart said as we walked past the vintage shops, boutiques, and art galleries of the Lambton Quay road. "The likes of Thomas Wise and Lord Rothchild are long gone, never to return."

"I know Rothchild cornered the market on eighteenth-century manuscripts, but I've never heard of Wise."

"Ah, Bevan, you have so much to learn. Thomas Wise presided over the Bibliographical Society and was a member of the Roxburghe Club, the most exclusive of all book-collecting fraternities. He was never rich, but his uncommon foresight, shrewdness, and acquisi-

tive skill made him more than a match for the likes of
J.P. Morgan and Huntington."

"I take it you've modeled your career on him."

"Indeed, as far as the new technology allows."

After that, we talked about Frances Steloff and the
grand old days of the Gotham Book Mart (he was
delighted to learn I'd encountered Edward Gorey
there) and followed that with a discussion of taste and
method, the distinction between fashion and style, and
the importance of obtaining a copy in the exact state it
was issued.

By the time we reached his hotel on Johnston
Street, I felt I'd earned an honorary Master of Arts
degree in book collecting. With a comradely wave of
his hand, he disappeared through the revolving door. I
wedged Gibson's journal in the small of my back
between my belt and waistband and headed for the
Duxton with a new lightness in my step.

A hundred meters later, on a quiet side street
between Johnston and Featherstone Quay, a stout
young woman with monstrous bosoms and the arms of
a linebacker popped from the doorway of a shuttered
building.

"Oy, big feller!" she gurgled, wiggling her bottom
in a way that would have made any self-respecting pole
dancer weep. "Want a piece of this?"

Even if my taste ran to practitioners of the ancient
trade (which, I hasten to add, it doesn't—not
anymore), I would have kept at the far end of the
bench from this one.

She was as common as an NBA tattoo, but what
she lacked in looks and charm she made up in
strength. I'd barely slipped from her lunging embrace
when she was back at it, clutching my crotch with

one viselike claw while the other mauled my backside.

I wasn't liking this one bit, especially when she rammed me up against a door and growled, "Okay, boys, he's all yours!"

Looking furtively over my shoulder, I saw two men materialize from the shadows like a pair of well-dressed rats.

They weren't particularly large, but wiry, and definitely not gangbangers. One even wore a sport coat—Harris Tweed, I think it was—a crisp white shirt and a tie with regimental stripes. The other man looked like all the other office workers I'd seen in the square before the ruckus began the previous day. My first thought was they had assumed I was attacking the fair maiden and were performing their civic duty to save her.

"Hold on, gents," I squawked while jerking loose of the harlot. "I'm an American!"

As if that had anything to do with innocence.

But then I noticed the knives. And the icy glint in their eyes.

I'm not exactly Bo Jackson in the forty-yard dash, but I can be quick for the first three strides off the ball, and there remained a dozen feet between us. I plowed into the first man with my shoulder, ducked his murderous swipe of the blade, grabbed his wrist with one hand and the seat of his pants with the other, then hurled him headfirst into the brick wall.

If you've ever smashed pumpkins on Halloween, you'd have a fair idea of the mess that made.

All well and good, but his partner, having determined I was no stranger to alley brawls, kept his distance without retreating. To turn and run in that narrow lane meant giving him a clear shot at my back. There was nothing for it but to grit my teeth, snarl something unseemly about his mother, and stare him down in a Mexican standoff. Not a brilliant tactic even if you have a weapon; ridiculous when you don't.

I still remember that grinning, feral face, studying me like I was just another ring in a straw target as he put one leg in front of the other and drew back his arm. A moment later, a ninja-style Boker blade whispered past my ear, close enough for me to foreswear close haircuts evermore. Before he could hurl a second knife, I snatched the journal from behind my back and flung it at his chest. He wheeled back on his heels as if struck by a brick. I was on him in a microsecond. Dodging the slashing blade, I countered with a series of short, fast jabs until his eyes rolled back. I finished the work with an uppercut, and he sank to the concrete like last week's laundry.

Funny how a touch of disciplined resistance can take the stuffing out of even professional killers. And professionals are what I figured they were, having defended enough of the species in Jackson County courtrooms.

The first man still lay crumpled by the brick wall. The lady, presumably paid in advance for having set me up, was long gone. I scooped up Gibson's journal and left the street feeling a little less light-footed than before.

Outside the federal government building that the locals call "the Beehive" (but looks more like an upside-down wedding cake) I summoned a police officer to give an account of the attack. When it came to my description of the perpetrators—"A heavyset, scantily clothed woman, and two clean-shaven, office-worker types, one maybe six feet tall, maybe a hundred-eighty pounds, mid-thirties, the other about the same"—she put away her pen, asked to see my passport, then suggested that I avoid whores and pimps for the remainder of my stay in beautiful downtown Wellywood.

Chapter 15

When Pillow picked me up in her rental car the next morning, I was still mulling over why two strangers would try to kill me. The only thing I'd decided was that I wasn't ready to share the experience with folks I didn't know all that well. For the time being, that meant Pillow and her uncle, as well as Adrian Hart.

"You've known for a long time that your father had the third journal, haven't you?" I demanded as she pulled into a parking lot in the suburb of Kelburn. On a hill high above us loomed the crenelated spires of the University of Victoria.

"No," she insisted testily. "I had no idea until Cattley mentioned the possibility to me."

"When was that?"

"The day before I introduced him to you at the rugby club."

"What about Adrian? He told me in San Francisco that he learned that a person in Hawaii likely bought the third from a Cotswold dealer, but he insisted the trail ended there. Do you think he lied to me? That he knew it was your father even before he left the UK looking for Bartow?"

She shrugged. "All I know is that he believes it now and intends for my uncle to confirm it."

The arrival of Hart on a moped cut her off from saying more.

"Hello, chums," he said, as pleased to see me as when we shared our walk from the library. "Let us seek enlightenment from Olympus."

His words conjured images of Sisyphus while we trudged up a hundred or more steps to the marble-arched entrance of the anthropology department. Naturally, the ancient elevator was closed for repairs, so I felt like we'd climbed Everest upon reaching the fifth floor.

While I gasped for breath, Pillow tapped her knuckles on the oak door numbered 551, and the now familiar voice of Cattley Middleditch invited us in.

The office was typical for a tenured college faculty member if, that is, your professor happens to collect shrunken heads, New Guinea penis gourds, and a delightful assortment of genital cuffs from the second-century Han Dynasty. These artifacts were artfully arranged on a ledge beneath a pane-glass window offering a fine view of Wellington and the harbor.

Hundreds of books on floor-to-ceiling shelves lined two adjacent walls. The professor hadn't bothered to display evidence of his academic degrees, but a small framed ribbon of the Order of St. Michael and St. George set atop the windowsill trumped any number of sheepskins he might have hung. An industrial-style kettle lamp hovered over a wide mahogany desk covered with papers, notebooks, and fifteen or so books wedged between a pair of iron ingots.

Middleditch rose from behind this desk as we entered, shook our hands, and urged us to sit in extra chairs that had been lugged in before our arrival. A coffee cup with a thin layer of clear liquid sat next to a laptop computer. I caught the whiff of mouthwash and gin, an oily combination reminiscent of Sunday mornings in the kitchen with my hungover old man.

Hart began the meeting with an obsequious attempt at flattery.

"Allow me to say, Professor, that I found *Farewell to Elysium* to be a fascinating book. Most extraordinary indeed."

Middleditch acknowledged this with a faint strain of the facial muscles. "Do you even recall what it was about?"

Hart looked as if he'd been pinched on the ass.

"Certainly," he answered defensively. "Your thesis was that the Hawaiians believed Cook to be super-natural."

"It's rather more than that. But, yes, the priests thought he was Lono, the incarnation of their fertility god in the flesh."

"Could they really have believed that mumbo jumbo back then?" Hart asked.

"As much as today's Christians believe Jesus was the son of God."

"I suppose it depends on which religion you're born into."

The professor nodded, but his eyes searched the Englishman's face across an abyss of distrust.

"Are you a nonbeliever, Mr. Hart?"

"Not necessarily. But I've always been one to hedge my bets."

"And you, Mr. Bevan?"

"I still have a lot of questions the nuns couldn't knock out of me."

Middleditch sniffed, then picked up the replica of a monkey paw—at least, I think it was a replica—that served as a paperweight on his desk.

"Penelope tells me," he began, shifting his eyes to Hart, "that you came to New Zealand to catch the thief who stole her journal."

Hart's stitched smile rapidly faded. "Also owned by me, Professor. I recovered Bevan's as well."

"Yes, of course. Congratulations to all." Middleditch shut his eyes in a sort of prolonged blink before adding: "I presume you'll return to your respective countries now you have what you came for?"

"On the contrary," Hart said. "We intend to find the third one, which Ivo Mackin possesses."

Middleditch's response was noncommittal. "Assuming he has it and would allow you access, what do you hope to accomplish?"

"What else," Hart said impatiently. "But to convince him to join us in publishing all three documents."

"Purely for the edification of scholars, no doubt? You've no interest in making money?"

Pillow jumped to Hart's defense. "We aren't entirely without financial motive, Uncle."

"Best to be honest in that regard," Middleditch said, scratching his chin with the monkey claw. "From my encounter with him, I got the distinct impression he never intends to share the journal. Not for you, Penelope, not for anyone."

"Are you certain he has it?" I asked.

"I didn't completely believe it then, but I do now. Undoubtedly, the thief who stole the first two believes it as well."

"Go on," Hart urged.

"Five years ago, I didn't give much thought to why Ivo was so obsessed with Cook. Then last December a student of mine, a very troubled lad who has since gone missing, claimed to have learned of the packet during his brief stay at the marae in the valley."

"Did he actually see it or hear what it contained?"

"No, Mr. Hart. Apparently, only Ivo and his chief adviser had access to its secrets."

"What sort of secrets?" I asked.

Middleditch returned the monkey paw to its original place on the table, then looked at me with those watery eyes. I could tell that he was struggling to control his impulse to pull a bottle from the desk drawer.

"As I told you yesterday, Ivo visited me in this very room after spending a year in Hawaii. While he never mentioned the journal directly, he made continual references to Cook's marine. That could only have been Sergeant Gibson, who witnessed as near as anyone the mental, physical, and, I dare say, spiritual deterioration of his captain."

Hart's glance reminded me that it was a person in Hawaii who had ordered the third journal from the Cotswold bookman.

Middleditch coughed before continuing. "Whatever Ivo discovered at Kealakekua Bay altered him profoundly. It made him susceptible to wild conjectures."

"Such as Cook planning to desert his men," Hart said, reiterating the theory he shared with me at the Marines' Memorial Club.

"Yes, but also that the great man had sexual intercourse with a daughter of the Hawaiian king."

Welcome to fairyland, I thought, as I exchanged incredulous looks with Pillow.

Hart, however, wasn't surprised. "Ivo Mackin may be bonkers, but there is a long-standing legend, mostly among Pacific Islanders of the lower orders, that Cook sired a Hawaiian child."

I looked to Middleditch for confirmation.

"Supposedly an exemplar of sexual forbearance when it came to any woman other than his wife, the captain may have succumbed to the entreaties of the Hawaiian king's daughter while off Maui. She reconnected with him six weeks later on the Big Island when her father's entourage met up with the *Resolution* at Kealakekua Bay. If it's true that the girl was pregnant, Cook would have learned of it just as the natives greeted him as Lono, their god of fertility."

"What a delicious irony," Hart crowed.

"I don't suppose the myth includes what happened to the mother and child?" Pillow asked.

"Within a year of Cook's death," Middleditch said, tamping tobacco into the walnut bowl of his pipe, "the young mother was banished to Kauai and her infant girl secretly whisked away to Maui. The child was raised by simple farmers, but the rumors persisted that the granddaughter of the gods of war and fertility walked the earth. This didn't bode well for the girl, who grew to womanhood during the reign of King

Kamehameha the Great. Her *tapu*"—he closed his eyes on the word—"was so great that no mortal could risk killing her. But neither could the new king afford to have her around."

The professor put a match to the edge of the bowl and sucked several times on the lip before getting it started. Satisfied with his efforts, he leaned back in his chair to watch the smoke curl toward the overhead fan.

"In 1791, the same year the Hawaiian Islands were united under his rule, she was put on an American whaling ship headed for the South Island of New Zealand.

"The young woman was adopted by a powerful tribe, married a warrior, and lived in the shadow of the Alps before dying in childbirth. The baby survived to become chief of the Ngai Kati Mamoe."

Pillow moved her eyes from Middleditch to me and back to her uncle. "Mamoe is my father's iwi, his tribe."

Middleditch relit the pipe. "It's only a myth, Penelope."

"What evidence exists to support any of it?" I asked.

"None, unless Gibson was aware of intercourse between Cook and the girl. Even then, I'd doubt he'd have had the gall to record it."

"Did this supposed love child have a moniker?" Hart asked.

Professor Middleditch took a final pull on his pipe before returning it to its cradle by the ashtray. "They called her Linea."

Pillow gasped. "That name has been given to women in my family for generations."

"Yes, Pen. Your father believes that he—and you—

are direct descendants of James Cook and the daughter of King Kalani'opu'u."

After several moments of silence, Hart rose from his chair, laid the palms of his hands on the desk, and looked directly into Middleditch's eyes.

"I can't believe you haven't tried to go up there to confirm this."

"It's a physical impossibility for me. The compound is within a mountain valley accessible by helicopter. To get there requires landing in a narrow gorge, followed by a difficult mountain trek to the Waipara River. Beyond that the area is controlled by Ivo's people. No one gets past the threshold to the marae without an invitation. I don't happen to be on that list."

Hart moved from the desk to place his hand on Pillow's shoulder. "But I'll bet she is."

She brushed his arm away, turned her head slowly, and looked at me.

I nodded.

"Then we'd best get packing," she said.

That evening we made arrangements to fly to Queenstown on New Zealand's South Island. Afterward, Pillow dropped me off at the Duxton. I'd just checked for messages at the front desk when I noticed an attractive redhead with shapely legs sitting in the lobby. She gazed at me with an amused look before I realized it was Beryl Cowper. The librarian had shed her owl-like glasses and dowdy attire for contacts and a low-cut black dress.

I approached, prepared to tell her how smashing she looked, but she spoke first.

"I thought you didn't want that man to see you."

"What man?"

"The man you were whooping and hollering with at the library."

"You mean Adrian Hart?"

"Well, if you say so. All I know is that he's the one who signed the ledger as Mr. William Bartow last week."

Chapter 16

That tidbit of information earned Beryl a steak dinner at The Green Parrot on Taranaki Street. Afterward we ended up for the craic at Molly Malones Pub near Te Oro Park.

The Celtic diaspora is everywhere in this world—you can find a Hibernian Club behind a barbwire wall in Kabul—but I didn't expect the Kiwi version to be so...well, Irish.

Downing two pints to limber up the old larynx, I stuffed twenty NZ dollars in the jar and challenged the locals on the vocals. "Foggy Dew" started a little shaky, but I hit stride with "Dirty Old Town" and had the place singing along by the time I closed with "Four Green Fields." Tommy Makem couldn't have done it better. After I told the barkeep to apply my prize money to rounds for the house, you couldn't have found a more popular man in Welly than yours truly that night. Just ask Beryl Cowper.

Alone again in my hotel room, questions and possible answers materialized in my beer-addled brain, then just as quickly faded. None of them seemed particularly heartening from my standpoint.

My first thought was that Hart had confronted Bartow in the garage off Molesworth Street as he had claimed, obtained the journals, and, for whatever reason, assumed Bartow's identity at the library. But why the masquerade, particularly after Hart had already recovered our journals from Bartow?

Maybe it was an effort by Hart to protect the dishonest, but relatively harmless, bibliophile, allowing him a few days to clear out of the country. After all, even if Hart was willing to forgive Bartow, the police, Clive Sexton, and the folks at Holt House (not to mention yours truly) might not be.

And yet.

Pillow had been drawn back to New Zealand, a place that clearly held only unpleasant memories for her, because Hart had gone looking for Bartow and the stolen journals.

Did Hart trick Pillow into coming, "letting" her accidentally find the email stating Bartow had been seen there?

But why would Hart do that?

I could think of only one reason. Hart had already discovered that Ivo Mackin had the third journal. And Pillow was the ticket to reaching her otherwise inaccessible father. Hart knew his partner well enough to know that she would stay at the Wellesley Club when in Wellington. What he hadn't figured on, however, was that Pillow would ask me to join her in New Zealand. That made me an inconvenient fly in the Englishman's ointment should he wish to take advantage of her.

So where was Bartow if not in New Zealand? And

how, when, and where did Hart come across the two stolen journals? I had no doubt Bartow had stolen them in San Francisco. The police told us that security cameras showed him entering the Marines' Memorial Club and getting on the elevator.

More questions, more fanciful answers.

I had given Hart my room number at the club. Hart was the only one who knew—until he told Bartow. Then it was just a matter of the little book thief sneaking into my room while I was sampling whiskeys in a snug corner bar at Ninth and Dash.

Okay so far. That left the question of what happened to Bartow after he'd delivered my journal to Hart.

I'm cursed by an active imagination. It sets up camp in my head and comes back whether I want it to or not, opening the door to ten more spirits, each more troubling than the next. Whether I liked it or not, the mind gremlins led to a conclusion that I dreaded.

Bartow had never left the United States. He was dead. Murdered by the man who had conspired with him to steal my journal—Adrian Hart. And those guys that tried to knife me in the side street? Was that a random mugging? Or had Hart paid them to get rid of me in the off-chance I'd be able to foil his plans?

Total conjecture, of course. Far-out speculation. All I had was a pretty librarian telling me that she thought Hart had signed in as Bartow, and off I go on these wild theories.

Certainly not enough to notify the San Francisco Police, let alone the Kiwi gendarmes.

I texted Josie Majansik instead.

She called me shortly before we left Wellington and

after she had contacted an old FBI colleague based in San Francisco.

"There's been no sighting of Bartow, dead or alive, but Customs doesn't show him having ever left the country."

"What about bodies discovered in the Bay Area over the past eighteen months?"

"At last count eighty-four," Josie said. "Half of them jumpers off the Golden Gate Bridge. Others were indigents who no one claimed. All but half a dozen have been identified. Of those, two were Hispanic males and another, a Cambodian woman, who was found buried upside down in the Berkeley hills. I'm waiting for the agent to send me a more detailed report of the three others. They were Caucasian, extremely decomposed. One of them, a male who washed up at Point Reyes last year, had been a meal for sharks. No head, arms, or legs. Only a trunk."

"Thanks for trying, Josie. In case your pal comes up with anything else, I'll have to get it by early tomorrow New Zealand time. There are no cell towers where we're going."

"I got it. But just so you know, Agent Henderson's going way out of bounds digging into working files outside his department."

"I understand. Are we still open for business?"

"The shop's hanging in there. How's the situation with Mrs. Wilkes?"

"Fair to partly cloudy."

"Do you trust her?"

"Not enough to share my suspicions with."

"Mike."

"Yeah, babe?"

"Based on what you've told me, Hart is a liar, a thief, and most likely a murderer. You don't trust the woman who coaxed you there. You located her scumbag partner and got your journal back. Mission accomplished on all counts. Time to come home."

"Wasn't it you who said something about 'stick-to-itiveness'?"

"Yes, love. And you've found what you went looking for."

"Not really."

"But…"

"I made a promise to Pillow that I'd help her."

"Oh, pleeeze. You don't know whether she's a damsel in distress or the second head of the dragon. Get your ass back here!"

"I'm going to see this all the way through, Josie. Access to Gibson's final journal could save Riverrun."

"What about us?"

"It's all about us, sweetheart. How better to prove to you that I'm not one to jump first onto any damn lifeboat?"

After a few seconds of long-distance sniffling, Josie said, "Me and my friggin' metaphors! They're going to get both of us in trouble one of these days."

"I'll be okay."

"Sure you will, Mike. I only wish I was there to watch your back."

"How's Feklar?"

"Miserable. He hasn't brought a dead mouse to our bed since you left."

Chapter 17

I always intend to check out the great landmarks, majestic cathedrals, and fabulous museums wherever my travels take me. But I usually don't.

There's always something else that grabs my attention, like a chance encounter with John Cleese in a Grasmere pub that nixed a visit to Wordsworth's Dove Cottage, or missing a tour of Evita's Pink Palace to watch an impromptu tango contest in the La Boca section of Buenos Aires.

I'm also not one to gush while gazing at Niagara Falls or the Grand Canyon.

Don't get me wrong. I love the outdoors. My soul lifts whenever I'm near a pristine body of water, forested hill, or open prairie. It's just that when I see those beauties, I figure that's how everything should be, then wonder why we tart up the areas we choose to live in.

But of all the countries I've seen in this world, there is one place where human beings have mostly managed to reside in harmony with their natural surroundings: the alpine lake districts of New Zealand's South Island.

Queenstown, the gateway to this beautiful land, lies atop an inlet at the southern end of a fifty-mile serpentine body of water. It's a neatly groomed community of flowered parks and handsome cottages surrounded by snowcapped peaks and verdant pine forests.

Think of the Scottish Highlands, except the mountains are bigger, the cascading waterfalls higher, the valleys greener, and the sun shinier. The citizens are a hardy bunch who regard weekends spent bungee jumping, parasailing, and extreme skiing preferable to playing golf. They're uncommonly friendly as well and more than happy to share their good tidings with strangers, as long as they don't linger too long.

Middleditch had secured one night's lodging for us at a bed-and-breakfast aptly named Bellissima. The century-old house was a converted water mill filled with aboriginal art, rustic furniture, and a well-stocked wine cellar. The owners were Australians named John and Melinda Pritchard, who gave up the bright lights of Sydney to settle in this sun-splashed Eden where even the air, infused with the fragrance of ripening fruit from the surrounding apple and peach orchards, was intoxicating.

That evening after dinner, we sat in Adirondack chairs next to a gurgling stream gazing at the Southern Cross and drinking wine.

Despite the ambiance of the setting, Pillow seemed somewhat subdued. Adrian Hart, on the other hand, was downright giddy, regaling our hosts with examples of the ignorance of American book collectors as compared to their British counterparts.

"Cynthia Clampton, supposedly the doyenne of

the New England antiquarian market, tried to pawn off on me a 1903 edition of Betty Grey as a true first even though the letter P didn't precede the author's name. Can you believe it?"

That sort of thing.

I could only imagine—there's that beastly word again—the reason for Hart's high spirits: he was near his goal of dispatching me, and maybe Pillow, in order to snatch the third journal for himself.

"So," John Pitchard asked Pillow after Hart had stopped yapping long enough for him to change the subject. "Cattley tells me you're going up to Ivo Mackin's camp for wayward Maoris. Any particular reason?"

"You know that Ivo is my father, don't you?" She seemed offended.

"Yes, of course."

"Forgive my husband," Melinda interjected as she laid a tray of cheese and crackers on a bench in front of us. "He's a former journalist and bad habits die hard."

"I'd just like to see him," Pillow said, softening. "It's been many years."

The couple briefly made eye contact with each other.

A few seconds of uncomfortable silence followed before John said, "Quite understandable. It's wise to take your friends with you, however. The terrain can be quite difficult, particularly if the weather closes in. A group of Chinese engineers were lost for three days recently before being found half frozen on the Bonar Glacier. I take it you've secured a guide?"

"Indeed, I have," Hart said. "A chap named

Daigleish Kildare. He'd already planned to take goods up there before I contacted him."

Now it was Pillow and me who exchanged looks. This was news to us.

"Interesting," John said, obviously unimpressed. "Who, may I ask, recommended him?"

Hart impersonated a blank wall.

"Enough with the interrogatories," Melinda scolded, tugging at her husband's arm. "Let them finish the wine and cheese so they can get their rest before heading into those lovely mountains."

The next morning, John drove us forty kilometers along a smooth asphalt road to the village of Glenorchy that sits at the top of Lake Wakatipu.

"What's with this area and the Maoris?" I asked John on the way. "We haven't seen many brown faces since arriving in Queenstown."

"Their Polynesian ancestors first settled on the coastal regions of the North Island where food was plentiful. The mountainous interior down here was considered too cold for people used to temperate Pacific islands. As time passed, however, the hardier members of the Ngati Mamoe and Ngai Tahu tribes migrated south seeking the highly valued jade called pounamu."

"What happened to them?"

"During the gold rush of the last century, they worked for pakeha-owned mining companies at near slave wages. When the mines tapped out, most of them, like Ivo's grandfather, left for jobs in Christchurch or cities in the North."

"That helps to explain his desire to reclaim the land," I said.

"Yes," Pillow said. "But I doubt that's the only reason."

Except for the scenery surrounding it, Glenorchy wasn't much to speak of. Past the Mobil Gas station, twenty or thirty prefab houses were clustered around a three-room schoolhouse. Main Street consisted of a general store, a weather-beaten pub, and a dingy post office. The only structure that looked built to last was a limestone library set in front of a tiny municipal park. There might have been a church and a cemetery somewhere in the vicinity, but I didn't see them.

At the edge of a marsh at the edge of the lake was a ramshackle trailer park where John said the transient population of backpack guides, jet boat drivers, and road construction crews lived. Kayaks and life jackets littered their weedy front yards, and wash lines groaned under a colorful assortment of bras, panties, socks, and men's heavy woolen shirts.

Robust guys and gals glided among the trailers, stopping to share the latest news, laughing, touching, and kissing before heading into town or to the boat dock. One or two women might have been pregnant, but there seemed a noticeable absence of children and older folk.

From the standpoint of its natural setting, Aspen and the ski villages of the Haute-Savoie had nothing on this jewel at the top end of the crystal blue, glacier-fed lake. What the area did not have, however, was reasonable proximity to major cities.

"Every decade or so," John told us, "a developer shows up offering to build a ski resort. It never gets past the city council. Adding traffic and froufrou resorts doesn't square with the locals, especially the sheep and cattle ranchers around Paradise Flat."

He turned to Pillow, adding, "Your mother's one of the more vocal ones on that subject."

She flinched as if he had mentioned a hanging. No more was said on the subject. For the rest of the way, she sat motionless, staring stonily ahead until John pulled the car up to a steel Quonset hut. A wooden sign with carved letters declared it to be the regional office for the Department of Conservation.

"Get your maps and permits here," he said. "I made arrangements for the jet boat to pick you up in half an hour."

As we got out of the car, John tugged on Pillow's sleeve.

"Go on," she said to Hart and me. "I'll catch up."

I followed Hart into the hut. A sturdy red-haired woman in a khaki uniform stepped from behind a curtain that separated the kitchen from the office. She held a steaming pot of tea in her right hand.

"Hello, gents," she said cheerfully. "Care for a spot of Glenorchy mud?"

"If it's Earl Grey," Hart said in a plumy accent that was exaggerated even for him. "That would be spiffing."

His attempt at humor, if that is what it was, didn't appear to cut it with the middle-aged guardian of the National Trust.

"Right then, Lord Windersphere," she said as she pulled cups from under the counter and poured tea into them.

"Sugar?" Hart asked.

"Afraid not," she replied. "No cream, neither. Now, what can I do for you?"

"We're heading northwest through Mount Aspiring National Park."

"You'll need a permit for that."

"And that, madam, is why we are bloody well here."

She put down her cup and with it, her smile. The color in her cheeks began to match her hair.

"I'll not have that language in this office," she said. "Climbing permits are fifty dollars. That's if," she added ominously, "I feel like issuing them to foreigners. It's a World Heritage Site beyond the Dart. We have to be selective about who goes there. Don't want disreputables messing with our scenery."

"Actually," I said in a tone meant to smooth troubled waters. "We intend to take a chopper to Pearl Flat, then trek over the Matukituki Saddle to the Maori compound."

"That's not a good idea," she said.

"Why on earth not?" Hart asked.

"Private property, for one thing."

"Since when does the New Zealand government pay you to be Mr. Mackin's private gatekeeper?"

She leveled her gray-green eyes at Hart, but his underlying threat cut through her intransigence.

"I can't stop you from going, but once you get past Pearl, you're on your own. We can't always be sending out rescue parties."

"Indeed, madam. I have procured a guide, a Mr. Kildare. Where might we find him?"

She looked at Hart quizzically. Her lack of enthusiasm for Kildare matched John Pritchard's.

"You'll find the possum trader next door."

"He sells roadkill?" I asked, completely baffled.

"Oh, they're not like your American possums," she said. "More's the pity. Their fur is quite soft and beautiful, a bit like mink, but they're an ecological nightmare. Since being brought here from Australia, they've practically destroyed all the birdlife in our forests. They have no natural enemies other than the trappers."

After paying a hundred fifty NZ dollars for three permits and dropping another twenty for topographical maps, we met Pillow outside and walked over to a log cabin. The sign on the door read DKGY —for "Daigleish Kildare, Glenorchy." I'd like to think it was a parody of Donna Karan's iconic New York fashion brand, but, having met the proprietor, I doubt it.

The interior of the building was filled with furs in varying shades of brown, black, and gray. They were pinned to the walls, draped on tables, and laid as rugs on the floor.

A lean, scraggly-bearded man scanned Pillow up and down from behind the counter with an undisguised leer. He filled the gap where his left incisor should be with the tip of his tongue.

"Daig Kildare," he said by way of introduction.

When he took his eyes off Pillow to look at Hart, he seemed to give him a dip of the eyebrow and something akin to a smirk.

"Mr. Hart, I presume?" he said, extending a hand that was ignored.

"Are you ready to go?" Hart asked him.

"You don't see any customers hankerin' for possum skin, do you?"

"All right then."

"Uh, Mr. Hart, there's the matter of my fee."

"I've already sent you a check for two hundred dollars."

"Down payment."

"Five hundred more now," Hart said, without

bothering to consult Pillow or me. "And five when you get us safely to the compound."

"In that case, I'm on."

The lout held up a board with novelty items that included penis gloves for the men and nipple covers for the ladies, all made of possum fur.

"It'll be mighty cold on the way up," he said, leering again at Pillow. "You'll want 'em to protect your privates."

"My, how very practical," she answered. "I take it you've been to the marae before, Mr. Kildare?"

"Plenty of times, missy. I take folks up there two, maybe three times every couple of months. I'm the only one allowed in."

"What kind of folks?" I asked.

"Young people mostly." He flashed that ghastly grin. "Girls even. Don't bring too many back. They like it once they get used to things."

"Take anyone else?"

"If you mean the Chinks, I suppose it's so."

"We heard some Chinese got lost on a glacier," Pillow said. "Were you leading them?"

"Not that bunch." Then, as if he'd said too much, added, "They was just tourists."

The possum trader put away the board, but the grin remained. "It's risky goin' off track. Plenty of folks get lost. If the fog or snow settles in, they stay that way."

"That's why I've hired you," Hart said.

Kildare's mouth twitched at the corners.

"Why you want to see that crazy place?" he asked. "Just 'cuz this lady's a *hine*, you boys ain't."

"I fail to see how that is any business of yours," Pillow said archly.

The trapper's grin turned to a snarl and just as quickly reverted back.

"You said five hundred."

When Hart pulled out a credit card, Pillow stepped between him and the counter.

"Hold off, Adrian."

Hart shot an exasperated look at her.

"Here now," Kildare blustered. "We have a deal."

"Not if Mr. Bevan and I don't accept your terms."

She looked at me.

"I'm with you," I mouthed.

"All right, then," Pillow said. "We prefer to take our business elsewhere."

"Aye?" Kildare sneered. "And where might that be?"

"I was recently informed that a man at the Paradise station knows the area."

The possum trapper's eyes narrowed.

"You don't want that fella. Hard codger. Done time at Rimutaka prison."

"If what you say is true about the backcountry"—Pillow rose to her full height to stare down at him—"this hine thinks we could use a hard man. Someone harder than you, at least."

Kildare hadn't finished sputtering when Pillow stormed out of the shop to where John Pritchard leaned against his Range Rover. I was ten steps behind her and anxious to find out why she'd suddenly decided to choose an ex-con to guide us through the mountain wilderness. Daig Kildare wasn't exactly Dudley Do-Right, but the alternative didn't sound like much of an improvement.

"You had better be right about this," I heard her

hiss to John. "Why didn't you mention Tane Craddock before we left Queenstown?"

"Trust me, you don't want Kildare."

"I've got history with Tane," she said in a defeated voice.

"He's not a bad sort. Not anymore."

"It's not so much him."

"I know," he said, opening the door and climbing behind the wheel. "But it won't hurt to spend time with your mother."

Chapter 18

At the Glenorchy General Store, we purchased backpacks, crampons, and nylon rope, among other gear to go with our anoraks and hiking boots. Following Hart's move, I selected a waterproof Aloksak pouch to protect my journal while Pillow loaded up on three days' worth of trail food for us.

They were both at the counter paying for their equipment and scroggin when I quietly slipped forty dollars to an assistant in the back of the store for a seven-inch hunting knife. It seemed prudent to take certain precautions without alerting my fellow travelers.

Heading to the pier after packing our equipment, I decided to get a rise out of Hart.

"I haven't properly thanked you for getting Bartow to hand over the journals. Still, it seems odd he was so complacent."

Hart shot me a quizzical look. "It suited us both," he said softly.

"Where do you think he's headed?" I pressed. "Surely not back to Sydney."

"Bartow could bloody well go to Reykjavik for all I fucking care."

Shortly before noon, a jet boat, its 526-horsepower Chrysler engine idling like a caged tiger, arrived at the pier to take us up the meandering Dart River to Paradise Flat.

A likable young boatman named Jeb gave instructions while handing out life preservers. Pillow sat in front while Adrian and I settled in the middle seats. The craft had an extremely shallow draft for navigating glacial rivers no more than inches deep. Instead of a propeller, it relied on a propulsion jet—basically, a powerful water pump capable of thrusting the boat forward at remarkable speeds against the current. It was extremely maneuverable, capable of turning or stopping instantaneously with a quick pull in either direction.

We motored slowly from the pier to enter the estuary where the river poured into the lake. Aiming the bow upstream, Jeb lowered his sunglasses, put his right hand on the accelerator, and said over his shoulder, "You folks might want to hang on."

Quite an understatement as it turned out.

I was watching sunbeams bounce off the pebbles through the clear water when the boat suddenly leaped forward with a deafening roar, shooting past sandbars and over inch-deep shallows at speeds over thirty knots. At midstream, things calmed a bit while Jeb deftly negotiated the ever-shifting channels, but when a sudden pivot strewed gallons of ice-cold water on us, Pillow laughed like a little girl who had never known pain or disappointment.

Magnificent peaks spread out on either side of the broad river valley, their glaciers gleaming in the sun under a cerulean sky, but Hart didn't seem to be enjoying the view or the exhilarating ride.

He was obviously not happy about Pillow's refusal to accept Kildare as our guide. But there was something different in his attitude toward me as well after I'd mentioned Bartow. Whereas before, he had treated me as a respected and, more or less, equal partner in this endeavor, the Englishman now watched me warily.

I wasn't about to acknowledge that he'd forged Bartow's signature at the Turnbull Library, however. Not yet, anyway. Best to let him squirm while I kept an eye out for myself.

After nearly an hour, we arrived at a point in the river marked by a red buoy indicating the river was unnavigable beyond it. Jeb texted our arrival, then guided the craft to a pebbled bank.

"Welcome to Paradise Flat," he greeted us as we climbed out. "The manager will be down soon."

Jeb didn't wait for our welcoming committee. After handing us a packet of mail he'd brought for the lodge, he guided the boat downstream. The gentle breeze rustling through eucalyptus leaves was a welcome reprieve from the pounding roar of the Chrysler engine.

A two-story pine and native stone structure lay beyond the stand of trees fifty yards from the edge of the water. Next to the house was a grassy meadow where a hundred or so sheep and a dozen cattle grazed on tussock grass. The elevation quickly increased after that, leading up a thousand yards to the ridges of the Earnslaw Burn. Three miles to the north, Mount

Earnslaw and its sister peaks gleamed in the afternoon sun.

Minutes later, a hearty Hercules sporting a handlebar mustache you could hang lanterns on ambled toward us. He wore a sweat-stained cowboy hat, a brightly colored check flannel shirt, and saddle-tweed trousers fastened with a plaited leather belt. A pair of heavy leather boots added another inch or two to his solid six-foot frame. Tied around his neck was a string that held a dog whistle.

"Greetings, folks." Dark eyes beamed under thick beetle eyebrows. "I'm the one-time only-time Tane Craddock, the station manager here. Esme's up in the hills chasing a goat that wandered away in the night. I'll get you settled in."

Craddock took a moment to help Pillow with her pack and I heard him whisper, "Nice to see you."

"Wish I could say the same of you."

"We were kids."

"I was a kid, Tane. You were almost sixteen. Let's not talk about it."

"Up to you," he said.

The pair moved slowly, silently away from the river, through the beech trees, on to the tussock area and toward the house. I followed at a respectful distance behind them. Hart purposely kept behind me, his eyes boring a hole in the back of my head.

The lodge seemed the kind of place you could settle in for a year and never draw an anxious breath. The front porch had a half dozen wicker chairs and small tables, the latter topped by wildflowers in clear glass vases. There were six bedrooms, four upstairs and two down, with a large central gathering area anchored by a stone fireplace at the north end. On the opposite side, a floor-to-ceiling window looked onto the Dart's turquoise waters and the snowcapped Humboldt Range.

Hart and I were given rooms downstairs; Pillow took the second-floor suite. After freshening up, we gathered on the front porch where Craddock greeted us with bottles of chilled white wine, cheese, and apples.

The station manager retreated toward the kitchen, but Pillow, smiling a little, said, "You might as well join us."

He turned and shyly pulled up a chair directly opposite her.

"She was the prettiest girl in Arrowtown," Craddock said to Hart and me as if she wasn't there.

"*E mai ana*, but not true," Pillow demurred. "I was tall and skinny. Clumsy as could be."

"She was like a thoroughbred colt, just coming into speed and grace."

"He called me names."

"'Sparky.'"

"Yes, because I wore braces. The other kids called me '*Kahiketea*' because of my height. 'Sparky' wasn't so bad, considering."

Craddock looked from us to her. She met his eyes with a kind of straightforwardness that made him uncomfortable.

Now it was Hart and me who were no longer there.

"I've gotten better," he said.

"As well you might have." Pillow's words sounded harsh, but her tone suggested forgiveness, even a rekindled fondness for him.

Hart, oblivious to the drama being played before us, shifted in his chair.

"Might you bring us another bottle, Craddock? I'd prefer a red to this pale plonk."

"Right away," the big man said, getting up. "Then I'd best search for Esme. Her goat thinks it's a tahr and took off toward Mount Richardson."

"What's a tahr?" I asked when he returned with the new bottle.

"A Nepalese cousin to the mountain goat some idiots brought to this country a century ago. In Asia, the snow leopards keep them in check, but they have no natural predators here, so they multiply like rabbits and chew up our alpine plants."

"Can't hunters weed them out?" Hart wanted to know.

"They come from all over the world to try, but the beasts are incredibly fleet and sure-footed, rambling up the steepest and most isolated peaks. Hunters bag no more than five or six a season, so the Conservation Society pays me to conduct aerial ops. If I spot a herd, the pilot flies close in and I use a gun net to corral a young nanny. Then I hop out to tag her with a radio collar."

"'Hop out?'"

"Sure," Craddock said. "I jump on her bulldog style from the chopper, sedate her, and put a tracking collar on the neck. It took me a while to get the hang of it, especially when the beast is on a narrow ridge with nothing but air on either side. Helps to have a steady pilot."

Once it became clear he wasn't joking, I looked at Tane Craddock with added respect. "What then?"

"I secure her to a winch connected to a wireline,

and the chopper hauls her to a release location close to suspected feral herds. Aircraft equipped with special location aerials monitor the 'Judas' nanny for six to eight months. Once a group has been located, the animals are shot from the air with a semiautomatic rifle. Not very sporting, but it's the only way to control the pests."

"Do you kill the nanny who led you there, too?"

"Yeah. She's no use to us anymore."

As if in protest to this description of animal slaughter, we heard the bleating of a disgruntled billy goat.

"Tane!" a woman shouted from the garden adjacent to the cliff. "Bring me a rope to secure Mortimer to the post. Make sure it's a Dynex that he can't chew apart this time."

"Excuse me, folks," he said, grabbing a nylon cord from a wooden crate on the porch. "Duty calls."

I looked in the direction of the meadow to see the tall, angular woman who had issued the order. Mid-sixties, I figured, with silver hair hanging on either side of her face in long braids. She wore a short-billed cap, a woolen shirt, and hiking shorts that hadn't protected her legs from being scratched while wading through the brambles.

She issued several more orders to Craddock while she secured the animal, but it was obvious that her commands were meant to hide her nervous anticipation at seeing her estranged daughter.

Hart and I got to our feet when she came up the steps, but Pillow remained seated, staring fixedly at her mother as if coldly studying the aging effects of the last ten years. I noticed she had pulled her collar down, exposing her neck.

After an awkward silence, introductions were made.

"I'm Esme," she said to Hart and me.

I saw a resemblance to Cattley Middleditch, including the evidence of alcoholism in her features. She had a few wrinkles about her mouth, but the rest of her gaunt face was remarkably smooth, as if the skin had been painted to the cheekbones. Her blue eyes were large and shining; her expression pleasant and candid.

"And what about you?" she said, addressing her daughter. "Or did London life strip you of civility?"

"Not at all," Pillow answered. "I've learned it's easier to polish manners than reform the heart."

Esme stared at her daughter without expression for a moment, but when Pillow stood up, she gave her a quick, motherly peck on her cheek.

Although there was little warmth in it, it melted a sliver off the glacier between them.

"You look well," Esme remarked, clasping Pillow's hand. "I'm very glad you came."

"Thank you, Mother." Pillow pulled her hand ever so tactfully away. "If you don't mind, I'm rather exhausted. I'd like to take a nap before dinner."

"Certainly."

After Pillow left for her room, Hart settled into a leather chair as if he owned the place and poured himself another glass of wine.

Esme caught my eye and tilted her head in the direction of the back door. I followed her there.

"Thanks for letting us share your lodge," I told her. "I suspect your brother and John Pritchard had something to do with reuniting you with your daughter."

"With you heading up to Ivo's compound, it makes sense. I doubt she agrees."

"Perhaps."

"Not a particularly good start to reconciliation," Esme said sadly. "Cattley and John had very nice things to say about you, by the way. Let me show you my garden."

We went out the back door onto a gradually elevated path.

"You were wise not to hire that beastly Kildare," she said as we passed through a pergola covered with yellow roses. "Knows the country up there, though."

"Doesn't Craddock?"

"Oh, sure. Tane will go up in the heli every other month or so with medical supplies and other necessities, but he's never been allowed near the marae."

"If you don't mind my asking, why did you hire him, particularly since Pillow had problems with him when they were younger?"

"I knew his mother, a remarkable woman. Old-time Maori lady. She helped me when no one else cared. That's all. When Tane was released from prison, I offered him a job as a sheep musterer. Low pay, hard work, but he never once complained. Promoted him after a few years and rely on him totally now. But I worry he'll leave. He's a fine man in the prime of life, and you may have noticed that females of the human variety aren't too plentiful here."

Esme kneeled and gently pushed aside a bouquet of waxy leaves. "These are my swedes. I guess in the States you call them rutabagas or turnips. Our winters are too bleak for most other vegetables. Here"—she pulled one from the hard, dry ground—"try one. The sheep love them as much as humans."

It was sweeter and milder than a turnip.

The golden leaves of the beech trees shimmered in the breeze coming off the mountains. I thought of Aspen and the glorious time Carol and I had climbing the Maroon Bells in the September before her death.

"Do you ever get lonely up here, Esme?" I asked impulsively.

"Too busy."

Then, as if to change the subject, she pointed east to the meadow where a herd of merino sheep were grazing. "Anyone who says those animals are dumb doesn't know them. They're deliberately uncooperative sometimes, as you would be at the bottom of the food predator chain, but they're not stupid."

"How'd you come to own this place?"

"Ivo bought it for me. I don't know if he meant it as punishment or to help in my rehabilitation. At first, the work nearly broke me, but I eventually got the hang of it. I quit drinking and learned to skin possum as well as shear sheep. It's getting tougher to hang on, though."

She stooped to pull a weed, shook the soil off it, and got back up. She fiddled with one of her braids.

"The long downturn in sheep prices has made it hard to survive. Nearly put me under last year, forcing me to take on off-station jobs. I work down at the library in Glenorchy part time, take in guests in the summer, and sell my paintings at a gallery in Queenstown. In the last six years, I've been beyond break-even once, but I'll never quit. This place has my heart."

It sounded like high-station ranching and the used-book business had a great deal in common.

"How much livestock do you have?"

"I run a hundred merinos and twenty cattle on two hundred acres. Besides Tane, I've five musterers and a couple of packmen. The snows have come early and already they're snow-raking in the high basins, struggling to get the sheep down where the food is. In summer the stock grazes on extensive tracts of tussock meadow. It's hard to keep control over the weeds and pests, but I'm keeping it natural that way. It's the only way to give the native plants and critters a chance."

We walked on, chatting among the roses while bees and butterflies flittered about our heads. Her voice was so matter of fact when describing the trials and joys of dealing with livestock and nature that I didn't realize until she turned her face up to me that her cheeks were streaked with tears.

"It must be difficult for you," I said. "Your relationship with Pillow, I mean."

"You saw the look in her eyes. She'll never forgive me for being such an irresponsible mother."

"Why not ask?"

"It's easier for a victim to forgive than for the offender to ask. Pillow is not that generous, and I'm not that brave."

"I understand, Esme. My daughter used to blame me for her mother's death. But things can change. Don't discount the pardoning power of the human heart."

She nodded politely, without conviction. A cloud crossed the sun. Its shadow made her face look all the more skeletal and forlorn.

We proceeded uphill in silence. At some point, not sure that my presence was still welcome, I stopped to admire the soaring flight of a falcon. The raptor made a startling cry, stretched back its wings as if it were an arrow, and dove in a direct vertical line to snatch a hare four times its size. Snapping the victim's neck with its curved beak, the bird began to pluck its quivering flesh.

Esme was far ahead by the time I resumed the uphill walk.

Ten minutes later, I found her standing on a ledge of crumbling rock, her toes hovering over the precipice and arms extended as if they were wings. The turquoise waters of the glacial runoff rippled like fluttering ribbons five hundred feet below.

Chapter 19

I'd have been too late to grab her had she truly intended to jump. As it was, my howl got her to turn away from the edge.

She stared at me without expression. I wondered if the years of drinking had addled her brain.

Finally, I said, "I thought you meant to harm yourself."

She blinked. Gradually, the color seeped back into her face.

"I'm terribly sorry," she said, walking toward me. "I wasn't in danger. It calms me to stand here and gaze out as if I were a bird, free and light as air. I didn't even realize you'd come up until you shouted."

She took hold of my arm.

"What do you think of Mr. Hart?" she asked unexpectedly.

"He's a first-rate bookman," I answered, shrugging, "but about as modest and trustworthy as Mussolini."

"I agree. The man's face has dishonesty written on it like a hieroglyphic."

"Pillow cares for him in ways I can't understand."

"She's a hard one, Michael. Not just with me."

"It's understandable."

Esme released her grip, sat on a small boulder, and motioned for me to join her.

"How much do you know about Penelope?" she asked.

"She's not been particularly forthcoming about her past. "

"That sounds like her."

"Cattley filled me in on some things—Pillow wasn't keen on seeing you again."

The skin under Esme's eyes turned even paler.

"An unwed mother who also happened to be a drunk wasn't exactly a formula for parenting success," she said softly.

How well I knew. Trade "unwed mom" for "widowed dad" and she'd described my relationship with my daughter.

"She jumped at the chance to escape, not only me, but New Zealand. Ivo provided her with everything she needed financially but not emotionally. The school was strong on scholastics and discipline, perhaps too much for a girl not used to either. Penelope rebelled, finding solace in trips to London, hanging out with toffs like Alistair Wilkes-ffolkes, fifth baronet of Dalhousie. Are you aware she was married to him?"

"Hart briefly mentioned it, but Pillow's trust in me apparently doesn't extend that far."

Esme paused, a painful recollection transforming her face into a bitter mask.

"Wilkes-ffolkes decamped for the south of France a

year after their wedding, having become infatuated with a South African fashion model. He left Penelope with a pile of gambling debts owed to a London-based oligarch named Goshenkin. When Wilkes-ffolkes ignored the threats, the Russian looked to her for payment. The amount wasn't insurmountable—fifty thousand pounds or so, a sum Ivo could have covered without a hiccup. But such was her embarrassment she didn't tell him.

"She agreed to settle the account by becoming Goshenkin's mistress. But after a month of that, the Russian offered her to an oil official in Azerbaijan with whom he was trying to close a deal. This time she refused. Goshenkin sent two henchmen to teach her a lesson. After raping her, they tossed acid at her face. She squirmed at the last second so that it splashed down the right side of her neck and chest."

Esme stood and returned to the edge of the cliff.

I started to speak, but she raised her hand for silence. For a long minute, the only sound I heard was the schuss of the wind as it spiraled up from the river.

"You see, Mr. Bevan," she said, gazing back at me. "It's not only physical scars that have made my daughter what she is."

"Has she had therapy?"

"I suppose her healing, such as it is, has been a result of part ownership in The Book and Bell." Esme's expression brightened. "Pardon me for asking this, but have you been intimate with Penelope?"

"She can be very friendly when the mood is upon her."

"Well put, Mr. Bevan. I'm glad that her taste in men has improved, but I do wish she would stop calling herself Pillow. It has such a negative connotation."

"All things considered—"

"Listen to me," she interrupted. "You've seen how fragile she can be. She needs protection, if not from Hart, from the people who surround her father. Something is terribly wrong up there. I've asked Tane to watch out for both of you. But he'll need help."

"I'll do what I can. I promise."

"Good. I once hoped this fellow Hart would be the antidote to her misery, but having met him, I know that isn't possible."

She picked some more wildflowers, and we started down the steep slope.

At dawn the next morning, Hart, Pillow, and I ate a breakfast of scrambled eggs, rack of lamb, and porridge while listening to Tane explain what lay ahead. It basically came down to a rugged two-day hike, weather permitting, once the chopper dropped us off at Pearl Flat. After that, he didn't know.

We drained our last cups of coffee, hit the restroom a final time, and grabbed our gear.

While the others proceeded down the stairs of the porch, Esme took me aside to deliver an odd-looking pendant. The flat jade object was three inches high and a couple of inches wide. The rudely carved figure carved on it resembled a human embryo. A leather string was attached to it through a hole at the top.

"Wear this," she told me as the helicopter approached. "It's a *hei-tiki* made of the most highly prized variety of greenstone. It has strong powers and will protect you."

She clutched my hand, then turned and walked briskly back to the lodge. I slipped the leather string with the jade object around my neck so that it rested against my breastbone.

Then, before joining the others, I checked my cell phone for the last time before losing service in the mountains.

On it was a text message sent an hour earlier:

> Regarding that headless trunk washed up at Point Reyes. A weird bow tie found around stump of neck. Rubber ducks on it. Mean anything to ya?

> Luv! Josie.

A sane person would have done an about-face to the lodge, rung up the jet boat for return service, spent another pleasant interlude among Esme's wildflowers, and speeded back to civilization before nightfall. But those damn words Josie had said back at the bookshop about lifeboats still rattled in my brain. I was going to see this thing through. For Riverrun. For Josie. For me.

I no longer doubted that Hart conspired to have Billy Bartow sneak into my room at the Marines Memorial Club. Afterward, he killed him and made up the story that his journal had been stolen, as well as mine.

Even if I believed Pillow wasn't in on the murderous business, I wasn't ready to share my suspicions with her. It was hard enough to conceal my own knowledge of Hart's guilt. Two of us could never pull off the charade.

Chapter 20

The bright red Twin Engine Squirrel helicopter, specially adapted for taking trekkers up to the remote valleys and glaciers, was piloted by a yellow-bearded pakeha from Christchurch named Lars Jensen. The man looked more suited to the prow of a Viking long ship than the cockpit of a flying machine.

"It's a short but bumpy ride," he said once we belted in and clamped on our earphones.

Seconds after receiving confirmation from the control station in Queenstown, the engines started, and the blades began to turn, slowly at first, then blindingly fast to form a solid blur above us. When the rotor speed indicator reached 200 RPMs, Jensen gradually pulled back the pitch lever and the machine leisurely lifted as if reluctant to leave the earth. At fifty feet, he checked clearance of the nearby trees, then pushed the joystick forward. The chopper lurched slightly before beginning its swift climb toward the towering peaks.

It was a six-seater with wide Plexiglas windows for

sightseeing. In my college days, I once spent a harrowing afternoon stuck on a knife-edge ridge below the summit of Mount Wilson in Colorado and would have conquered the Grand Teton in Wyoming had I not broken an ankle near the summit. Although I felt an aversion to enclosed spaces, ballroom dancing, and texting teenagers, fear of heights wasn't one of my phobias. I love the mountains.

Interspersed among the high ranges, massive glaciers spread below us like the rumpled carpets of giants. A spiderweb network of cascading waterfalls, streams, and deep valleys filled every crease. I pressed my face to the window and, between glances to my map, matched names to the summits and ice plateaus as we scuttled past them at 140 knots: Whitbourn, Snowball, Mercer, Bonar, French Ridge, Aspiring. Smaller locales read like a litany of past adventures and disasters: Shotover Saddle, Shovel Flat, Rough Creek, and Gloomy Gorge.

The service ceiling of the Twin Squirrel was eleven thousand feet, so that we weren't flying so much above the peaks as between them. Even then, the Squirrel's rotors struggled to maintain height in the thin air as the pilot skillfully maneuvered through the gaps on an east-northeast course toward the Haast Range. The crown jewel of the chain was the massive snow-bedecked triangle of Mount Aspiring, known to the Maoris as Tititea.

At one point Jensen turned his head to me and said, "You say your name is Bevan?"

"That's right."

"You've got something in common with that peak six clicks ahead."

At a mere seven thousand feet, Mount Bevan's

cone of snow and rock was cloaked that morning in the shadow of the larger Aspiring, but it was impressive enough to claim as a good omen.

Two kilometers south of my namesake mountain, we began a stomach-flopping descent into a mist-shrouded canyon where the helicopter battled cross-winds whipping down the gorge from the higher elevations. Jensen maintained control, however, feathering the propellers above the cobbled river stones of Pearl Flat. He let the machine hover for a moment before its final direct descent. Then he worked the joystick, and within a minute, we settled gently next to the rushing waters of the Matukituki River.

The rotor arms slowed gradually to a stop, and after our pilot's warning to mind the back blades, we stepped out and unloaded our gear.

"Good luck," Jensen called before revving up the rotors again. "I'll see you here in twelve days."

Protecting our faces from the spray churned up by the ascending helicopter, we shrugged on our packs and gathered around Craddock, who had unfolded his Ordnance Survey over a boulder. The map's sharply meandering contour lines—orange for the mountains and blue for glaciers—were tightly spaced, indicating dramatically steep elevations on either side of the river.

"We'll head up the valley for a bivouac at the Scotts Rock hut," he told us. "In the morning we'll ascend sixteen hundred meters to the Matu Saddle and, if the weather holds, cross over and descend to the lake."

He pointed on the map to a blue oval far below the Bonar Glacier. It was a mile long and a quarter mile wide at either end, but so isolated it didn't warrant a name on the map, only its elevation: 517 meters.

"Then what?" Hart asked.

"We follow the western edge where the Waipara River flows into it, then follow the rapids up the gorge for four or five kilometers to where I've unloaded supplies in the past. I expect we'll be met by scouts from the compound. After that, we'll just have to see if we're allowed to go further. I've never been allowed past that point."

We arrived at the Scotts Rock shelter hut after a leisurely four-hour hike swatting sand flies the entire way. It was a good warm-up for the grueling vertical ascent that followed, taking us from the valley floor through moss-covered beech forests to the tree line.

I was in the lead, breaking the path through knee-deep snow when I edged around a jagged escarpment to come face-to-face with a simian-faced demon straight out of a painting by Hieronymus Bosch. Balanced on a six-inch ledge, the creature peered down at me with wide-set orange eyes beneath a pair of stumpy horns. Completing the satanic image was a mane of reddish fur that extended from neck to cloven hooves.

I shouted out my discovery, but the tahr bounded away before the others rounded the corner.

It was late afternoon when we spotted the Matu Saddle still high above us. The ground ahead involved verglassed rock slabs and a thin coating of snow that blew away with every gust. Hard to manage under any circumstance, but not the kind of ground you can get four people over safely with daylight fading.

It was Adrian Hart who led us in these worsening

conditions. He may not have had the classical physique of an athlete, but he had shown remarkable endurance and agility on the rougher patches.

At one point, we encountered an extremely narrow and exposed ledge where the steep slope seemed to angle outward. There was an alternate route, but this one was considerably shorter, and with night approaching, we wanted to get to the relative safety of the saddle. Roping up, we watched Hart inch along the tapered shelf. It went well for about six feet until his axe struck a crack in the wall hidden by a thick sheet of ice. It gave way abruptly, causing him to teeter backward toward the void.

We braced for the belay, but he pivoted on a thin outcrop of rock and leaped back to where we stood.

It was a move worthy of Baryshnikov.

"Indeed," he said with no more irritation than if he'd stepped in a cow patty. "Perhaps it's best to take the other option."

The other option was only slightly better. Sidestepping on slippery crusts of ice that crumbled beneath our crampons, it was close to midnight when we staggered into the lee shelter of a ten-foot-high slab of rock. Although exhausted, we got little sleep as we lay huddled in a snow cave listening to enormous chunks of ice crashing off the Bonar Glacier.

Toward sunrise, I noticed Pillow had laid her head against Craddock's shoulder. When she thought no one was looking, she used her glove to affectionately brush off a crust of frozen snot clinging to his mustache.

The next morning rose clear except for a high white cloud approaching from the north in an otherwise blue sky. After linking up with the half-inch thick static rope, we headed upward with heads down, keeping ten yards' distance between us.

Craddock opted for a route that had looked promising the day before, but by noon we were questioning that decision. We clawed our way seven hundred meters up a steep scree slope, gaining two meters for every one sliding back. It was like skating uphill on ball bearings, amplified by exposure of a thousand meters on either side.

My lungs felt packed with concrete for the first hour, and my calves were burning from the steady exertion over the loose surface. But when I caught my second wind, something strange happened—I suddenly felt downright exhilarated, as if I'd been injected with a powerful drug.

It must have been a combination of the altitude and lack of sleep that caused the hallucination, but "floating on air" began to take on a literal meaning for me. Sparked by the weird adrenaline high, I heard myself demanding to take the lead from Craddock.

His judgment must have been suffering from the altitude as well. Over the irate objections of Hart, he agreed to switch positions on the rope. We stopped on a reasonably comfortable ledge to slip the hundred-fifty-foot-long rope through the harnesses around our waists and clipped our carabiners to it. Pillow maintained her place behind me, with Craddock linking his oval 'biner behind her. Hart remained at the rear.

I surged ahead, keeping the line taut as the others struggled to match my pace. We were less than a hundred meters from the ridge marking the col when I paused to look over my shoulder at my fellow climbers.

"What's with you, feather merchants?" I shouted.

"Can't handle a little exercise? Why once on Mount Wilson, I—"

And that's when a powerful gust of surprisingly warm air launched me off the slope as if I were a character in Marvel Comics.

Chapter 21

They've named it the foehn in Europe. It's the chinook or snow-eater in our Rockies. New Zealanders call the warm hurricane-force wind that rolls without warning over a summit the Nor'west Arch.

The hundred-mile-per-hour hammer inflated my rucksack cover like a sail and sent me flying through space. The rope made a zinging noise as it ran through the carabiner attached to my waist harness until the freefall abruptly ended with an excruciating jerk.

I briefly passed out. When I awoke, my legs were moving as if there was something under them other than fifteen hundred feet of air. It didn't take long to realize the situation had changed. One second I was falling to my death, the next I was assaulted by sickening waves of pain while twisting on a half-inch-thick cord.

A forty-pound pack is not the kind of anchor you'd want with a harness squeezing the base of your ribcage. I was no stranger to torn cartilage from my rugby days, but this was different. At least two ribs were broken. There was a real chance of internal bleeding and suffocation. With every desperate exhalation of breath, I moaned like a bankrupt banker.

Even worse than the pain was the feeling that the jagged ends of bones were edging closer to my left lung. Every swerve of my body on that nylon rope brought me an eighth of an inch closer to dying. Gritting my teeth, I forced myself to disregard the injuries, real or imagined. Instead, I focused on countering the centrifugal force of the spin.

I accomplished this by spreading out my arms, which left me dangling like a field-dressed deer a dozen feet from the side of the mountain. The rushing wind had passed so that I could hear voices shouting above me. Stretching my neck as far back as the pack would allow, I saw I'd fallen about forty feet. The line had snagged on an outcrop of rock, catching my fall in time to save my life.

For the time being, anyway.

It doesn't matter if you're Edmund Hillary or Reinhold Messner: nobody lasts long hanging at the end of a rope.

I spotted Craddock and Hart sitting on a thin ledge not far above the overhang. Their backs were braced against the slope, and their arms extended in front of them as if in a tug-of-war contest. Their gloved hands clung fiercely to the line.

Twenty feet below the outcrop and an equal distance above me, Pillow hung like a broken doll. Her head was slumped forward, her arms straight and motionless. The harness had slipped high under her right armpit, causing her shoulder to appear horribly out of place.

The two of us had fallen on opposite sides of the outcrop so that our lines straddled the rock, running parallel to each other. With each sway in the wind, the rope threatened to snap under our combined weight. Craddock shouted a warning that he and Hart couldn't maintain the belay much longer.

Ignoring the pain in my chest, I reached over my backpack and pulled the ice axe from the strap holding it. Then I began to swing back and forth as if on a pendulum, each time coming closer to the edge of the wall. With the fourth try, I managed to slam the axe into the rock, gaining a tenuous hold. Quickly, I swung my left foot onto the slope, adjusted my shoulders to shift the weight of the pack, and let gravity pull the rest of me onto hard ground. The pressure on my ribs lessened considerably. I was still in agony, but I could breathe freely again.

I shook off the pack and evaluated Pillow's situation. Even if Craddock and Hart had the strength to pull her up, the fulcrum of the rock and the condition of the frayed rope wouldn't allow it. It was up to me to get close enough to pull her onto the slope.

Because the surface was mostly rock, I removed my crampons and clawed upward, inch by inch, gasping with each painful breath. It took ten minutes to get to where I was directly across from Pillow. My platform was a ledge about two meters wide.

Using my ice axe to anchor me to the rock wall, I stretched over the void, keeping my left leg on the slope and my right suspended in the air. Pillow hung tantalizingly just out of my reach.

I brought my right leg back to the slope to replant the axe in the rock a few inches closer to the edge. Then I stretched out again.

It was enough to snag a loose strap of her back-pack that was fluttering in the wind. When I turned her toward me, I was shocked to find her face covered by a thin carapace of ice. It looked like a death mask.

I tugged on the strap. It brought her closer. I pulled harder, risking that the strap would come loose. And again, until I was able to secure both of my feet on the mountain while still tenuously connected to her.

I yelled for the men to slacken the rope on my count of three. Then, bracing my feet and with my left hand still clinging to the ice axe, my right hand released its grip on the strap. I grasped the front of her anorak.

At my command, the rope slackened. I heaved her across my body onto the ledge.

There was no time to catch my breath. I slipped the carabiner from her harness and gently turned her over. Her right shoulder hung like a puppet's whose arm had been caught in a hopelessly snagged string. I loosened her collar to get to the carotid artery. Although the pulse was feeble, she was alive.

Craddock was at my side within seconds. One look at Pillow and the hard lump of muscles of his neck tightened. He took over, pressing his thumbs in the small hollow space behind her ears.

Her eyes popped open as if she'd been shocked by a cattle prod. She gazed furtively into our faces as if confused as to time and place. When she shifted her weight to get up, the unexpected explosion of pain caused by the movement caused her to scream.

Hart appeared with the frayed rope looped in circles over his shoulder. As was the case with Craddock, blood from his fingers had seeped through his mittens.

"Her shoulder's dislocated," he said. "It has to be put back into the socket."

Craddock and I nodded in agreement. If the muscles and ligaments were torn, tugging on the arm might cripple it. But, given her unbearable pain, we had no choice.

Pillow's shrieks had subsided to pitiful groans by the time we got her to lie flat on her back.

While I held down her legs and Craddock cradled her torso, Hart kneeled by her right side. Grabbing her wrist, he placed his left foot under her armpit for leverage, then began a slow, steady pull on her arm directly away from her body. Her howls were unnerving, but after a few long minutes, the joint slid into place. The pain seemed to magically vanish.

We sat her up to remove her anorak and get her arm stabilized. From my backpack, I pulled a thin foam pad—great for keeping backsides dry on wet ground, by the way—and slipped it between her right arm and chest. Using a pair of nylon crampon strips for a sling, we slipped the anorak over her and let her rest.

If any of us had any doubts as to Pillow's toughness, they were soon dispelled when we resumed the climb an hour later.

We reached the Matukituki Saddle without further incident, Pillow stoically matching our every step without complaint. I, on the other hand, muttered an occasional whimper whenever something brushed against my ribs.

On the downward slope, we made good time glissading on our butts down the hard-packed surface of a snow gulley. After a quarter of a mile, the snow petered out, and we had to clamber over a boulder-littered moraine. This was particularly painful for Pillow and me, but we soon reached a beech forest devoid of rocks and with eye-popping views of Mount Aspiring.

After our rest, we scrambled down a barely visible deer path to the crescent-shaped lake with no name. The sand flies and sharp tips of sword grass soon drew blood from everyone, but the flat ground was kind to our aching muscles.

Sitting around a campfire next to the rapids of the Waipara that night, Craddock informed us that in the morning, we'd hike up the gorge to where the Cat O'Nine Tails cascade met the river.

"After that, I'm pretty sure Ivo's scouts will find us. Do as they say and it will be all right. We'll pass among topuni, sacred sites of the Kati Mamoe iwi, so watch where you spit. And, for God's sake, if you need to relieve yourself, ask to make sure it's not on ground that's tapu."

I felt like a sodbuster listening to Kit Carson warn the wagon train before it entered Apache country.

Sometime before midnight, three of us still remained by the dying fire. Craddock had crawled into his sleeping bag an hour earlier.

Pillow, cradling her damaged arm, gave a mighty yawn and got to her feet.

"I need to hit the loo," she explained before wandering toward the river.

I figured it was as good a time as any to again stir the ashes with Hart. I began nicely.

"You were impressive on that belay."

He swiveled his head toward me. His eyes had a red glare. "Have you a question for me, Bevan? You've seemed full of them since we left Queenstown."

Looking back on it, maybe I should have just come out and told him I knew he killed Bartow. We would have settled things one way or the other right there. But there remained too many unknowns—one of them concerning Pillow's involvement.

And truth be told, after surviving one harrowing incident with cracked ribs, I didn't fancy tangling in the wilderness with a former SBS man. Hart may have been what romance novelists call a "popinjay," but he was no pansy.

Instead, I said, "You knew Ivo Mackin had the third journal a long time ago. Why didn't you tell Pillow? She's your business partner, after all."

"I didn't want to involve her at the time."

He looked over his shoulder to make sure Pillow hadn't started back. "She was involved in certain, shall we say…difficulties."

"Such as?"

Hart didn't answer at first. Instead, he remarked, edging closer to me, "She's an interesting woman, don't you think? Smart, strong, attractive."

"Yes. So what?"

"Fancy her?"

"None of your business."

"She was married, you know."

"So I heard."

"He's dead now."

"I wasn't aware of that."

"Don't you think it odd she never mentioned it to you?"

I didn't answer. But I thought it just as strange that her mother and Cattley Middleditch hadn't either.

"And the Russian?"

"Esme told me. Having to testify at the bastard's trial must have been traumatic for Pillow."

Hart grinned at my naiveté.

"There was no need for the Crown to file charges. Another form of justice intervened. The girl may be only one-eighth Maori, but Utu—the hereditary will to avenge—courses through her blood."

"What are you saying, Hart?"

He drew uncomfortably close to my face. Light years from the nearest Macy's, the guy stunk of cologne. Lavender, I think it was.

"Only what I read in the London Observer. Goshenkin was a collector of books on big-game hunting and erotica. One day he received a letter from a dealer on Cecil Court asking if he might be interested in a privately printed edition of *Les Cent Vingt Journées de Sodome, ou l'École du libertinage* by the Marquis de Sade.

"The next day, he showed up to inspect it and was never seen again."

Hart got up to throw another log on the fire.

Returning to my side, he whispered, "Who would have thought that lily of the valley steeped in warm water and added to a cup of tea could have such devastating effects?"

"Where were you during this time?"

"At the Boston Antiquarian Fair, all by myself."

"And her husband? How did he die?"

"Lost at sea shortly thereafter. Mysteriously fell from his yacht one night while sailing off the Côte d'Azur. The presumed suicide made all the papers."

"I don't suppose you were on that boat?"

"My dear boy, I was in London setting up our booth at the Olympia Book Fair."

"And Pillow?"

"In Cassis."

"Cassis?"

"Oh, yes, a lovely place down the coast from Marseilles. Pillow has oh-so-many friends in the yachting community there. Some are rather notorious."

"Why are you telling me this?"

"Because," he said, getting to his feet upon hearing Pillow's return. "You should know more about your gal pal before leaping to conclusions about me."

Chapter 22

Low-flying clouds off Mount Aspiring brought flurries of snow mixed with sleet the next morning. It was the kind of dreary weather that made you want to pull up the covers and dream of Barbados. But Craddock had us on the trail by seven with only oatmeal and raisins in our bellies. At least the pain in my ribs had subsided to a dull throbbing.

After tramping through a long, narrow ravine gouged by the river, we reached the Cat O' Nine Tails cascade at mid-morning, where we encountered a most extraordinary-looking young man.

He wore a kilt-like garment between his waist and knees and a flax cloak over his upper body. Traditional cold weather Maori gear, I reckoned, except for the Nike hiking boots and woolen socks.

He was a handsome, well-built kid whose long plaited hair was tied at the top in a knob adorned with white-tipped feathers. But it was the head of a live juvenile kea squeezed through a hole in his ear that caused me to do an Oliver Hardy double-take. The parrot must have been accustomed to the treatment because the brilliant olive wings and gray legs hung listlessly down the left side of its master's neck. Only the yellow-ringed eyes seemed alive. Nervously, they followed our every move.

In addition to the bird, our greeter carried a flat quarterstaff five feet in length. The weapon looked from a distance to be made of hard wood and seemed remarkably light. He began to twirl it like a baton, increasingly fast, alternating it in his right hand and his left, spinning it horizontally over his head, then in front of him and vertically on either side of his body. With his hands and arms thus engaged, he hopped from one foot to the other, his body twisting, head jerking from side to side, tongue extended, and eyes bulging like a drum major stoked on ecstasy.

He hopscotched that way before careening to a stop five yards in front of us, standing stock still, right foot in front of left, the weapon held over his head primed to thrust.

Craddock cautioned us to not move.

After a few tense moments, the youth cocked his head sideways, twisted his spear horizontally so that the tip pointed away from us. Slowly, he removed a bone knife from the woven belt around his waist, took four cautious steps forward, and laid it on the ground.

Craddock waited for him to retreat four steps back to his original position. Then, cautiously, he moved toward the object, shouted something in Maori, and stooped to pick up the knife by the blade. He was so deliberate in grasping it by the sharp edge that I got the uneasy feeling our subsequent relations might not have been so amicable had Craddock reached for the handle instead.

Whatever, it did the trick. The boy relaxed noticeably. He performed some kind of waving motion with the hand that did not hold the spear, and addressed Craddock, mostly in English.

"*Haere*, Tane Craddock! What brings you here without supplies?"

"*Kia ora*, Ngati! I'm taking these people to see Watere Mackin."

The boy he called Ngati looked perplexed.

"The Ariki has made no mention of this. You must go back."

Craddock's amiable attitude suddenly changed. He thrust one foot forward, forcefully crossed his arms and jutted his face forward. His eyes bulged comically and his tongue shot from his mouth to an extraordinary length until it reached below the cleft of his lantern jaw.

Snapping his tongue back but maintaining his fierce stance and glare, Craddock spoke Maori in a deep guttural voice that was totally alien to his previously amiable nature.

"*E moe! E moe!*" he snarled. "*Ko te po nui, ko te po roa, ko te pi i whaka—aua ai to moe, e moe! Mackin tamahine, Te Rangihaeta!*"

The boy shot a startled look at Pillow, who met it with a haughty stare. He assumed a defensive posture with the spear drawn over his right shoulder while Craddock harangued him for several more minutes.

When the verbal barrage finally ended, Ngati assumed a respectful, almost sleepy, attitude, then motioned for us to follow him.

"What in the world did you say?" I asked Craddock.

"I recited my ancestry, threw in a bit of hocus-pocus, and, by my command of the high Maori language, let him know I was not to be messed with at the risk of offending certain spirits. This wouldn't have worked in the city, but these lads are different. You'll see. It's good that I didn't have to threaten to take the *hau* of the boy."

"The *hau*?"

"When a person's *hau* is affected, his body perishes because his intellectual and spiritual forces desert him. It would have been overkill in this situation."

We followed Ngati at a respectful distance, gaining altitude until we crested a minor peak and descended to a grove of fir trees where five Maori women squatted in the snow. Covered head to toe in brown and gray cloaks, all five peered between the folds with disinterested eyes, humming strange incantations that unsettled Craddock. He motioned for us to steer clear of them.

"Who—what—are they?" Hart asked once we had passed through the trees onto an open field.

"*Memgas*. Witches," Pillow answered matter-of-factly as if she'd known of them all her life. Unlike Craddock, she didn't seem worried by them.

Since the encounter with Ngati, she no longer used the sling. It made for a subtle difference in her bearing; one that exuded a cool, aristocratic poise, as impersonal as a queen. It was as if she was returning to her people, to a past that had meaning for her.

"I haven't seen their kind in many years," Craddock said of the crones. "My magic is not as strong as theirs. It's good the boy led the way for us."

No sooner had he said this than Ngati reappeared, accompanied by four fearsome-looking men dressed in traditional Maori mountain capes made of bird feathers and dog hide. Like Ngati, they wore their long hair pulled back and tied at the top of the head in a knot. One of them had stuck a feather through the septum of his nose so that it spread horizontally from cheek to cheek like a mustache. Two were heavily tattooed from forehead to chin.

With a nod from Craddock, we followed them over a hill and eventually into a fourteenth-century Maori version of Brigadoon.

Another circle of women, less ominous than the witches, sat under a spare four-post shelter. They fed strands of flax fiber between their toes to their fingers and onto looms, nimbly creating new capes. Another group, similarly clothed in long black cloaks and so intent upon their work that they scarcely noticed us, plaited floor mats from reeds of saw grass.

By noon, the mountain mists and snow were replaced by clear skies, and we stuffed jackets and woolen sweaters into our rucksacks. At the far end of the meadow was a gravel path that seemed to peter out in front of a granite crag soaring several thousand feet. Ngati motioned for Craddock to join him where two jade boulders stood.

I could barely hear their voices—in any case, they spoke in Maori—but the exchange was extremely animated, and I assumed that we weren't to continue until word arrived from a higher authority.

An hour passed before we got our answer. It came in the guise of an oval-faced woman who materialized like an apparition between the giant rocks. She might have been fifty-five, stood five and a half feet, and was plump as a stuffed goose. Her nose was broad and her skin was the color of slightly burnt toast. Long strands of silver hair had been braided into four serpentine plaits topped by a bone comb and a black feather. She said her name was Medusa.

My first impression was of a rather innocuous middle-aged Maori woman until I noticed her eyes. Direct and unblinking, they were filled with a callousness that was chilling; the empty eyes of a Gulag guard.

She walked directly up to Pillow, studied her face for a full minute. Then she caressed the scar tissue on Pillow's neck with the tips of her clawlike fingers.

"You claim to be Te Ranginui's daughter?" the woman demanded.

"Yes."

"Raise your arms."

Pillow blushed but did as directed.

The woman, her wet lips parted, reached under Pillow's sweater and slowly drew it up, exposing the scars from belt to collarbone.

"Why have you come?" she asked when finished with the inspection.

"Simply to see my father," Pillow said, readjusting her sweater. "And to offer gifts."

The woman sneered. "And what can that be for a man who wants for nothing?"

"The lost words of Captain Cook's marine."

The yellowish eyes narrowed.

"Give them to me," the woman hissed.

Hart and I exchanged looks, but there seemed no alternative if we were to proceed further. We pulled from our backpacks the plastic pouches containing the journals. Then we stepped forward to place them in her crabbed hands.

When I handed mine over, the woman studied me for a moment as if to mark me. She hadn't done that with Hart. Silently, she placed the journals in a pocket of her woven flax cape, swung around, and returned to wherever it was she had come from.

Once again, it seemed like the stones had swallowed her.

"What now?" Hart asked Craddock.

But it was Pillow who answered, her eyes gleaming.

"What else? We follow the bitch to hell if need be."

Chapter 23

The granite wall of the cliff turned out to have an enfilading fissure.

The path inside it meandered between towering slabs of rock that allowed little sunlight to penetrate to our level. Flashlights proved useless because of the constant turns in the labyrinth, so we felt our way along the walls, ears alert to the tapping sounds made by the woman's staff, keeping within arm's length of each other. The farther we walked, the more enclosed our tunnel became. It became warmer as well. The air filled with the stench of sulfur.

We stumbled for a mile or more through the ribboned maze before arriving at a stupendous chamber set in the heart of the mountain.

It was fifteen stories high at its apex. Stalactites dripped from the ceiling in unicorn spires and undulating curtains as if designed by Gaudi. Sun rays piercing through a dozen keyholes in the upper reaches struck calcite formations to create a subterranean version of the northern lights. With the Technicolor light show dancing above, it took me a while to notice the long, thick seams of emerald basaltic rock that streaked the massive limestone walls.

"Pounamu," Pillow murmured next to me. "I didn't know it existed in such quantities."

Less entrancing were the numerous fumaroles, each bubbling and belching globs of glutinous, evil-smelling slime. We were in a postcard mash-up of heaven and hell.

"Keep moving," Craddock ordered, nodding toward the sun-splashed mouth of the cave a hundred meters away. "The lady's getting impatient."

Treading lightly past the sulfurous pools like acolytes in Dante's Inferno, we arrived to where the woman stood at the bottom of a rock-strewn incline. Twenty feet above her was the tantalizingly close exit from the cavern.

Pivoting to face us, Medusa recited an incantation in Maori.

Craddock raised his hand palm outward to acknowledge the significance of the spell. To Hart and me—Pillow apparently understood already—he whispered, "She has taken our hau to protect the land we are about to enter. As strangers, we are considered tapu—unclean—until we are officially accepted at the marae."

Seemingly satisfied with the explanation, our guide led us from the stygian floor into brilliant sunlight and fresh air.

Granted, the physical exertions of the last couple of days, not to mention my cracked ribs, may have affected my critical sensibilities. But when I recall the marvel I beheld that morning—a winding emerald valley six or seven miles long, wedged between towering perpendicular cliffs and filled with every beauty nature can offer—I doubt that Wordsworth could have done poetic justice to the scene before us.

Even Hart gasped at the view.

However, from the standpoint of accessibility, this miracle of nature had a lot to be desired. Although stunningly beautiful, the steep cliffs guarded the jigsaw-shaped valley like a vise. Nothing that could remotely be called a road was within fifty miles and the erratic winds funneling down the perpetually snowcapped peaks of the Haast Range made it impossible for helicopters to land. That meant the only entry into Ivo Mackin's fiefdom was by foot through the maddening labyrinth of tunnels, dead ends, and toxic fumaroles under Shipowner Ridge. And, unless you had wings, the route through the cavern was also the only exit.

Prior to entering the cave, the ambient temperature had been below freezing and the ground covered by varying depths of snow. But here, the temperature felt no less than sixty degrees Fahrenheit. Where the rays of the sun escaped the continual shadow of the mountains, acres of vegetables had been planted at an elevation not normally conducive to plants. It was a microclimate straight out of Lost Horizon, in which waterfalls tumbled from velvet heights into turquoise pools, sheep grazed contentedly on lush grasses, and willow-laced bridges covered fast-flowing streams teeming with trout.

I've seen some mighty fine places in my time—the U-shaped canyon of Telluride, England's Lake District, and the Swiss Lauterbrunnen Gap—but this wind-sheltered vale combined the best of them all, with the balmy fragrance of Napa Valley to boot.

The beauty did nothing to soften our guide's

demeanor. Bogs, drizzle, and darkness seemed to be Medusa's natural milieu. But I wondered how the Maoris who once dwelled here could have called this terrestrial paradise The Land of Tears?

We followed her on a pebbled path past rows of sweet potatoes, taro, spinach, and cress, and a field where the honeyed reek of marijuana permeated the air. A dozen lightly clothed young men and women—all seemingly buzzed and oblivious to our presence—lazily filled their baskets with the flowering tops and leaves from tall stalks of cannabis. In an adjacent meadow, thousands of red and orange poppies swayed in the gentle breeze.

It was a mile from the cavern to a wooden arch covered with elaborately carved designs that signaled the entrance to the marae. A lodge-pole fence extended from it for a few yards on either side. Behind this ran a shallow trench filled with smooth rocks. The fence and ditch seemed there for appearances only, a nod to the traditional fortress or pa that once served a very real defensive purpose in the days of warring tribes.

Within the border was a cleared rectangular compound about half the size of a football field. It was lined by plank-sided houses and sapling huts, interspersed with lean-tos where women huddled over looms and men executed remarkable spiral designs on wood using chisels made of sharpened greenstone. At either end of the village were storehouses in which people came and went carrying baskets filled with berries, vegetables, and grain. Sullen, foxlike dogs with thick tails roamed freely between them.

Beyond the arch stretched a walkway leading to a large A-frame building that Craddock explained was the Wharenu, or meetinghouse. Facing to the east to greet the morning sun, it was covered with beautiful carvings representing the history of the Maori people. Each spiral notch represented a paragraph, every concentric swirl a chapter to a legend. Next to the Wharenu was a slightly less imposing structure that was the communal eating place, the Whare Kai.

The center of the compound was open except for a raised stone circle. Five men stood in front of it carrying wooden staffs.

The woman, having led us this far, beckoned us to advance toward the center of the open space while singing in a haunting, high-pitched voice.

As if on cue, a dozen young men and women streamed from the meetinghouse. They formed a semi-circle in front of us. They were dressed in cloaks, capes, and kilts of woven flax and bark cloth with kiwi feathers. All were barefooted, and both sexes had some type of facial tattoo. Our guide shouted a command. They began to sway their bodies as if in some hypnotic trance.

The dancing continued for a few minutes, followed by speeches from two older men, one of which was delivered in English for our benefit. After reciting their ancestry, tribe, and subtribe, they greeted us in the name of the dead who had come before and would come after, and the importance of remembering tikanga Maori—their culture and traditions. The Archbishop of New York couldn't have delivered the Litany of the Saints any better.

When the homilies finally ended, Craddock told us that an offering was required. He gathered a ten-dollar note from me, earrings from Pillow, and half a bag of trail mix from a miserly Hart, and laid them at the foot of Medusa.

Once she had picked up our offerings, the only thing left to complete our initiation was to formally meet with the welcoming party. It took a couple of clumsy efforts, but I finally got the hang of the *hongi*— touch forehead of target lightly, press (don't rub!) target's nose, introduce yourself by stating your name and the mountain, river or lake nearest to where you were raised. In my case, the Muddy Missouri.

Most of the greeters seemed friendly enough, but, despite the genial words, I didn't feel any closer to being a member of their fraternity, let alone family, than I had before we entered the compound. Most of them, women as well, had a glazed look about them, looking only slightly less stoned than the workers we'd seen earlier.

With the *powhiri* ceremony over, a sinewy man in late middle age approached us with the precision and posture of a grenadier guard. He wore a beautiful cloak made entirely of kiwi feathers draped over his left shoulder, leaving his right shoulder and muscular arm bare. His long black hair was brushed straight from his forehead and tied in the usual knot at the top of the head, and a greenstone pendant dangled from an earlobe. A trim white mustache and goatee framed his mouth. His face, except for the bridge of his nose and his cheeks, was adorned with tattoos consisting of linear and concentric lines.

He studied us with interest and not a little amusement. With a start, I realized he was holding our two journals against his chest.

"I am Wiremu Tako," he said with no trace of a Maori accent. "If it's easier for you, call me Witako. I was known as Terence Robertson in the world below."

Craddock stepped forward to exchange the hongi. "Are you the Ariki of this compound?"

Chief Witako nodded. "Ora, Tane Ne Teome. I knew your mother years ago in Otematata. She was one of the great storytellers and a powerful seer. She would have been most welcome here."

He then approached Pillow. Instinctively, she bent her head toward him. He responded in a like manner for the ritual nose press.

"It is good to meet you at last, Penelope. The Ranginui speaks of you often."

"Why call my father 'Sky God'?"

"Merely a term of respect."

"When will I see him?"

"That is a delicate matter. I suggest that you take a few days to gather your strength. I have assigned people to assist each of you. Hopefully, you will learn some of our ways and see what we have accomplished here."

Hart stepped forward and pointed to the journals.

"How about giving those back now that you've seen them? Not that I...we...don't trust you."

The Ariki maintained his courteous formal demeanor but made it clear we were going to play by the home team's rules.

"For now," he said after barking orders that brought two young men scurrying from a nearby hut. "They shall remain in my care."

I didn't see them spirit my fellow travelers away because by then a stocky young woman, foregoing the traditional greeting, had pulled my head down to plant a kiss on my lips.

"I am Aronui," she said, flashing a coquettish smile above her tattooed chin. "I asked to be your host. Do you agree to have me?"

"Have I a choice?"

Her mouth curved downward. "I do not please you?"

"It's not that. I just don't think I need a babysitter."

Aronui let out a silvery laugh. She purred, "I think you'll like me."

Well, thinks I, if a buxom girl wants to put it that way, who am I to protest?

She led me by the hand to a hut on the eastern side of the marae.

I had to duck to get through the door, but the floor had been excavated so that the overall height inside the structure allowed me to stand upright. Aronui lit an oil lamp with an old Zippo, and I saw what would be my digs for the next week.

Coarse grass mats covered the otherwise dirt floor. The bed was marginally different from the mats in that it was woven of a thicker, finer material and stuffed with straw. There was a hole in the roof, twelve inches or so in diameter. Directly beneath it were sticks of kindling and matches for making a fire, but it would have to get plenty cold for me to risk asphyxiation lighting it. In the corner was a pottery bowl that Aronui shyly suggested could be used as a chamber pot.

It wasn't exactly the Dorchester, but it was snug enough, and after the arduous journey, I wasn't complaining.

When I turned to inform Aronui that, despite the lack of a television and a minibar, the room would do, I saw she had taken off her cloak and was kneeling on the bed mat with nothing on except a tiny grass apron. The minx didn't look in my direction, but there was no getting around her intent.

It was late afternoon and the temperature had dropped twenty degrees, but watching that apple-cheeked girl with the up-turned breasts and milk-chocolate eyes playfully pretending to adjust the feathers in her hair, had me sweating like an Algerian stevedore.

Nonetheless, I'm proud, if not a little surprised, to report that I declined her invitation to grapple in the buff.

"Here now, what's the problem?" she demanded when it became apparent I wasn't succumbing to her charms. "You like boys instead maybe?"

"No problem at all, Aronui. I find you extremely desirable. It's just... Well, it wouldn't be gentlemanly, my being a guest of the Ranginui and all."

She found that amusing.

"He doesn't mind. No one here minds. It's expected of us."

"'Us' who?"

"Comfort hine," she said, demurely draping the cloak over her shoulders. "Not all the girls, just the ones who plied the old trade before. This isn't a monastery. Me, I come from a knocking shop in Hamilton up north. Things got too rough, and I let an *arioi* know I wanted to put my talents to use elsewhere. Got me away from my uncle and his dirty friends. Been all right, all things considered. They teach me Maori stuff. I don't drink gin no more. No chance for meth up here, neither. Only the hashish and poppies, which are brilliant! Like you never had the likes of."

"What's an *arioi*?"

"A wanderin' type. They go about the country lookin' for folks the Ariki can help."

"How long have you been here?"

"Going on three years. That's why I talk Maori so good, although I was always hearin' the words from my nana before she died. Most of them cuss words, mixed in with the old tales."

She looked at me before securing the cloak pin at her shoulder.

"*Ka mahi ai?* You sure you don't want to lie with me? I ain't got the pox."

"Not today," I answered, not too convincingly. "I still don't quite see how your trade fits in with the Ranginui's plans for a Maori rehab center."

Aronui considered this very seriously.

"What I do is very much part of *whanaungatanga*. That is, to teach and guide, working to maintain harmony with what skills I have. I can't weave, but I'm good at fucking, and I don't mind if it's with someone I don't especially like or even know. I make happy the blokes who need sex so they won't take it out on others, upsetting the *hau* of the village."

"Why did you think it necessary to offer your body to me?"

"Witako said it would be proper."

"That's the only reason?"

She smiled. "It would have been a nice greeting for me as well. Now, take off your clothes."

"But I thought…"

"Pah, not for that." She went to one of the baskets and pulled out a kilt, a woven belt, and a cloak made of dog skin similar to the one she wore with the hair side out. "You aren't to wear *pakeha* clothes while our guest."

In deference to my tender feet, Aronui handed me a pair of sandals plaited from strips of leaves. Coyly, she averted her eyes when I pulled off my skivvies and climbed into the kilt. Once I'd secured the garb with a woven belt, I dipped my head so that she could drape a long cloak over it. Then she handed me a rectangular garment to be placed around my shoulders, pinned the two vestments together at my right shoulder, and stood back to admire her work.

"*Pai. I iwi humarire.*"

"Pardon?"

"I said, 'You look handsome.' Like an old-time warrior."

"I feel like I've been rolled up in a bearskin rug."

"You'll get used to it."

"Are my friends going through the same rigmarole?"

"Yeah."

"When can I see them?"

"Soon enough. There are some things you must know now that you're a guest of the marae."

She motioned for me to follow her out of the hut.

Chapter 24

I t took a while, but I eventually learned that Hart was lodged on the western edge of the marae. Pillow was kept isolated outside the compound in a hut by the river, watched over by a pair of Medusa's harpies. She might as well have been on the moon. Because of his mother's reputation and command of most things Maori, Craddock had the advantage of being the teacher's pet. He asked and got Witako's permission to pitch his nylon pup tent in a spot conveniently near the cannabis field. He also had free run of the place as long as he stayed away from the cavern.

As for me, I was reasonably comfortable in my *wikiup*, and the delightful Aronui proved to be a natural tour guide. During the next three days, she showed me enough of the ways of tikanga Maori to fill four issues of *National Geographic*. More importantly, because of her willingness to answer my questions, it didn't take long for me to understand which way the wind blew in this Down Under version of Oz.

Most of the hundred-fifty or so inhabitants were in

their late teens or early twenties and had been enticed to the marae to escape their dreadful home environment. When not farming, fishing for trout, or stoking on joints laced with opium, they practiced martial arts, woodcraft, and other old-time skills.

Their paid instructors were well-versed in tikanga disciplines. But while some appeared dedicated, I saw little evidence that the primary goal of the training was to rehabilitate troubled Maoris. The more I observed, in fact, the more I thought Professor Middleditch's instincts were correct—the marae was nothing more than a Potemkin village established to fool the Inland Revenue and the Ministry for Maori Development; a ruse to grant Ivo Mackin full title to the land.

For one thing, I saw no evidence that the Ranginui cared a hoot as to what went on in the village. Aronui said that his whare was in an isolated grove a quarter mile outside the compound where only a select few were allowed to see him. They apparently included Medusa, a few scouts to keep people at a distance, and, of course, Witako, who had been Ivo Mackin's former chief operating officer at TransNational Metals, Ltd.

The former Terence Robertson ran the compound with an iron fist encased in a velvet glove. He encouraged access to opiates and sex as a means to controlling his young charges, but anyone asking too many questions or caught snooping around forbidden areas paid a harsh price at the hands of a dozen gang-bangers hired to police the area. Aronui said they barracked in one of two concrete blockhouses a half mile past the village.

"Who stays in the other blockhouse?" I asked.

Her cheery face suddenly turned opaque. "Others," she said in a way that meant she would say no more for the time being.

It was raining on the morning that an eighteen-year-old kid named Koro brought Tane Craddock and me to the martial arts center. Inside were a dozen young bucks sitting on their haunches waiting for their lesson to begin. Ngati, the scout who discovered us by the Waipara River, went to the front of the class.

He spoke in Maori, but with Craddock translating, I got the gist of the instruction.

"The *taiaha*!" Ngati exclaimed, holding up a long quarterstaff. "It is everything—it is your protection, your genealogy, your bearing, your prayers, and life force. It is the language of Tu, the war god, this *taiaha*!"

He dropped the weapon and picked up a short, flat paddle-like object made of stone.

"The *patu*," Craddock explained quietly to me. "For use in close fighting. The *taiaha* wounds, but the *patu* delivers the kill."

Ngati swung the short weapon expertly back and forth, forward and backward, in quick-footed feints and draws as his eyes bulged and his tongue extended to absurd lengths.

Soon the class was pairing off, going at each other like wolverines, thrusting and dodging with their weapons in mock but furious combat. They were so charged with adrenaline that even when the blows inadvertently connected with a limb or chest, the pain didn't appear to register.

Twenty minutes of that was enough for me. Craddock stayed, but I slipped away before someone invited me to become target practice.

Aronui was waiting patiently for me outside.

"When do you plan to leave this place?" I asked as we walked past through the arch toward the river.

She seemed bewildered by the question. "I don't want to go back. This is my *whanua*. My family."

"What 'family'? I don't see any kids, nor many old folks."

At this, the first tiny crack appeared in her devotion to the cause. "Wouldn't be right to have little ones," she said. Her eyes avoided mine.

"Don't you ever get tired of the isolation and all the rules?"

"Rules must be followed."

"*Tapu*, for instance?"

"That's only another word for self-respect. It is every person's responsibility to maintain their own while respecting the dignity of others. But it can't only be about human beings."

I must have looked skeptical.

"The Ariki expects us to be spiritual," she explained, taking my hand and leading me to where eels swam near the surface of the stream. "We all come from one source. See how even the water celebrates my image. My eyebrows are like the wingspan of birds, my forehead the crown of a great tree."

"Oh, come off it, Aronui! You don't really believe all that stuff. It makes you sound like a New Age hippie."

Her cheeks flushed. "Maori tradition teaches that everything is connected. We aren't supposed to believe in separation."

"What about good and evil? Can they be one and the same?"

"Is there a good tree, an evil tree?"

"You've got me there."

We passed a bush covered with long strands of shiny black berries that looked delicious. When I reached for a handful, Aronui slapped my hand away.

"The tutu berry," she said. "Its seeds will freeze up your lungs."

"So," I said. "There are bad trees in this Arcadia of yours."

She frowned at this but soon had a rejoinder.

"The seeds protect the berry. But the juice makes a tasty jelly when boiled properly and can even treat illness. Certainly nature can be dangerous, but there is sweetness as well."

We moved silently into a pine forest where Aronui again started spouting feel-good Maori philosophy in which bushes and whales were cousins, boulders and oceans brothers, birds the bearers of seeds that created mighty forests—all the claptrap one hears when justifying a traditional way of life long past its usefulness.

I was half-expecting her to show me a unicorn when an A-frame house materialized as if out of nowhere in a clearing of the woods. Lavishly decorated with swirls, ferns, and weird creatures, it looked like something out of Terry Gilliam's *Time Bandits*.

In the center of the front wall, above a door you could drive a tank through, was the last thing I expected to see on the backside of a mountain in Maoriville—the giant anchor of an eighteenth-century sailing ship.

"Who lives there?"

"The Ranginui," Aronui said, moving hurriedly past. "We've come too far. They may see us."

"They?"

"The Mongrels. Or, worse, the Chinese fellas."

Chapter 25

Aronui wouldn't say more until we had retreated back to the river, but once there, she opened up full throttle.

"At any given time, there are five or six who work in the cavern. They live in the other blockhouse. They are tapu to all but the girls chosen to service them."

"Have you?"

"Yes. Once. But no more. I'd kill myself first."

"Do you know what they do in the caves?"

She shook her head. "When the first group arrived, they brought with them a lot of fancy tools and hand-held machines with spiky antennae and such.

"None stay more than a few months. Then they're replaced by a new crew brought up by Daig Kildare. They're like walking skeletons by the time they leave. I don't know how any of them survive the return over the mountains. Maybe they don't."

"It's important I learn what they are doing here," I pressed when she had described all she knew. "Will you tell me when the next group is brought up?"

"Yes," she said.

"Promise?"

Aronui touched the greenstone around my neck. "I promise."

We returned to a grove outside the marae where people were gathered for the midweek communal supper. While some stood patiently in line, others placed clay bowls of fruit and woven baskets of sweet potatoes and corn on long tables. Scattered behind the tables, people knelt in front of charcoal fire pits frying eels, fish, and small birds that were then scooped onto wooden plates.

If you disregarded the clothing, facial tats, and food implements harkening back to the Bronze Age, you might think you'd stumbled onto a Labor Day picnic in a small town of one of our western states, only without children scampering about.

I was piling soggy corn, squash, and some brownish slithery thing onto my wooden plate when I spotted Adrian Hart. He stood near a clump of trees, nose in the air as usual despite looking ridiculous in a kilt that was too long for his short legs.

Alternating between bites of bread and smoking a huge ganja joint, he spoke earnestly with a muscle-bound brute straight out of central casting for the movie *Once Were Warriors*. The man's arms were thicker than my thighs. His head was ghastly, with black eyes that shined like a cobra's beneath a heavy unibrow. Long ringlets of curly hair framed a tattooed face that even in this übertraditional Maori setting seemed excessive. Ferns and scrolls ran alongside the flaring nostrils of his widespread nose. A pair of lizards were intertwined in some kind of mating dance around the wide, purplish lips.

But what made his markings truly unusual was that they seemed to have been chiseled on rather than punctured by a needle. His darkened skin was covered in grooves that must have taken months to heal.

The traditional dress code didn't apply to him. He wore a pair of filthy, ragged jeans and hobnail boots. A black leather vest struggled to cover a bare chest the size of a Nevada dam.

"That ugly devil with my friend—is he a guest as well?"

Aronui shook her head. "Kahoura has been here over a year. He's a Mongrel."

"Why is he with Hart?"

"Your friend liked the looks of him."

Witako suddenly appeared by our side. Aronui shyly acknowledged his presence, then slipped away.

"You've caught the attention of someone," he warned, looking over my shoulder.

I turned to find Kahoura staring in my direction. Hart remained next to him, checking out the crowd as if at the Ascot Races. The Mongrel's face was devoid of any light and his pitiless eyes exuded such malice that I dropped my gaze like a convent girl having witnessed her first exhibitionist. When I forced myself to look back, he snarled something, and I felt my chest explode as if a wrecking ball had struck my solar plexus.

I stood stock still for a moment gasping for breath, a blinding pain ricocheting within my skull. Then the scene before me went topsy-turvy. I dropped to my knees, a quivering heap of disconnected molecules. Limbs numb. Throat burning. Senses approaching meltdown. Temporal lobe just a pile of undercooked spaghetti.

Kahoura had disappeared by the time I awoke on my back, my lips flapping like a landed carp mouthing for air. A grim-faced Witako kneeled beside me, chanting, "*Kaitoa! I tahuna mai ahaou kit e ahi whakeane Ki mate te wairua!*"

As he spouted this gibberish in my ear, Aronui was busily cutting a green lizard into pieces with a pounamu blade and tossing the bits into a charcoal fire.

I know it sounds ridiculous, but as soon as I heard the sound of that sizzling reptile, the agony vanished. It left me limp as week-old lettuce, but only the ribs I'd busted during the fall on the mountain hurt.

"What just happened?" I asked, practically weeping with relief.

"Kahoura sent the lizard," Aronui replied. "The *moko kakariki.*"

"The lizard bit me?"

"No, and even if it did, it isn't poisonous. But *kotipu* is an evil omen."

"You had an experience not many would survive," Witako told me. "Only by performing the *whakautuutu* rite were we able to banish the curse. You should rest this afternoon; perhaps take a bath in one of the hot springs.

"I'm sure," he added as he helped me to my feet, "that the soothing waters will have you feeling like the king's own rooster."

After thanking the Ariki, I asked why Kahoura would want to harm a guest of the marae.

Witako didn't answer. By the look on his face, I'm not sure that he knew. But he did say something that got my attention.

"Perhaps it is time for you to meet the Ranginui. If all is well, I'll make arrangements for you to see him this evening."

left time or leave...

But he's just that if you leave me tonight it's all over. I'll make arrangements for you to see this evening...

Chapter 26

That afternoon I took Witako's advice and went to soak in one of the hot springs near the center of the valley. I wanted privacy, not only to restore body and soul, but to go over what I'd say to Ivo Mackin. After all, calling on someone who considers himself a god requires some thoughtful preparation. But there was no getting rid of Aronui, who skipped after me like a frisky puppy as soon as she saw me leave the hut. After eliciting a promise that there would be no hanky-panky, I allowed her to lead me to a bubbling spring next to a waterfall straight out of Rivendell.

It was just past four p.m. and the sun had dipped behind the western peaks, covering that part of the valley in a deep purple glow.

I should have known the hussy had no intention of following orders when she slipped out of her kiwi feathers to settle, naked as a jaybird, into the pool. Sitting upright against the side, her brown breasts gleaming in the moonlight and the tip of her pink tongue sliding ever so slowly above that tattooed chin, Arounui was enough to make a eunuch's mouth water.

Muttering the Lord's Prayer, I primly shed my cloak—but not my kilt—and climbed into the bubbling cauldron a few feet opposite her. Although hellishly hot, it was remarkably soothing, too. I was just beginning to relax when I felt her toes tickle my nether region.

"Hey!" I yelped, nearly levitating out of the water. "Enough of that!"

"Don't you find me attractive?" she pouted as the steam engulfed us.

I felt like Adam prior to bashing the leather with Eve, but remembering how that turned out—not to mention what happened to Abelard—I willed myself to remain chaste.

"Of course I do, but if you recall our agreement…"

Aronui answered with the other foot, confirming that she was not only a liar, but ambidextrous as well.

"Whoa! That's not fair. Stop it now!"

She flew at me then, wrapping her legs around my waist like a monkey on a stick, sobbing endearments, nibbling at my ear, and begging for a platinum-grade lesson in what Canadian ruggers call "a Chesterfield scrum."

Mind you, I've been locked in enough randy embraces to know that, despite one's purest intentions, there comes a point when old Nebuchadnezzar won't return to the barn.

And yet.

This time.

Somehow.

He did.

Counting the cold shoulder she got the first time we met in the hut, Aronui was batting 0 for 2 in the series. She wasn't used to it and didn't like it one bit. I can't say I did either, but I realized that if I hoped to succeed in finding the third journal, sexual abstinence was the one virtue that must be heeded.

But just try to explain that to a feisty siren who misinterprets prudence for rejection.

After she'd called me every nasty Maori word learned at her uncle's scabrous knee, she pulled on her clothes and stomped back to the compound.

Alone at last, my thoughts drifted to home and of my conversation with Josie Majansik the night before I left for New Zealand.

I forget what our quarrel was about. Ever since her return from Wyoming, we'd been peeved with each other most of the time. Touchy and argumentative. Maybe that's because when I'm right on some issue she disagrees with, I get angry. Josie gets angry when she is wrong.

"You have three main topics of interest," she said later as we got ready for bed. "Books, rugby, and Michael Bevan. It gets rather old."

"You forgot sex."

"Wisecrack all you want, Mike. You know the lyrics to every song, the punch line to every joke, but you lack the courage to follow through on anything. You'd rather ruin it before someone or something else can do it to you first."

I'm not sure what brought this sudden condemnation on—it might have been due to Feklar having rejected the new litter box—but Josie was right. My inability to stay the course in the law, my marriage, fatherhood, and a hundred other things was self-inflicted.

I kept my pajama bottoms on as I crawled under the covers. So did she.

"Is there anything you do like about me?"

"Aside from your body, I suppose it's your boyish enthusiasm."

"Some would call that immaturity."

"Yes," she said. "But in your case, it's been a saving grace."

"Who's the wiseacre now, Josie?"

"I'm not joking. I thought I knew you after our terrifying experience with Martin Quist. But the more we settled in, the more I realized you're like the layers of an onion. Pull one away, there's always another until I'm left with a question mark."

"Am I that unpredictable?"

"Yes, darling." She shifted so that we were face-to-face, sharing one pillow. "I love you, Mike, but I don't want us to stay together if it means continually repairing differences just to be able to say at the end, 'We endured.'"

"I don't either. I saw what it did to my parents. It's just that I feel there's a piece of the jigsaw missing."

Her fingertips caressed my face. "That's why you need to go to New Zealand. Find what you seek. Bring it home to complete the puzzle. I'll be here to help. I promise."

Chapter 27

The moon had risen over Mount Aspiring when I got out of the hot spring, donned my dog-hair tuxedo, and walked back to my hut to find Pillow lounging provocatively on my mat.

She wore something made of black and white feathers arranged in horizontal stripes that would have done justice to Alexander McQueen. Her hair was bundled on the top of her head with falcon quills. The backpack straps we'd used to immobilize her injured shoulder had been replaced by a binding of flat leather strips securing her right arm against her chest. Aside from its practical functionality, the wrap was an exquisite design of complicated concentric knots.

"Well, if it isn't Xena the Warrior Princess," I said, sitting beside her.

"And her best pal, Barney Rubble," came the wry response.

"Who wrapped your shoulder?"

"One of Medusa's ladies. Amazing how comfortable it is."

"Seen your father yet?"

She shook her head, leaned back seductively, and tickled my chin with the index finger of her left hand. "Witako will be by in an hour to take us to him. I've missed you, Michael."

It never rains, but it pours.

The promise I'd made to myself was again being severely tested. It was hard enough declining Aronui's entreaties. Now Pillow was hankering for a replay of our Wellington tryst.

But Veronica Lake, Lady Godiva, and Bettie Page rolled into one couldn't have brought me up to the plate. Things were getting too weird, what with green lizards and mysterious Asians about—not to mention a meeting with the Sky God looming.

There was only one thing to do—look serious and stall.

"Been keeping busy, have you?" I asked with wide-eyed innocence.

Ignoring the question, Pillow stopped the teasing. She sat up and, with a stare that could have frozen Genghis Khan, demanded, "What were you doing before coming here?"

"Enjoying the waters," I answered truthfully.

"While a certain strumpet was enjoying you, I suppose."

The remark caught me off guard, not because she'd thought I'd been up to something with Aronui, but because it implied a real feeling of jealousy. Without bothering to counter her charge, I put on a perplexed Howdy Doody grin and repeated my question.

It was enough to stop her inquisition. She sat up, all thoughts of passion gone for now. I adjusted my kilt and crossed my legs. (Ironically, now that I'd quelled her ardor, mine was beginning to act up.)

"Until now," she finally answered, "I've practically been a prisoner. Whenever I asked to see my father, I was told the time was 'inconvenient.' If it hadn't been for Tane dropping by every day, I might have gone crazy."

"Speaking of whom," I said. "The last time I saw him was two days ago when we watched some young bucks at their weapons practice."

"It's been a while for me as well."

"What is Tane to you, Pillow? Why did he apologize to you back at Esme's?"

Her lips twitched a little.

"My friends and I used to play in a cave outside Arrowtown," she began. "Being the skinniest, I usually was the one sent to check out the tightest spots and got stuck in a hole once. Tane was too big to get in close enough to pull me out. His brother Hemi wasn't, though. Saved my life really."

"And you paid accordingly?"

"Yeah. I didn't want to, but Hemi insisted. It was his first time. Tane was older and could have stopped it, but he just walked away."

"Is that why the Craddocks went to prison?"

"Lord, no! Testifying would have just meant my being totally shunned."

She shrugged off the memory.

"Anyway, no baby came of it. Given the rest of the blokes in that family, Tane wasn't so bad. Three of the Craddocks got sent to prison for robbing a grocery store a few years later. Because he talked Hemi out of killing the clerk, Tane received a lighter sentence."

A number of secrets had come to light in the past

couple of days. Alone in the semidarkness of the hut, I sensed the time was right to tell what I knew of her past.

"I heard that your husband left you holding the bag on a debt."

"Congratulations," Pillow retorted warily. "Our financial problems were hardly unknown in certain circles of Edinburgh and London."

"I know about the Russian, too—what he forced you to do."

Silence. Complete silence.

I withheld the urge to shake her.

Slowly, emptily, she said, "I take it Adrian told you?"

"Yes."

"And how I dealt with it."

"I'm not judging you."

She stared back at me with stone-cold eyes. "How very considerate."

"Sorry, Pillow. I didn't intend a Sunday school lecture."

Her eyes, so hard before, now were pleading. "I'm not evil."

"Of course you're not. I'd have fricasseed that Russian and goosed him on his way to hell."

She pressed her body against mine.

"Adrian threatened to tell the police."

"And that's the hold he has over you?"

"Yes. Once he learned that my father had the third journal, Adrian knew I was the only way he'd be able to gain access to it."

"So why drag me into this?"

"At first it was because I wanted added protection."

She was trembling. "But the more I came to know you…"

"What is it?"

"Will you stay with me when this is over?"

My response to this astonishing request—I knew she'd given top marks to our one and only tumbling session, but I never imagined true romance might enter the equation—was to answer with a kiss.

I'm not proud of it, but since it seemed neither the time nor the place to confess that Josie Majansik was my one true love, I saw no way around the situation. I already had enough enemies.

Pillow was an odd one, to be sure: a victim of a terrible crime who had taken it upon herself to exact revenge in her own very personal way. Part Amazon, part little girl, and part something else, I wasn't sure I could trust Pillow any more than I could Adrian Hart.

I might have learned more had Witako not arrived to take us to meet his boss.

Chapter 28

We walked along a graveled path for twenty minutes before arriving at the steeply roofed house that I had glimpsed earlier with Aronui.

Hart, who had exchanged his Maori getup for his clothes from the real world, was waiting impatiently for us by the door under the iron anchor. Pillow scarcely looked at him, and when she did, it was with a Gorgon stare for having spilled her secrets.

Every inch of the walls of the sparsely furnished space we entered was covered with beautiful carvings. A buzzing generator in a corner powered half a dozen electrical lights hanging from overhead beams. Except for matches and running shoes, they were the only nod to the modern era I'd seen since arriving at the compound.

A second room beckoned. On the lintel above the entrance was carved a Latin inscription: *Adsum. Arcamun arcanorum.*

I knew *Adsum* meant "I am here," but my grammar school Latin wasn't up to the rest.

Pillow's classical education, however, was.

"*Arcanum Arcanorum*—Secret of Secrets," she told me. "To alchemists in the Middle Ages, it meant the ultimate key to the unknown—the secret of nature."

Witako pressed his finger to his lips before motioning to follow him.

God knows I'd had enough surprises since landing in this country, but considering what we encountered in the next room—a full-size replica of the Great Cabin of the *HMS Resolution* complete with a pantry, cupboards for scientific and botanical equipment, ship lanterns, and a stuffed dodo—is there any wonder I felt trapped inside a maniac's dream?

A man whose long gray hair was tied back in a sailor's rattail sat in a spindle-legged chair with his back to us. He scratched words onto a sheet of parchment with a feather quill.

The broad oak table he wrote at was covered with old charts weighted down by a barometer and an old brass sextant. Some things had escaped the eighteenth century: a table lamp fed by a generator, books with contemporary titles, a front-loading steel safe.

Without turning, he acknowledged the sound of our presence by raising his left arm and extending two fingers. Another minute passed before he set the quill into a copper ink pot and rose to face us.

The Te Ranginui, hereditary leader of the Kati Mamoe iwi, champion rugger, and former billionaire CEO of TransNational Metals, wasn't the type you'd find at Costco sorting through the sale bin.

He was lean, with long arms and immense hands, and tall, taller than me, but with a slight stoop as if used to bending over to hear others of lesser stature. His face browned to a rich chestnut, was slightly pitted from some childhood disease. Silver-rimmed spectacles perched perilously on the end of a broad nose that tilted a quarter inch off center then back to square one. A jagged three-inch scar creased his forehead.

Despite these imperfections, it wasn't an unpleasant face. Credit goes to the hypnotic eyes, the strong jaw, and a wide, sensuous mouth.

His getup, however, was another matter. It looked like something out of a J. Peterman catalog whose fashion statement for the month was Mutiny on the Bounty. The white linen shirt with billowing sleeves, tucked into twill trousers fronted by exposed buttons instead of a zipper, must have come in the same box as the mauve silk brocade vest. His footwear consisted of bucket boots with the obligatory brass buckles.

There was something else that didn't match the man who had been a world-beater in everything he tried. Despite a face befitting a Comanche chief—or godfather to the Corsican mafia—he had the dazed manner of someone who had suffered a mental illness and was fearful of it returning soon.

The inner tension became even more apparent as he tentatively ran the fingers of one hand through his hair. He seemed at a loss as to who we were.

"How do you do?" he finally said as if greeting us in the lobby of the Ritz-Carlton. Then, before we could respond, he turned to Witako, who had moved to his side like a solicitous caregiver. "And why do I have the pleasure of their company?"

"These men have brought your daughter to see you."

"Ah, yes." He turned to Pillow, adjusting his glasses for better focus. "Leslie, is it?"

"No, Rangi," Witako corrected gently. "Leslie is in Auckland. This is your Penelope who now lives in London."

"The burned creature?"

"Yes, Father," Pillow answered stoically. "Your little monster."

Ivo Mackin glanced at the rest of us for confirmation that this person was his bastard daughter.

I felt the smile that had frozen my face getting another glazing. Adrian Hart shuffled his feet with impatience. Pillow chose to emulate a wooden Indian, albeit one with flushed cheeks.

"Perhaps we should come back later," I suggested, following the long, awkward silence.

My words were mostly for the benefit of Witako, who seemed aching for an excuse to end the meeting.

"Come back?" Mackin echoed. "Come back from where?" He leaned against his desk. "Who are you again?"

I introduced myself while Pillow remained silent. Hart, ever the charmer, had lost all patience.

"Look here, old man; we know you possess a journal relating to Captain Cook. We intend to see it."

Mackin stared questioningly at Hart, but something had registered in his clouded brain. He tipped backward on his heels, crossing his long arms as if locked in a straitjacket. A gleam emerged from behind the glasses.

"See it, you say? Another word for 'steal,' perhaps. I'm not sure my people would allow that. Let me give you a word of advice, sir…"

A peculiar expression suddenly swept across his

face. Collapsing in his chair, he stared blankly at the ceiling and shuddered uncontrollably in the beginning throes of a seizure.

Instantly, Witako took charge, grabbing his shoulders from behind while he chanted, "*Ka rere te ringa kit e ure...Kai ure nga atua...Kai ure nga tapu...Kai ure ou makutu...*"

Within seconds the spasms stopped, bringing about a transition in the Ranginui's appearance and demeanor. The mists of confusion departed. They were replaced by a piercing recollection of who we were and what Witako had explained to him earlier of our mission. It was remarkable to watch his recollections flutter like butterflies back to his consciousness.

"Penelope, dear child!" Mackin gushed, rising and extending his arms. "How gratifying to see how beautiful you have become."

The blank mask on her face held firm for an instant before she walked around the table and fell into his embrace.

"I trust your journey from London was pleasant?" he said after the happy exchange.

"Yes, papa-*hakora*. I've stayed away too long."

Then, turning toward the rest of us, Mackin asked, "And the hike over the col? Not too strenuous?"

"A bit," Hart answered as he reshelved a book he had pulled from a cabinet. It was titled *Metallurgy and Geological Findings of New Zealand* by G.S. Woodcock. "Indeed, the journey proved to be most invigorating."

"Delighted to hear it," Mackin murmured, returning to his chair. He scratched his nose with the quill. Then he motioned for us to sit.

"Forgive me for seeming confused when you appeared. Apparitions sometimes invade my brain—

terrible images of grotesque beings climb through the walls and ceiling, threatening to take me away with them. It's a bit of a bother distinguishing what's real and what isn't. When you first entered, they were my reality and you were the apparitions. It helps to write about them. Only by the Ariki's intervention can they be dispelled. I meant no discourtesy."

"Understood," Hart said brusquely. "But Witako might have warned us and saved us all the embarrassment."

Ivo Mackin's placid smile remained steady.

"A drink, Mr. Bevan?"

"Yes, thank you."

"Mr. Hart?"

"If you insist."

Pillow declined.

Witako brought out a bottle of single malt whiskey —another nod to the present—from the pantry while Mackin motioned for us to sit in the other three saddleback chairs at the table.

"To your journey," he said, raising a glass.

I drank to that. Then, taking advantage of Mackin's civility, I asked, "I understand some Chinese technicians are in the caves? Are they taking samples or—"

"Bloody hell, Bevan!" Hart blurted impatiently. "If you won't get to the point, I will."

He turned to Mackin.

"I—we—demand that our journals be returned immediately and that we be allowed to fully inspect yours as well."

Pillow jumped to her feet. "For God's sake, Adrian, show some respect to my father!"

Mackin raised his hand. He looked directly at Hart, not unkindly.

"While I appreciate the diligence that you have shown to find me, I must question the reasons for your request. Assuming," he added mildly, "that I have what you wish to see."

"It's quite simple," Hart said. "Years ago, I came across Gibson's journal of Cook's second voyage. Recently, Bevan here discovered that he possessed the first. We've spent considerable time and expense to share ours with you. It seems perfectly reasonable that you reciprocate."

"In what manner? For what purpose?"

"I should think it apparent," Hart rasped, warming to the demand. "It would be an insult to scholarship, not to mention British heritage, to deny the world of that last, and I suspect most important witness to the final months, days, and hours of the great James Cook."

"But what if..." Mackin countered, maintaining his noncommittal smile. "The journal contained secrets the world was better off not knowing?"

"Assuming you have beheld these mysteries, I find that attitude to be not only presumptive but incredibly arrogant."

"Rather strong words, Mr. Hart." The Sky God no longer smiled.

That was my cue.

"Excuse me, sir, but do you believe what Gibson wrote was based on honest observation?"

"Yes, Mr. Bevan, I'm sure it was done in good faith."

"And you believe it to be accurate?"

"I do, but it presents an unhappy, uncharitable

revelation. I see no reason that a single lapse, largely due to illness brought about by incredible stress, should define the whole of a great man's life."

Pillow joined the debate with heartfelt emotion.

"Adrian has presented our case too bluntly, Father. I realize that for you, this is a very personal matter."

"As it is for you, my dear."

Pillow looked at him curiously before continuing. "But none of us will live forever. Don't you think there is a moral obligation to inform the world?"

"It is not a lie if no one asks the question."

Hart again: "It's no secret that by the end, Cook might have been insane, tormented by sickness and stress. What can Gibson add that's harsh enough to alter the image of this man?"

Mackin eyed the Englishman as if sizing up an unbroken horse. "I simply intend to let him rest in peace, Mr. Hart. There is no need to add further calumny to his reputation. Like unwise love, the unnecessary delivery of cruel facts is best avoided."

"If anything," Pillow said, "it will show that he was a normal human being, subject to the usual frailties that beset even the greatest heroes." She leaned forward to emphasize her point. "And, with all due respect, Adrian is right. You are being selfish by keeping it to yourself."

At this, her father's face assumed a most unforgiving look. "Selfish, am I? I've spent years and the remains of my fortune to help young Maoris sickened by pakeha culture!"

"Come off it, you old fool," Hart sneered. "If you're so keen on instilling native traditions, why wear that ridiculous costume as if you're the reincarnation of James Cook?"

Before Pillow could again apologize for her partner's boorishness, the Ranginui shakily rose to his feet. "Who," he said, the word slowly dripping from his lips. "Is to say I am not?"

And that, as Galileo once remarked, certainly put a different spin on things.

Chapter 29

"What are you saying, Father? Surely you don't believe…"

Mackin's eyes darted from Pillow to me and back to Pillow, showing all the symptoms of a man bursting to share his secrets.

"Actually," he said. "I do believe it."

He pulled a key out of his jacket pocket, brushing past Witako to reach the steel safe. His shaking hands caused him to fumble with the lock, but eventually the door opened and he removed a grotesque figure of a Maori tiki. It was three feet high and two feet wide. The wood had been carved to represent a head with shell eyes, a short neck, and a cylindrical torso without arms or legs. It looked identical to the image of the embryo on the greenstone pendant Esme had given me.

Returning to the table, he placed the object on the surface and fiddled with a latch on the back. Then, ignoring the Ariki who glared at him like a constipated undertaker, he told us a story within a story.

"After Captain Cook was killed at Kealakekua Bay in February 1779, his body was dissected on a flat stone according to custom. The priests parceled out pieces of flesh among themselves but granted King Kalani'opu'u the skull and a femur. The king kept them in a wicker basket covered with red feathers. For years afterward, these sacred relics were used to collect tributes throughout the Hawaiian Islands.

"Honored as the living avatar of Lono, the fertility god, Cook became even more revered in death. But when Hawaii came under the sway of the United States, Calvinist missionaries considered the natives' adulation of him to be the worst sort of blasphemy."

While Mackin spoke, his daughter sat motionless, hands folded tensely in front of her on the table. A sort of expectant melancholy had settled on Pillow's face. Witako stood in the corner of the room, shaking his head, silently seething. As for me, I studied the cuticle of my left thumb while wondering what the hell this history lesson had to do with the mysterious influx of Chinese in the area.

Hart, fidgeting with impatience, spoke through a yawn. "You've told us nothing that isn't available in the official narratives and subsequent histories. But you are wrong concerning his skull. Lieutenants Gore and King were quite specific as to which of his body parts the priests returned to the ship: a thigh bone, a hand that had been damaged years earlier, and his skull."

If Mackin was bothered by the interruption, he didn't show it. His eyes gleamed with renewed energy.

"His left hand, yes. Because it was the one thing that could be identified as Cook's. The extremely long thigh bone was likely his as well. But the head that had been boiled clean was of a marine who died by his side. Cook's skull was too much of a prize for the king to relinquish."

"How on earth do you know that?"

"I'll get to that in a moment. Now, where was I? Oh, yes, the missionaries. In the 1830s, they convinced the Hawaiians that diseases and even the catastrophic eruption of two volcanoes were God's revenge on those who clung to such pagan beliefs. As a result, the reverential treatment of Cook's remains came to an abrupt end.

"The bones would have been tossed in the sea, but a grandson of King Kalani'opu'u secretly hid them in the high cliffs overlooking Kealakekua Bay. When the king died, the same young man placed his grandfather's bones there as well."

"You went to Hawaii, didn't you?" I said.

"Yes. Six years ago, I stayed in a village above the bay where I met—"

That was enough for the Ariki, who clearly had not foreseen this turn of events. He rushed to the table, nearly setting it over.

"Stop this talk! It's tapu to mention these things to outsiders!"

Shaken by the outburst, Mackin appeared to reconsider his course. Just as the blabbing was getting interesting, too. But after gazing once more at Pillow, he said to Witako, "Please leave us, old friend. My daughter deserves to know the truth."

"*Kotahi loe ki reira!*" the Ariki shouted as he stormed from the room. It didn't sound like an invitation to dance.

Mackin waited a few moments for everyone to catch their breath, then sat down.

"Shall I continue?" he asked mischievously, his eyes shining behind the spectacles.

"Bloody hell," Hart growled. "Get on with it."

"At Kealakekua, I met an old man of pure Hawaiian blood. He noted my Maori features and proceeded to ask me many questions about my background. Then, perhaps in exchange for hearing my history, he related not only what I have told you so far, but something rather more surprising: It was his paternal forebear who had placed the bones there.

"After he had told me this secret, known only to direct descendants of the old king, I asked him why he shared it with me. His answer was that *Kapena Kuke*, meaning Captain Cook, had enjoyed relations with the king's favorite daughter, *Ka-maka-helei*. Following the captain's death, or perhaps even before, it was found that *Ka-maka-helei* was with child. Cook as Lono had usurped the king, the earthly embodiment of the war god Ku."

Hart's laugh was mocking.

"Double bloody bollocks! If that's the case, I'm the queen of the fairies. Cattley Middleditch warned us you might claim something like this and I thought he was nuts. You may have the journal, old boy, but this really is too much. Come on, quit your jabbering about a crazy old Hawaiian who thinks you're the gods' gift to mankind and show us what Gibson had to say."

Ivo Mackin fell silent during this harangue, gazing absentmindedly into the distance. I feared that whatever curse Witako had talked about was coming true. If the mind beasties came for the Ranginui again, it would be days before we would learn more of the story, even if it was a bunch of hooey.

His focus soon returned, however, and this time he directed his words to Pillow.

"It began with the old man's intuition as to who and what I was. Listening to him, I began to understand that a mystical power had brought me there. How else to explain it?"

If Dr. Oliver Sacks had been in the room, he might have suggested hallucinations derived from the onset of Parkinson's disease. But I held my tongue.

"He led me to the top of the cliffs," Mackin went on dreamily. "Using a rope ladder, we climbed down to a small cave that had been dug in the rock. Within it was the wicker basket."

He placed his hands on the wooden statue of the grotesque tiki figure.

"And this. Do you know what it is?"

"A small casket," Pillow said. "Used in the old days to contain the femur and lesser bones of a warrior."

Mackin nodded, then opened the lid and began unwrapping something within a cloth.

We edged closer to the table.

I heard a muffled gasp. Whether it came from Pillow or Hart, I can't say. Christ, it might have come from me. What I do remember is feeling, after that first dreadful realization, that what we gazed upon was real and that we had fallen down the rabbit hole for sure.

A thigh bone and clavicle, yellow with age, lay before us.

"But it's impossible," Hart protested.

"No more than this." Mackin tenderly removed from the tiki a larger object that was bundled in a linen bag. He placed it next to the bones. With all the drama of a State Fair conjurer, he untied the ribbon at the base. Pausing for a moment to offer Pillow a strange little smile, he lifted the cloth.

For a moment I couldn't make out what it was. The light from the table lamp cast half of the thing in shadow. But once my brain accepted the inconceivable, the image became quite clear.

It was the mummified face of a middle-aged man with an aquiline nose, a low brow, and a jutting jaw. The remaining strands of brown-gray hair were tied in a bow at the back of its skull. The skin color was nut brown, perhaps from some tannic solution used to preserve it, but it didn't hide the resemblance to the portrait I'd seen on Admiral Herndon's wall long ago in Newport.

I was staring into the empty eye sockets of James Cook.

Chapter 30

Y ou must admit, Ivo sure knew how to cap off a monologue.

After a stunned silence, the ever-practical Adrian Hart said in a choked voice, "Now can we read what Sergeant Gibson had to say about the matter? Promise not to tell."

Ivo's smile matched the grin on the skull. He again reached into the tiki coffin. This time, he withdrew the three journals. He handed the first to me and, avoiding Hart's outstretched hand, gave the second one to Pillow. Then he opened the third journal to a page marked by a feather and began to read aloud:

"26 November 1778. There has been much happiness now we have returned to warm waters and to a mountainous isle the Indians call Mowee…"

We listened to the words of Sergeant Gibson describing how the crews of the *Resolution* and *Discovery* were besieged by friendly natives climbing aboard to trade fruits, fish, and, in the case of some women, themselves for iron. Interesting stuff if you're sitting in a leather chair by a cozy fire with no football games to watch, but damn frustrating if you're grinding your teeth waiting for the man to get to the juicy bits.

The wait wasn't long.

"30 November 1778. Fearsome surf has kept us from going ashore, but we were visited today by a chief named Kalani'opu'u. He is portly, covered with the Pox and smells like a cod three days dead. With him are two priests, five warriors, a wife, and a fetching girl he called his Daughter. His child she might well be, but the disgusting way the old letch pawed her—this in front of us all!—did not seem filial.

"He and the Captain talked well into the afternoon. When at last the king was hoisted like a lumbering walrus from the Ship onto a canoe, it was close to sundown and the Wife and Girl were still aboard. The crew not on duty retired below decks to sup and rest for the next day departure to the next island. The natives on Mowee called it Owyhee and said it was bigger than all others with peaks so great that snow covered them...

"And now it is two hours since penning the above. What I now report I do so with a heavy heart, but it must be told.

"The last canoe had yet to depart by eight bells. Lieutenant Clerke told me to summon the Captain as he had yet to issue ship's orders for the next day. Not since June of '70 after running aground on the New Holland reef had he missed this nightly meeting with his officers. He had not been well for many weeks and I was sore afraid for him. I tapped upon the hatch and getting no response, opened it a crack to make sure all was well. Would I have never opened it! Would I have never had eyes to see or ears to hear!

"The room was in darkness but for a single candle. I opened the door wider and heard moaning followed by a low grunting sound. I stifled the urge to rush in, to stop the madness. The Captain lay naked upon the maiden who gasped in pain, his pale white bum pounding up and down while the heathen mother of the maid urged him on with muted fervor.

"This, three days after issuing the order that any who tried to bring women on board, let alone lie with them, would have twenty-four lickings from the cat.

"I backed away unseen and retired to my hammock, sickened by our captain's hypocrisy, and left it for Clerke to find him…"

Our attention remained riveted as we heard how, after the ships dropped anchor in Kealakekua Bay, Cook was worshipped as the fertility god, Lono; how the ships departed at just the right time in the worship cycle; and how a broken mast in a storm forced the ships to return, leading to misunderstandings and death. All this is in the history books, of course. But hearing it from this primary source made it seem as if the events had occurred the previous week. Having the ghastly skull of the captain looking on might have had something to do with it as well.

Aside from the shocking revelation of the captain's lust, the most interesting details were during the first two weeks of February, when things really began to disintegrate. But the last entry of Gibson's journal that Mackin read is what really rang the bell for the three of us. It was dated 22 February 1779, eight days after Cook's death.

"This noon, having reached a sort of peace with the Natives, enough to obtain a few more provisions and more brackish water without incident and getting the confounded repaired mast up and fully rigged, we left this unhappy isle. Before departing and with due ceremony, hindered only by the uncontrolled coughing of Lieutenant Clerke, the small box that contained the few pitiful remains of our captain was dropped into the bay. Afterward, I retired to a private corner and read the last written words of Captain Cook that I had found hidden beneath his bedding."

Mackin pulled a folded loose sheet of rough paper from the journal and handed it across the table to his daughter.

Pillow studied it for a few seconds.

"My god," she gasped. "It's true."

"Well, go ahead," Hart urged. "Read it aloud."

Pillow shook her head and slipped the paper to me. I looked at the script—it was written in a far more legible hand than Gibson's—and began to read.

"The king's daughter will bear my child. Of that, I am now certain—whether for good or ill is not for me to say. They think I am a god, but my lust has merely made me a Puppet to Fate. I am now part of their world as foretold long ago by their sages. I pray that whatever results from this will be for the good of these innocent People to whom we have introduced the Pox and our insidious English ways. May God have mercy on my Soul."

Thus endeth James Cook's final sermon.

Perhaps one day I'll encounter an evening as startling as that one, but I doubt I'll ever again experience the way I felt after reading that great man's mea culpa.

As disenchanting as it was to learn the saintly discoverer had succumbed to the cardinal sin of lust, I couldn't help but calculate how much that single paragraph would bring on the open market.

We three were pirates at heart. And while it didn't surprise me to see Hart practically frothing from the mouth with the gimmes, Pillow, too, had the wolfish look of the plunderer. Neither intended to share the prize with a guy from Kansas City.

My suspicions seemed confirmed when my gaze shifted back to the captain. I could have sworn one of the empty eyes in that wretched skull winked.

The history lesson over, Ivo Mackin grew agitated. Twitching and gabbling about the "beasties," he slumped into the chair. A thread of saliva appeared at the corner of his mouth. When the drool slipped onto his chin, he did nothing to remove it.

"They're coming for me," he cried out. "Get Witako!"

But the Ariki had already returned, accompanied by Ngati and another youth armed with *taiahas*. Rushing to the chair, he poured a green concoction down Mackin's throat that sent him straight to la-la land.

While the young men carried their Ranginui to a cot, Witako turned to us. His face was filled with contempt, but his voice was cool, commanding.

"You will not divulge what you heard today. Ivo's foolish preoccupation with his ancestor would destroy our mission were it to get out."

"We'll be the ones to decide that," Hart blustered. "Mackin chose to tell us of his own free will."

Witako's response was all the more disturbing for its quiet certitude.

"That's debatable, given his illness. At any rate, he most certainly did not authorize you to share the information. As I recall, you prompted him by promising not to repeat what he said. Respect his wishes until such time as he is able to decide."

Pillow looked at me, then to Hart.

"Fair enough," she said, but only I nodded in agreement.

There was nothing more to discuss. As we walked out, I looked over my shoulder. Witako was returning the grisly relics and the journal with Cook's piece of paper to the tiki coffin.

The three of us said little on the way back to our respective huts, each of us wondering how to proceed should Ivo be incapacitated before it was time for us to leave. Hart was uncharacteristically quiet. I knew it wouldn't be long before he'd make a move to try to steal the journal.

Having finally met with her father, Pillow was now free to roam the compound. For the next two days, she and I searched for Tane Craddock throughout the valley. People in the marae acted as if he had never been there. Medusa simply shrugged her shoulders when asked.

We got to know a few more of the young people working and playing in the fields. They weren't a particularly talkative group. Few were older than twenty-one; all had been associated with gangs. None of them acknowledged having known or even seen Craddock. When they weren't practicing their craft skills, they bonded in groups of three or four to smoke the potent hashish and opium cocktails that were in abundance everywhere.

In the late afternoon, we eavesdropped on three girls romping in a sylvan pool like naiads from a Greek myth.

"This truly is paradise to them," Pillow said wistfully. "I wish there had been a place like this when I was that young."

"You would have been a prime candidate," I told her. "But a life without consequences is never good."

"It's better than the alternative for people abused by parents and bullied by peers. At least they feel protected here."

"They can't live like this forever. They're being used."

"Used? That's ridiculous, Michael!"

"Is it? When I asked Aronui what she intended to do when back in Auckland, she looked at me as if I was an idiot. Neither Ngati nor Aronui plan or expect to leave the valley. They're woefully unprepared to meet societal pressures outside. A few months here ensures they could never hack it in the real world. They'll become—how do you say it in Maori?"

"*Kaipaoe*."

"Right. Vagrants, drifters like a fellow I saw on a curb in Wellington. It's as if the witches have cast a spell on them—with a little help from the drugs, of course. Even if they wanted to leave, I suspect guys like Kahoura are paid to make sure they don't."

"Kahoura? Who's that?"

"Someone you only want to see in a nightmare. He may belong to the human race, but just. Kahoura's the ugliest devil I've ever seen, an enormous brute with a face from The Chamber of Horrors."

"Pardon?"

"Never mind. Kahoura's a Mongrel gangbanger who doesn't bother with the dress code. His face is a roadmap to hell."

Her face brightened.

"I know who you're talking about. A huge man, his face covered with mokos?"

"Yeah, the kind applied with a chisel, not a needle."

Pillow bit her lip. "The last time I saw Tane, he was talking to him by the river."

"Talking or arguing?"

"They were too far away to see their expressions. But when they'd finished, they headed toward the cavern."

I didn't respond immediately. My mind was racing.

Finally, I took her hand. "We've got to assume he's gone."

She turned very pale. "Tane wouldn't desert us."

"I agree."

"You don't mean…"

"Some men are so evil, so beyond the snickering savagery of your garden-variety sadist, they'd make Vlad the Impaler nervous. My only encounter with Kahoura was brief and at a distance, but what I saw in him fit my template for the devil."

She pulled her hand away from mine; tried to find words again but couldn't.

"I don't know what happened to Tane, Pillow. But even if your father agrees to let us have the journal, Witako doesn't intend to let us leave this valley."

"But the only way out is through the cavern."

"So we need to do a recon of it. I've been meaning to find out what the Chinese are doing in there anyway. Are you with me on this?"

"Yes," she said. "But I'm not sure I want to be."

Chapter 31

We approached the mouth of the cavern shortly after dawn, keeping close to the cliff wall to avoid detection by gangbangers and Medusa's roaming harridans. As before, silver bars of light streamed diagonally to the floor through natural apertures hundreds of feet above.

Beyond the no-man's-land of belching fumaroles were a series of fissures in the limestone walls. Each appeared to lead to innumerable vaults and passages. Using flashlights purchased in Glenorchy, we entered a ten-foot-wide crease in the rock that seemed as likely an exit as any other.

Inside was a twilight zone where natural light barely penetrated. Yellow sumps, interspersed among spiral stalactites, hung like crystalline pumpkins from the ceiling. Nothing looked familiar. We followed a slight, slippery decline to a flowstone. Its globular bulk of shimmering calcite deposits looked like a giant ice cream cone carelessly stuck upside down. In the center of it was a shaft just wide enough for a grown person to slip through. This was definitely not the way we had traversed before.

"Care to explore?" I asked Pillow.

Her face was very pale. "Up to a point."

We edged sideways through the cleft for about twenty feet before coming to a small chamber. Tens of thousands of tiny flickering lights clung to networks of silk threads dangling from the rocks and calcite formations.

"*Arachnocampa luminosa*," Pillow told me. "They're glowworms, the larvae of the two-winged gnat fly found only in New Zealand's caves."

"Those pretty things are maggots?"

"Yes, and they're territorial buggers as well, not opposed to eating one another when battling for space."

We turned off the flashlights and stood on the edge of a shimmering pool of water, its border of crystal bouquets infused with the turquoise luminescence of the innumerable insects.

"It's so beautiful," she began. "Don't you think…"

I expected her to continue waxing poetic about the wonders of nature even in its subterranean depths, but she stopped mid-sentence, clutching my hand.

The man sitting straight up in the pool looked to have been dead a week or more; long enough, anyway, to start rotting but not enough to expose bone. The blue maggots performed their mating light show within the mouth and eye sockets, but there weren't the myriad legions of ants or other insects that normally make short work of the flesh. That's not to say there weren't other things feasting on him.

One creature clung to the chin like a shiny goatee. The forklike pincers stemming from either side of its head steadily worked on what remained of the man's lower lip without seeming to disturb the glowworms. I thought it might be a mutant cricket, but Pillow told me later that it was a cave weta. Like every insect in the cavern, the weta was unique to New Zealand and, having been around a hundred ninety million years, it's the oldest original species in existence. It also wins top honors for being the heaviest bug in the world, weighing more than a sparrow.

What I had first thought to be the man's lacquered black hair turned out to be a bloated spider sitting atop the skull. The spider's torso was five inches long and almost as wide. Eight legs, covered with bristly hairs, gripped either side of the head past the ear lobes. It looked like it might pounce any second on the larger weta.

Sections of the man's neck and shoulders visible above the water were covered with boils as if he had suffered some sort of chemical burn.

We'd started to back away from the ghastly scene when we heard voices and hacking coughs outside the chamber.

Peering through the opening, we saw Medusa leading five Chinese across the floor of the cavern. The woman bridled with impatience as the grim procession padded past the fumaroles toward openings in the far wall.

The men wore hard hats affixed with mining lamps, orange jumpsuits, and thick-soled boots. The ends of metal instruments stuck out from the top flaps of their backpacks. All carried lunch boxes, most of which were generic green or black, except for one that featured a collage of Hello Kitty characters. Two of them had trouble maintaining the pace.

It seemed obvious that they were scientists or engineers looking to identify a resource. But if the gold and silver had been tapped out long ago, what could they have been seeking?

Whatever it was, I didn't intend to risk being discovered in the cavern.

When the Chinese disappeared into the fissures, and before Medusa reemerged, Pillow and I ran for daylight.

Early that same afternoon, I left Pillow in the communal dining whare and took the path down to the river. After crossing a stone bridge, I entered a dense pine forest where I walked a mile, maybe more.

It was silent as death in this section of the vale where everything was cast in shadows. In a clearing at the far edge of the woods, I spotted the pair of bunkhouses tucked at the base of a tussock-covered hill. I turned to see if I'd been followed, then tiptoed for the last fifty yards across a carpet of needles and moss.

Each of the single-story buildings was about thirty feet long and twenty feet wide. Slanted corrugated roofs topped the pitted concrete walls. They looked more like horse stables than bunkhouses, which is probably what they had been originally.

In contrast to the elaborate Maori designs found on structures in the marae, the only decoration here was the crudely carved figure of a naked lady on the door of the first hut. The barely legible name of Lucille—undoubtedly a fond memory for a tracker or miner from gold rush days long past—had been etched above her head.

A small plastic Buddha, evidence of more recent guests, squatted inside the first building behind a filthy windowpane. Tin cans and chicken bones lay strewn in front of a steel drum that had been used recently as a cooker. Woolen socks, gloves, cotton shirts, and pants hung on the limbs of a dead tree. There were Chinese markings on some of the clothes.

Behind the buildings were copper tubs, washbasins, and four poles with wooden buckets for showering. A bit farther, four primitive outhouses tilted at angles, perilously close to collapse. Here and there lay evidence of the mining days that had ceased in the 1920s—rusty crowbars, pick heads, a huge anvil, and a massive cog wheel.

I was wondering how the things were ever transported through the cavern when I suddenly froze. Behind me, at the edge of the wood, a deer scurried into the underbrush.

After vainly straining my eyes and ears to determine what had frightened it, I crept up to the door of the first building. It wasn't locked—probably never had been—and I entered into a dark, evil-smelling lair filled with sleeping bags, various heavy packs, and scientific equipment. The stench of wet wool, kerosene, and sour body odor permeated the place.

The windows, ten to a side, were covered with so much grime as to be nearly opaque. A makeshift shelf held tins of sardines and boxes of rice next to a wood-burning potbelly stove. Unlit kerosene lamps hung on hooks from wooden rafters. A calendar with Chinese characters was pinned to a center post. Porn and movie magazines, all in Chinese, lay scattered on single-mattress beds.

On a table lay a heavy notebook filled with equations, universal chemical element designations, and hand drawings of various minerals. I turned on my flashlight hoping to determine what the formulas might be about, but the writing, except for the company name on the cover, was in Mandarin. Below the logo of a red cube and the company's Chinese hanzi characters was the title in English: Baomong Iron, Ltd.

I left the bunkhouse nauseated by the stifling atmosphere but slightly wiser. From the paperwork I'd seen, I figured Mackin and Witako were looking for a Chinese partner to revive TransNational Metals. Again, I asked myself what the Baomong engineers could be seeking in the cavern where the gold and silver had been tapped out long ago. As impressive as the pounamu strains were, greenstone wasn't the type of mineral to interest an international conglomerate.

Blue jeans, sweatshirts with Mongrel Mob symbols, and other clothes hung on clotheslines in front of the other building. My stomach hadn't sufficiently recovered, however, for me to investigate the gangbangers' lair. By then, anyway, I'd noticed the sunken foundation of another structure partially hidden by gorse and bracken. Rotted planks of quarter-sawn wood lay within the rectangular border along with forks, spoons, rolling pins, a coffee pot, metal chairs, and something that didn't harken back to the 1920s—a lead canister topped by a screw valve.

I wouldn't have noticed it except for a hook-beaked kea bird that had pulled back the corner of a tarp to feast on a dead rat. The tube was three feet long with an eight-inch diameter. It looked like a pressurized gas container for beer kegs, except it was stamped with a black trefoil on a yellow background—the universal symbol for radiation. I pulled off the canvas and counted fifteen more tubes.

With the shadows deepening in the valley, I placed the tarp back over the canisters and headed for Ivo Mackin's whare I determined to get some answers.

Twenty minutes later, I was under the iron anchor and, to my surprise, found the entrance unguarded.

Inside, Ivo Mackin sat at his table reading J.C. Beaglehole's biography of Sir Joseph Banks.

"Ah, Mr. Bevan!" he said, sounding pleased to see me. He appeared weak but lucid. "I was told you had gone."

"And Pillow as well?"

"Yes. I was rather disappointed she didn't stop by before leaving."

"Your daughter's still here, sir. She'd like nothing more than to see you again."

Hearing our voices, Ngati rushed into the room from the sleeping quarters.

"Ranginui, you are not to have visitors. The Ariki…"

"Yes?"

"He says you must have your rest."

"I understand, but now that Mr. Bevan is here, I wish to challenge him to a game." Mackin eyed me.

"You do wish to play, don't you, Bevan?"

"Sure," I said, taking a seat across from him.

A beautifully carved wooden box with brass fittings, burl wood inlay on top, mitered joints, and a lustrous finish lay in front of him. Its lid was open, revealing thirty or forty small wooden balls, half of them a tan shade and the other half a darker brown. They lay sprawled on a green velvet cloth. Affixed to the inside of the lid were seven empty channels.

Mackin picked up a brown ball and dropped it into the first chute.

"On each of his three voyages," he said, "Cook played this deceptively simple game to relax. Given the intellectual and reasoning challenges, he usually invited Sir Joseph Banks as an opponent. Cook spent so much time playing the game that it came to be known by crew members as the Captain's Mistress. The rules are as simple as tic-tac-toe, but the strategies are practically endless. The aim is to get four of a player's balls side by side in a row, diagonally, vertically, or horizontally. Should all the balls in the set be played without either player having a consecutive, uninterrupted line, a draw results."

He selected a tan one off the cloth and handed it to me.

"Are you sorry to have told us?" I asked him.

"I have many regrets, Mr. Bevan, but not for that. Penelope needed to know."

I placed my ball in the first chute and watched it clatter to the bottom. Mackin countered by letting his darker ball fall on top of mine.

As play progressed, I found it increasingly difficult to concentrate. Mackin's moves were extraordinarily fast, while I struggled to anticipate his moves while plotting my own. The game had seemed so childish at first, nothing near as complicated as chess or even backgammon. But, having second-guessed myself on every move, I was forced to concede after fifteen minutes. At game's end, he pulled the bottom retaining board—or, as he called it, "the gangplank"—and the hardwood rounds dropped into the velvet-lined cabinet.

When we began a second match, Ngati retired to the front room.

"Simple, yet deceptively challenging," Mackin told

me. "That's how things are here. The old ways we teach are very basic, primitive, in fact, and of no use in the outside world. And yet in the art of weaving, lineage chanting, singing, carving, there is much value."

He hesitated a moment before focusing his eyes on me. His hands trembled slightly. "If you haven't noticed, Bevan, I am going mad. It's not just the phantoms and dementia that plague me. Lono and Ku, the gods of love and war, battle for my soul."

"Cattley Middleditch thought you might have Parkinson's disease," I told him bluntly. "The proper drugs can control the hallucinations. Pillow and I will go with you to Queenstown for help."

He slowly inclined his head.

"Drugs cannot control *titiro makutu*, the evil eye. Only Witako understands the art of *matapuru* and has the mana to ward off the demons. At any rate, it's far too late for me, Bevan. All I wish to do is seek redemption before I die."

"Sir?"

"Your move," he said loudly. Then, nodding toward the room, he muttered, "Let him think we're still playing."

I dropped a ball in the third chute.

"What are the Chinese doing here?" I asked quietly.

"Confirming that what lies within is worth destroying."

"I don't follow."

Ivo Mackin countered my move, opening a new chute.

Chapter 32

Later that evening, Aronui visited my hut. She looked out of sorts and not a little disgruntled to find Pillow with me.

"Yes?"

"Sorry, I see you're busy."

"What is it, Aronui? You can speak freely."

"You asked me to tell you if Daig Kildare came up. He brought in more Chinese fellas tonight. But not just them."

"Who else?"

"Five or six more bikers from Poirua. A new girl came with them, too. She looked scared."

"Where are they now?"

"They left the marae for the bunkhouses. Kildare wants me to entertain them there."

I got off the mat and fastened my cloak.

"What are you doing?" Pillow asked.

"I've got to find out why they're here."

"I'll go with you," Aronui said.

"I know where it is."

235

"But you'll never find it in the dark."

The moon had not yet risen over Mount Aspiring when we reached the far section of the forest near the buildings. Hearing voices ahead, we dropped to our knees and peered through tangled brush. A large group of men huddled around a roaring fire between the two buildings. Half of them were thugs armed with chains, bats, and knives. They wore dirty leathers with the Mongrel Mob colors. In addition to them were a dozen Chinese and a pair of the youths I'd seen training with their long taiaha staffs with Ngati. Some of the Chinese looked decidedly nervous and out of place. I figured they were the new arrivals.

Daig Kildare sat at the top of the circle. The new girl Aronui had mentioned lay shivering beyond the warmth of the fire. She wore a tattered parka, wool trousers, and canvas tennis shoes.

It was obvious the newcomers hadn't arrived to learn the intricacies of basket weaving.

Initially, all I heard was bitching and moaning from the bikers about having to sleep outside the hut following their hard trek over the mountains. Then one of the youths asked when he could have the girl.

That brought a howl of obscenities from two leather-jacketed devils, leading one of them to toss the kid headlong into the fire. Sparks and ashes flew everywhere as he rolled out, howling and clawing frantically at the embers clinging to his legs, to the general merriment of the others.

"Now, calm down, lads!" Kildare shouted above the din while the girl was dragged by another Mongrel into the light of the fire. Like Aronui, she might not have been a stranger to the sex trade, but by the look on her terrified face, it was clear she hadn't signed up for this party.

"Here's what's waitin' for you if you do your jobs right," Kildare said, tearing off her jacket and lifting up her sweater. "Some of you youngsters will have to wait your turn when the time comes, but there are plenty more bints at the marae. We've got work to do first."

Aronui clutched my arm. She was trembling.

"Go back," I whispered. "I'll join you as soon as I find out what these brutes are up to."

She slipped away and I turned my attention back to the campfire, glad to be responsible only for myself.

Someone sitting directly opposite from Kildare had not found the horseplay so amusing. He was too far away for me to see him or hear what was said, but his words silenced the others, even the members of the Mongrel Mob entertainment committee.

With quiet restored, Kildare proceeded to set out the agenda.

"At dawn, we take the last of the canisters to the caves so the engineers can begin releasing the gas. Should anyone get in the way, you know what to do."

"What about the Ranginui?" someone asked.

"Leave him to me," a voice answered. "For I have his hau."

The words were met with grunts of approval.

The voice belonged to Witako, who now stepped from the shadows. Accompanying him was Kahoura, all two hundred sixty pounds of butt-ugly brawn.

I remembered what Elsdon Best had written about the power of makutu. To take one's hau meant stealing the essence of life so that a person's spiritual and intellectual force no longer had substance. Without a countercharm to the spell, the victim simply wasted away. It sure sounded like that was happening to Ivo Mackin.

Whether it was the menacing words being bandied about or my natural reaction when close to danger, I was starting to feel a bit addled myself. I'd heard enough. It was time to leave.

In the midst of turning, however, I detected a faint silhouette in the trees behind me where there had been none before. I froze. Peering into the darkness, I tried like mad to stop the chattering of my teeth. Then I heard a branch break.

I reacted as if a starting gun had gone off, bolting blindly toward the cover of a murky thicket twenty yards to my right. Had clouds not covered the moon, I might have made it. But it was dark as Pluto's palace, and five paces later, I plunged headlong into a pit. The only reason I didn't break my neck was because a bed of plantain leaves cushioned my fall.

I started to scramble out, but the sound of approaching voices forced me back into the hole. Hurriedly covering myself with the long fronds, I stopped breathing and waited for the threat to pass.

Only it didn't. Not right away. The footsteps halted directly above me, oblivious to my quivering presence. Two men—Mongrels by their voices—belched and farted and bragged about what the women would soon have coming to them. My blood froze when I felt what I thought were small stones being tossed onto my leafy cover.

I couldn't imagine what the men were doing, but one must always consider the positives of a situation. In my case, while the temperature above had dipped considerably, my hiding spot felt downright warm. Rather cozy, in fact, as if I'd fallen onto a mattress heated by an electric blanket. I was prepared to stay there all night if need be.

But what goes up must come down—and vice versa if you're talking about degrees of temperature. While the two yahoos above continued to yap and shuffle their feet in the cold, I began to feel downright feverish. A natural inclination, one might say, given the stressful situation I was in. As I soon learned, however, it wasn't only anxiety causing the sweat to pop out on my forehead.

Suddenly two hundred pounds of something hard and stinking of manure landed on my back.

I groaned to high heaven, but the mass of whatever it was, plus the bushels of dirt quickly shoveled onto it, must have muffled the noise.

Only after I reached up to feel the gristly snout of a boar did it dawn on me that I was trapped in a traditional hangi oven. The burning charcoal beneath the stones and leaves was just beginning to heat up. And those weren't rocks the men had been tossing— they were cabbages, sweet potatoes, and other veggies.

As any boy raised in the barbecue belt of America can tell you, it's an exquisitely slow process that requires utmost patience. The heat builds steadily, then rapidly increases after an hour or two, causing the smoke to infuse the meat with that delicious flavor Arthur Bryant's is famous for. Given any luck, I'd suffocate long before my tasty flesh began to loosen from my bones.

There was nothing for it but to climb out of the pit, issue apologies, and sprint for the woods, hoping that my zombielike resurrection would discourage the chefs from pursuit. If that didn't work, at least I wouldn't become a surprise dish on that evening's menu.

Trouble was, I was trapped in a situation that only a Carnival Cruise comedian could appreciate. The combined weight of pig and dirt had packed me in as tight as a Monday morning commuter in Tokyo. Only my left arm had any play at all, allowing just enough motion to create a hole for air.

While the men made their culinary preparations and I struggled in vain beneath a mound of assorted vegetables, a chicken or two, and that damn hog, my brain erupted in utter terror in anticipation of the agony to come.

You may guess what my thoughts were as the minutes crept by, but you'd most likely be wrong. With the singeing heat of the steam attacking my body like a thousand razor cuts, I didn't think of Josie, my daughter, or the bookstore. Not even rugby. And for damn sure, I didn't waste time asking forgiveness for having wasted much of my life on drink, drugs, and fornication.

With my lungs bursting, my throat and dirt-clogged nostrils scorched from the steam, my only thought was that it wouldn't be wise to hurl the contents of my gut into the limited air space in front of my nose. Reptilian instinct was all I had left. My spastic efforts were only good for buying a few more miserable moments of existence. If I'd been trapped underwater, I would have taken a final gulp, but I was denied even that.

Billy Graham can preach all he wants about it, but there was no bright light at the end of the tunnel, no heavenly voices calling me home. Nothing but blinding pain, suffocation, and pure terror.

Charming, eh?

It was close to checkout time, but something in me made a last desperate effort to get free. With the muscles of my neck straining, my head exploding with the pain in my legs and ribs, I thrust my arm as far up as the space allowed.

Like people who have favorite colors and animals, I have a favorite word. It is "serendipity." The writer Horace Walpole first coined it in a letter to a friend in the 1750s to describe a pleasant surprise. He took it from a Persian fairy tale called *The Three Princes of Serendip,* in which the royal characters continually discovered delightful things they weren't looking for.

I didn't expect a helping hand to remove me from that pit. I didn't expect anything, in fact, only to die. But as soon as my hand emerged from the dirt, I felt the great weight of the hog lift. A moment later, someone grabbed my wrist and jerked me like a gigged catfish out of the crater.

Serendipity.

The launch nearly dislocated my shoulder, almost cracked another rib, and the rush of oxygen ignited the smoldering coals to set my kilt on fire. Not that I'm complaining, mind you. The skin was only slightly seared, thanks to my benefactor's quick action of rolling me in the dirt, but the muscles in my arms and legs were another matter. After the slow roasting in that hellish steam bath, they felt like deflated beach balls.

So did my brain, which—having recognized the immediate danger was over—decided that it was time to take a little nap.

I emerged from my swoon to find myself in my hut with gentle Aronui spreading upon my burns a salve made from boiled bark of the rata tree. Tears ran down her chubby cheeks when I opened my eyes and she practically knocked me out again with the nose pressing that followed.

It's odd how being resurrected can recharge certain batteries. While my major appendages felt all but worthless after the harrowing event, there was another that seemed remarkably robust. It might have had to do with breathing real air again.

Any carnal thoughts were promptly dashed, however, when I noticed Pillow standing by the door. Steely-eyed and with arms crossed, she seemed poised to pounce should Aronui's ministrations extend to areas unaffected by flame or steam.

"Feeling better, are we?" Pillow asked, tossing my civilian clothes to me.

"Yeah. Thanks for the rescue."

"It wasn't us."

"Huh?"

"At least, not the physical part," Aronui chimed in. "I'd started back to the marae for help when I spotted four men hauling the pig toward the bunkhouses. I figured they'd be joining Kildare, so I ran back to warn you."

"And you saw me fall in the pit?"

She nodded. "With the men standing around the hangi, there was nothing I could do. Soon, however, only one of them remained to stir the coals. Our friend surprised him with a swipe of the patu. He pulled you out."

"Your friend?"

"You'll meet him soon," Pillow said.

"What happened to the guy who got whacked?"

Aronui lowered her eyes. "We knew the others would be returning soon."

"Yeah?"

"He was big. Must have weighed eighteen stone. Maybe more. We didn't have the time to hide him in the woods."

"Yeah?"

She looked up at me. "He took your place under the pig."

"Oh."

"I'm fairly sure he was dead already."

"That's comforting to know."

"Does it really matter?"

"I suppose not."

"I wish it had been Kildare," she said sweetly.

Aronui might have looked like an angelic teddy bear when she was teaching me cat's cradle or the back-knuckle game, and she could certainly be a charming little fox when the mood was upon her, but I'd misjudged her capacity for revenge.

I glanced sideways at Pillow, expecting her to be shocked, but her face exhibited as much emotion as a stone idol. She and Aronui were two of a kind when it came to *Utu*, the Maori word Hart had applied to Pillow when describing her retaliation on the Russian oligarch.

Depending on the circumstances, it can mean the reciprocation of kind deeds or the seeking of vengeance to restore balance. In the old days, when a Maori, man or woman, set out to avenge a grievous wrong the first person they met, whether friend or foe, was slain—just to get warmed up, I imagine, for the later innings. I reminded myself it would be wise not to make either of these women jealous. Their penchant for Old Testament justice would have made Delilah blanch.

"How are you feeling?" Pillow asked.

"Sixty percent."

"That will have to do." She turned to Aronui. "Leave us. Michael and I have something to discuss. Alone."

A petulant look flashed across the girl's face, but after pressing her forehead to mine, she gathered up her lotions and disappeared into the night.

Pillow turned back to me. "I understand you visited my father this afternoon. Has he changed his mind about the journal?"

"We didn't discuss it. There was something far more important on his mind."

"I think I know what it was," she said, walking toward the opening and drawing back the flap. "You can come in now."

I got up to see who she was talking to when I suddenly found myself staring into a face that was even more grotesque than the late, great Captain Cook's.

"We need to talk," Kahoura said.

Chapter 33

Talk? This from was the ruffian who'd sent me to my knees for just looking at him; the same monster who commanded a pack of the worst motorcycle thugs I'd seen this side of Oakland. Considering the knuckle-dragger's size, however, and the encouraging fact that he'd literally pulled my ass out of the fire, I saw no point in objecting.

Anyone who's read my earlier exploits knows my middle name is Malachy, not Dauntless.

"Get out of the way, bro."

I did as ordered and he ducked inside. With a great sigh, he plopped onto my bed mat and began rubbing the back of his leg.

"I'm Special Constable Richard Kahoura Carlton, New Zealand Federal Police."

You'd think I'd be inured to shock by now, but this astounding pronouncement had me wondering when the next bus to Bedlam would arrive.

"Eh?" I squeaked.

"Been on assignment for the Conservation Department," the brute continued. "Before that, it was three years in Hawke's Bay establishing my creds with the Mongrel Mob."

The cobwebs cleared from my muddled brain. He had my attention. I sat next to him.

"Why—how—did you put me on the ground at the food line the other day?"

"What are you talking about?"

"That curse or whatever it was. Hit me in the chest like a lightning bolt."

"Ahh!" he roared. "You think I sent you to your knees with just a look? Must have been the saintly Ariki who jabbed you. A pin coated with tutu juice works like a Stone Age Taser. In higher doses, it's fatal. I wondered what happened when I saw him chanting the mumbo jumbo over you. Should have known when I saw him chop up the green lizard and have Aronui pitch it into the fire."

"Witako?

"Just another nasty trick he's played on you."

"You mean the Ariki's behind all this?"

"Who bloody else?" Kahoura said, rubbing his chin with the blood-caked patu. "That crafty bugger's been manipulating Ivo Mackin for years, ever since Ivo began showing signs of the irrational behavior that led to the bankruptcy of TransNational. Even though he was chief operating officer, Terence Robertson couldn't prevent the downfall of the corporation, but he discovered another way Mackin could regain their fortune through ownership of this valley. In a few months, the Ngai Kati Mamoe tribe that he controls through Ivo's provenance will have full title to this area."

"Is Ivo aware that the tikanga Maori is more or less

a charade? It doesn't seem worth the effort to con the Inland Revenue for a tax write-off."

Kahoura narrowed his eyes—hideous-looking things—but his deep voice was amazingly soft. He was articulate, too, in the way that polymorphs usually are.

"It's more than that, Bevan. This is a sophisticated scheme to get control of minerals that are worth billions."

I've heard some peculiar things in my time, but this absurd claim caused me to forget I was within patu-clubbing distance of a man whose looks would make a Neanderthal mother weep.

"That's ridiculous," I blurted. "The gold and silver deposits were tapped out in these mountains decades ago."

Instead of bashing my head, Kahoura smiled, displaying a row of metal teeth.

"That's true," he agreed. "But a century of mining resulted in vast amounts of tailings from those metals. Once thought worthless, they're far more precious than diamonds now. Ever hear of rare earth elements?"

"The stuff they make cell phones with?"

"And iPods and laptops, color TVs, wind turbines, medical imaging, you name it. They represent the fifteen elements having atomic numbers fifty-seven through seventy-one. Modern life wouldn't be the same without them. To meet future tech demands, it's going to take thousands of times the amount of the stuff currently being extracted. China controls ninety-seven percent of the world's output. Russia and Brazil most of the rest. Your country is totally dependent on REE imports from them."

"Surely America can find deposits of its own."

"It did in the eighties and early nineties, but to maintain its monopoly, China undercut its prices to make it economically unfeasible. It takes ten years to develop new mines once deposits are discovered. They're usually difficult to quarry and the risks to the environment are enormous. Only China, with its lack of regulations, has been willing to make the sacrifice."

It's not often one finds oneself standing in a straw hut being lectured by a tattoo-faced heathen on geological physics as if he were Lord Kelvin. But there it was. The man knew his stuff way beyond what appearances—and his pay grade—would indicate. It wouldn't surprise me to learn he could play a Bartok concerto on the kazoo as well.

"But given their lock on the market," I said. "Why are the Chinese bothering with New Zealand?"

"You have to understand something," Kahoura answered, bristling at my ignorance of macroeconomics. "The Chinese always look decades ahead. Demand for rare earth materials is growing exponentially. A future New Zealand government will no longer be able to ignore the untapped treasure within these mountains. Saudi Arabia's oil wealth pales in comparison to what this little country could reap. Underneath us are enough rare earth oxides to cut China's production by twenty-five percent, maybe more. Even more importantly, it's of a much higher grade and would be relatively easy to extract."

"Says who?"

"Says Jiang Tsao, a former guest of Witako. He was one of the Chinese geologists brought in to confirm the extent of the deposits."

"Former guest?"

"He had moral qualms about what was going on.

He was last seen being taken into the cavern last week, but not before secretly passing me his notes."

"We saw what was left of him," Pillow said quietly. "So why aren't Kiwi geologists crawling all over the place? Not to mention the Army?"

"You know how isolated this place is. Nobody leaves without Witako's permission, and that's only if you're on his payroll. I could never figure the way out through that limestone maze."

"But how do Kildare and scouts like Ngati navigate it?" I asked.

"With guides like Medusa. There are six of them who trade off. The rest of the time, they sit outside the green boulders with their black cloaks pulled over their heads weaving or chanting."

"Craddock said they were witches. They spooked him."

"Craddock was right to be afraid. They'd prick you with a tatu-poisoned needle as soon as they look at you."

Then the big man turned solemn as he looked at Pillow. His voice was soft again.

"I'm afraid Tane is dead. With time running out, I needed a strong ally. I took the chance—as I am now with you—of telling him what I'd learned. He set off to explore the cavern, looking for an exit before coming back to get me. Somehow, Witako found out. He sent Medusa and three of the Dogs after him…"

"I knew he'd never desert us," Pillow said tonelessly.

I thought of the man who had been such a help to Esme, who had been so touched when forgiven by Pillow. Who held the rope when I was blown off the mountain.

I've known a few like Tane Craddock in the Marines and on the rugby pitch, but none better.

"I still don't see where China's interests figure in this," I said after an uneasy silence. "If New Zealand regulators aren't about to let its own companies mine the deposits, they damn sure won't allow foreigners."

"It was hard for me to understand as well. But two months ago, I discovered something Kildare's boys brought up and stored behind the tracker buildings. Inside it were four dozen tubes with the markings of a chemical component. I shouldn't have touched them without rubber gloves. Ever hear of polonium-210?"

"No, but I saw the canisters myself today. You say you saw forty-eight? There were only fifteen this afternoon."

"The Chinese have moved them into the cavern. There must be hundreds in there now, and as your friend Hart would say, they are very bad, indeed."

He looked at Pillow. "What do you see in that *te kaihau* anyway?"

"It's a long story," she replied. "Tell us more about what's in the tubes."

"It's intensely radioactive—two hundred fifty thousand times more toxic than hydrogen cyanide if inhaled or absorbed through the skin. The containers I saw weren't properly sealed."

For a moment, I was confused. What the devil did those deadly canisters have to do with anything? Then I saw it with blinding certainty—all Witako needed to do was poison the tailings in the cavern. If and when other geologists became aware of the REE deposits, as they inevitably would, no New Zealand corporation would ever be able to exploit them. Nobody would. And that was the point.

China, desperate to maintain its global monopoly on REEs, must have been willing to pay hundreds of millions just to neutralize the value of the minerals. TransNational, if Witako so chose, would then have the funds to continue exploiting the earth in more traditional ways.

"We've got to do something," I said. "They're planning to release the gas in the morning."

Kahoura nodded. "Witako intends to secure the compound before the engineers move in to open the valves. We can't count on more than ten lads to support us. He has at least four times that many, plus the latest pack of Mongrels who Kildare brought up today."

"At least we have the element of surprise."

"We did until you fell into that pit, Bevan. If we're lucky, they won't find the body of their friend for another two hours."

Kahoura stood up.

"A single gram of Po-210 can expose twenty million people to cancer. If Witako succeeds in contaminating the deposits, a huge portion of the South Island could be uninhabitable for generations."

After he left to gather volunteers for the upcoming struggle, Aronui reentered my hut.

"The Ranginui wants to see you both."

"Anyone with him?"

"Just the Ariki."

Chapter 34

Witako eyed Pillow and me warily as we entered the great room. Ivo Mackin, looking like death warmed over, sat in front of a wooden dish piled with mashed sweet potatoes, various vegetables, and slices of pinkish-brown meat.

"Here," the Ranginui said, pushing the plate toward me. "I'm not hungry."

I'd hardly eaten the entire day and dove in with knife and fork. I was astonished at how delicious it was, particularly the cutlet, which was tender and rather sweet tasting.

"Is this veal?" I asked after the first two bites.

"It's something Witako brought over from the blockhouses," Mackin mumbled. "I prefer pork, however."

The Ariki smiled disingenuously. I gave the steak a closer inspection. Along a marble of fat, barely visible on the charred ends, was part of an inked circle. I put down my utensils.

"You have something to tell us?" I asked, looking up at Mackin.

"I've reconsidered the matter of the journal," he said, apparently oblivious to the provenance of my dinner. "While I'm not prepared to share it with the world, I recognize there must be some purpose for it to have survived this long."

He motioned for Witako to go to the safe.

"Sergeant Gibson's tale is as much your legacy as mine," Mackin said to Pillow. "Do with it as you wish."

Shifting his attention to me, he added, "She'll need your help."

"Do we have your permission to leave, then?" I asked, trying not to sound too eager. "The helicopter is scheduled to meet us at Pearl Flat in three days. We can make it if we leave in the morning."

"Yes, of course." He turned to Witako. "Make sure Medusa takes them through the cavern first thing tomorrow and have Ngati guide them over the mountains. I don't suppose that Craddock fellow has shown up?"

"He has not, Ranginui."

All this was news to make my day—aside from the Tane-still-missing part—but I should have known better. You'd have to be a pretty hard case to deny that I'd had my share of tribulations on this trip. But it had all been a walk up Daisy Hill compared with what was to come.

"All right, then. Be a good man, Witako, and bring out the journals."

The Ariki took his time opening the safe as if savoring the moment to come. When he paused to look over his shoulder at me, I knew what he'd say when the door opened. All I could do was sit and wait uneasily.

"They're gone, Ranginui!"

Sure enough, the safe was as empty as an Eskimo's wallet—the journals, the captain's bones and skull; all gone.

Ivo Mackin reacted as if he'd been harpooned. His roar brought Ngati and another youth scrambling into the room with raised *patus*. Witako, of course, got on his high horse to noisily declare that I was the thief.

"I caught him sneaking into the whare yesterday," Ngati added cheerfully, jabbing his finger at me.

"And for one reason only!" cried the Ariki. "To extract the combination from a confused Ranginui!"

Once, during my semi-illustrious law career, I found myself arguing a case before a crooked judge and a bought jury in Peculiar, Missouri. There wasn't much use in citing legal precedent, let alone evidence favorable to my client, the sleazy owner of a rural porn shop. But, as an officer of the court, I was expected to put on a good show. For some reason, however—it might have been the snarky look the foreman of the jury gave the judge—I withdrew from the case midway through the trial. It cost me five days in the county jail for contempt, but the judge was forced to declare a mistrial and the case reassigned—with a new defense counsel—to another court where the defendant was promptly convicted, fair and square.

Need I mention that my scumbag client stiffed me on fees?

If you're wondering what's my point in telling this, I suppose it's to show there was some precedence for my having the balls to laugh in Witako's face at his accusation. It must have been the first time anyone had ever done that to him, because his jaw dropped like a broken marionette. It didn't take long, however, for him to recover. And this time, his rage was real.

Looking back on that evening, I'm convinced the only thing saving me from a boiled brain was the sudden return of Mackin's hallucinations.

The Ranginui's mouth stopped in mid-bellow as he gaped in horror at the opposite wall. Thrusting out his arms to ward off imaginary demons, spasms racked his body until his bulging eyes went empty and he slumped in the chair.

During the eerie silence that followed, the marks of stupefied anguish departed from Mackin's face. The only motion that remained was a slight fluttering of his nostrils from ever-decreasing exchanges of air.

For an instant, his eyes opened as if he was startled to still be alive. Just as quickly, the light within them dimmed. There came a hushed exhalation of breath, followed by the slacking of the jaw. It pulled his lips back, giving him the painted grin of a circus clown, the teeth gleaming yellow in the rictus of death.

It was Pillow who played the role of coroner, callously confirming her father's death by pinching his nostrils, then pricking his cheek with a pin. She avoided my eyes when Daig Kildare and his pack of louts from the campfire conference entered the room. I might have handled the two youths and escaped to the woods, but not six gangbangers armed with chains and bats.

They tied my hands behind my back and dragged me outside just as Adrian Hart approached the whare.

"Is the deed done?" he asked Kildare.

"Aye. The crazy bastard's gone down the stairs for good."

Facing me, Hart held up the three journals in his stubby hands.

"When Witako lost control over Ivo, it threatened to blow his deal with Baomong Iron, Ltd. Ms. Wilkes and I offered to help in exchange for these and safe passage."

"Are you aware of what they plan to do?" I said.

"No. And I don't give a damn. Whenever circumstances are in my favor, I find it wise not to ask too many questions."

That said, he turned and walked into the whare whistling a sea shanty.

"Haul Away, Joe," I think it was.

Chapter 35

The Mongrels who manhandled me were in a foul mood, having learned they would be hauling the rest of the canisters into the cavern the next day. Not only that, Witako had forbidden them the fun of raping and pillaging until after the Ranginui's funeral.

The fact that one of their own had been barbecued didn't seem to have bothered them in the least.

It must have been past midnight when they dragged me into the cavern. Immediately, the guards' flashlights startled thousands of long-tailed bats and soon had us ducking to avoid their frenetic, screeching dives.

In the midst of the chaos, a loud crack resounded close to me, followed by a horrible shriek. The Mongrel who had been pulling me by a leather leash staggered heavily against my chest, his skull cleaved nearly in half. As I recoiled, he went limp and crumpled to the ground, leaving a trail of warm blood on my shirt. An instant later, Kahoura used his gore-covered patu to cut the cord binding my hands. Then he tossed me a five-foot-long taiaha while the other Mongrels warily surrounded us, one of them holding back to keep us in his light.

I countered the first assault with a jab to the man's solar plexus, followed by a downward slice to his collarbone that brought a satisfying scream. Kahoura had similar success with his patu until an axe swung from the blind side cut off his left arm at the elbow. As he toppled over, growling in agony, another blow struck his spine. It must have severed the chord because everything below his neck stopped moving. His eyes went blank and the veins on either side of his thick neck swelled and his lips opened but no sound emerged from them.

I swung my weapon wildly over the constable's limp body, keeping the murderous bastards at bay until a machete sliced my stave in half. There was nothing for it then but to stagger backward from the melee while they, like jackals sensing the kill, tore Kahoura apart—literally.

The only positive thing to come from the Mongrels' bloodlust was that it gave me time to slip away. Had I dallied a moment longer, I wouldn't be telling this tale because additional Witako loyalists were streaming into the chamber holding their weapons aloft like a bunch of pissed-off Transylvanian villagers.

As my old drill instructor once said, "A Marine fights with all he's got, but when Johnny Turk overruns the ramparts, it's best to get where the enemy ain't until reinforcements or the next sundown arrives."

Pulling the flashlight from my jacket, I sped over the rugged ground, dodging calcite formations, fumaroles, bats, and God knows what else, never breaking stride, praying like Moses to add distance between me and those hounds of darkness.

Upon reaching the limestone wall, I popped into the first cleft available. The passage was wide but ended after twenty meters. It contained a narrow flowstone hole, however. I knew that these deposits of calcite created from seeping water could lead to new chambers. Even if it led nowhere else, it would provide temporary cover.

The thought of crawling into that slimy vent caused my heart to palpitate like a premature bunny's. But what choice did I have?

So in I went, scrunching down the cavity using my back against one side and my feet pressing against the other. Aiming the tiny beam of light between my thighs, I could see that the hole went down another five or six feet before opening into a wider pocket.

To descend farther meant I wouldn't be able to shimmy back up. Fighting panic, I decided to climb out while I could.

But approaching voices and the light of torches reflecting on the ceiling above put a stop to that. They would soon be right above the flow hole and would surely look into it. My only option was to slip farther down the cold, wet tube and hope I'd be able to get back up when the danger passed.

It took less than ten seconds to drop into a small chamber, but that was enough for one of them to have seen the beam of my flashlight. Treading along another slippery path, I groped along the face of the walls until I found another opening, four feet high and about as wide. Cool air streamed into my face, accompanied by the sound of rushing water.

I took a deep breath and plunged forward, keeping my head low to avoid it scraping the ceiling. The roar of the underground torrent now blocked the sound of footsteps and voices, but the flickering light from behind made it clear my pursuers were not giving up. I was sprinting now, hunched over to avoid banging my head on the ever-lowering wall with only instinct to guide me—instinct and hope, for there was no turning back.

Another twenty yards and I was on my knees, crawling in the narrowing tube, encouraged only by the breeze that continued to caress my face. There were neither beams of light nor voices behind me now. I lay still for a minute or two, gasping, desperately wondering how long they might wait.

It was a mistake.

The longer I thought about it, the more my faith in going forward dissolved. The walls and the darkness began to close in, gripping me in the horror of claustrophobia. Having scrambled into a space no wider than a coffin, I tried scooting backward. But my toes, knees, and elbows couldn't gain traction on the smooth, water-slick stone. I was trapped.

It was Esme's green jade pendant that saved me from succumbing to panic. I swear I heard the thing speak to me just when the screaming meemies began to take over.

I steeled myself to crawl as far as the tunnel allowed.

Five meters later, the walls were touching both shoulders. My chin brushed the slippery wet floor, but there were less than three inches of clearance above my head. My knees had no room to maneuver. With my arms extended in front of me, I could only push forward with my toes, inch by inch.

But I still felt that breeze.

A few more feet and the floor of the tunnel began to slant. I moved a yard, then another, and suddenly I was sliding without effort toward the rushing sound of water. Water and air, the elements of all life.

I glided headfirst into a pool warmed by some thermal influence in a chamber infused with the turquoise luminescence of the glowworms.

Sharp-edged crystals surrounded most of the lagoon except for a flat limestone slab at one end. I swam to it and pulled myself onto the slippery rock by grasping a pair of spiral stalagmites. I sat there for a long time, marveling at the myriad display of tiny lights dotting the grotto's ceiling and giving thanks to every patron saint Sister Mary Agnes pounded into my skull at Our Lady of Perpetual Anguish Grammar School. After I'd sent regards to Saint Bonaventura (bowel disorders) and Saint Lidwina (skaters), I found a relatively smooth ledge and caught some much-needed sleep.

It must have been close to dawn when I got to my feet and began looking for a way out.

Moving under low-hanging draperies of calcite, I made my way along the pool until coming to an opening twice my shoulder width. The light of the glowworms barely penetrated there, but it was just enough to see a cataract of white water plunging into the abyss of the mountain.

White-water rapids are fearsome enough aboveground. Pour a rampaging river into a dark limestone shaft with the velocity of a freight train and it becomes something altogether more terrifying. The torrent looked to be flowing fifteen feet below where I stood. Even if I wasn't drowned or pummeled to death, I would die from decompression in water that, from the sound of it, plunged hundreds of vertical feet.

But I couldn't climb up. And I wasn't partial to dying a slow death in that beautiful sepulchre. The only option was to go down while trying to avoid falling into the deadly vortex.

It's strange, looking back on it, how calm I felt at the time. No, not just calm—more like exhilarated. Anything, after all, was better than being stuck in that narrow crawl space. Plus, I had the strangest feeling that, given any sort of luck, I would find a way out. I guess you can say I'd finally found in myself, when everything seemed against it, something to trust.

I touched the pendant one more time for luck. Then I climbed slowly into the sinkhole, wedging my back against one side while using my knees and arms against the other for the first ten feet until the shaft opened wider. I dropped the remaining five feet like a convict down a prison wall onto a flat stone surface. Outside the shaft, the ceiling was slightly above my head. The rapids roared two or three yards to my left, but some of its icy overflow swirled around my calves.

I began to shiver uncontrollably. The racing, frigid water which had risen above my knees made it almost impossible to stay upright. I walked briskly with the current, however, using my right hand to feel my way along the wall. After three false leads, I reached an opening with a fresh breeze flowing from it.

By stretching my hands over my head, I felt the top of the entrance of what I hoped was a lava tube. That meant no rocks to cut and bruise me, just a smooth cannon barrel six feet or so in diameter cutting through the mountain. Putting the freight train din of the rapids behind me, I pushed away from the wall and drifted into a tributary with a powerful but surprisingly gentle flow.

I was soon floating around a curve where the stream intersected with a larger subterranean river. Scrambling to keep my head above water, I felt like I'd been dumped in a giant washing machine, but I saw a pinprick of light in the distance.

The gleam became brighter and brighter as I propelled faster, ever faster, until I shot out of darkness into the early morning air, my heart nearly bursting with joy. I had become an element of the Cat O' Nine Tails cascade and, seconds later, landed headfirst into the Waipara River.

Thankfully, the river was slow-moving at this juncture and deep enough so that I didn't break my neck. After drifting a hundred or so feet downstream, I was able to swim to the pebbled shoreline. It took my eyes several minutes to fully adjust to the sunlight after getting out, but when they finally did, the first thing I beheld was the glistening pyramid of Mount Aspiring.

I didn't have long to admire the view because I was shivering again. But one thing New Zealand has is plenty of thermal springs, and my nose detected the strong sulfur odor not far away. The steam-shrouded pond was just temperate enough not to scald, and I stumbled in, letting the warm, mineral-laden water work its magic.

The meadow where we had first encountered Ngati was less than fifty yards away. There was considerably more snow on the ground now. Another mile beyond would be the green jade boulders, but I had no intention of going back.

I got out of the pool, shook off as much water as possible, and began the upward trek toward the Bonar Glacier. Soaked to the bone, the odds weren't good that I'd get over the Matukituki Saddle without freezing to death.

But I needn't have worried. Tane Craddock and two squads of New Zealand Special Air Service troopers found me four hours later, shivering under a ledge on the leeward side of the Hector Col.

Chapter 36

After getting kitted out in proper alpine winter gear, it still took a couple cans of Sterno and an extra pair of fleece socks to get circulation back in my feet. I had no trouble keeping up with the soldiers once we got going, thanks to two civilian radiation containment experts whose curricula vitae didn't include mountain climbing in winter.

At midday, we halted at the westernmost end of the nameless lake to rest and make final plans for the approach to the compound.

It didn't take long. You don't need much when you have twenty-five elite fighters armed with Heckler & Koch submachine guns going against an assortment of axes, baseball bats, chains, and taiahas.

The strategy was for Tane Craddock to guide the party through the winding labyrinth of the cavern. Once in the valley, the first squad would surround the marae, and the second, again led by Tane, would rush to the bunkhouses in order for the radiation experts to secure the deadly containers of polonium-210 still above ground. I was to go with Captain Slaughter in the first squad to identify friend from foe as much as possible, with the bikers being in a different category from the taiaha-carrying youths like Ngati. The troopers already had photos of Witako and Daig Kildare. I also made it clear that my first priority would be to locate and secure the safety of Pillow Wilkes, Aronui, and, if possible, Adrian Hart. Under no circumstances were the troopers to use their weapons on anyone unless in immediate bodily peril.

After our briefing, Tane and I warmed our hands over a small fire. It was the first opportunity to talk since our reunion on the mountain.

"How'd you get through?" I asked, after describing my desperate struggle to escape via the flow-hole subway.

"The same way we came in. My mother knew the secrets of the Waitaha, the first wave of people who discovered and settled this mountain region seven hundred years ago. You saw the way I controlled Ngati when he first challenged us in the meadow?"

"I remember how you threatened to send some nasty spirits after him. It certainly put him in his place."

"My mother passed on more than that to me. The early iwi hunted and found shelter in the caverns and created an art form exclusive to the South Island. Using charcoal and red ochre mixed with bird fat, they drew fantastic images onto the limestone walls. Some are extremely beautiful and complex. My mother said these had enormous spiritual qualities, a link between man and the supernatural. Others are simple stick figures, but they, too, had a valuable purpose—as sign-posts to direct people through the caves."

"And that's what you used?"

"Yeah. I'd noticed the moa bird drawings when we were first led in. The flightless creatures are extinct now, but they held a special place in the hearts of the people because they represented deliverance from suffering. Most have faded to pale images over the centuries, so you have to know to look for them. My mother told me that if ever I found myself lost in a cave, they would guide me home. One bird means turn right, two means left. Basic as that but extremely effective. A couple of Witako's men saw me enter the cave, and the chase was on, but they didn't know about the signs."

"What do you think will happen to Pillow now that we know she was in with Hart?"

"I'm suggesting the government put her up for the Order of St. George."

"What do you mean?"

"Kahoura informed Pillow of our mission shortly after her arrival. The plan had to be kept secret, or Hart and subsequently, Witako might have suspected something. The polonium threat was too important to risk letting even you know I'd escaped."

Captain Slaughter interrupted Craddock's story, barking orders to move out. After gathering our gear, we went to the head of the patrol and slogged for three hours in heavy snow before reaching the twin greenstone boulders.

There was no one at the portal. The area was deserted. Even the haystack witches were absent. Tane led us at a quick-time pace through the labyrinth and across the great chamber. At the mouth of the cave, the captain reiterated his plan of attack. Then we fanned out on our designated assignments.

When we arrived at the marae, we saw that most of the people in the valley had gathered for Ivo Mackin's funeral ritual.

Slaughter, who was a quarter Maori himself, quietly ordered his men to block any potential exits but to make no other attempts to stop the sacred rites. His men showed their prowess by swiftly and silently surrounding the compound.

Witako stood stoically before the bier where Ivo Mackin lay. The Ranginui's corpse had been trussed according to ancient custom. The knees were drawn up so that they touched the body and secured in place by a cord. He wore a beautiful cape of kiwi feathers and an elaborately detailed kilt. His hair had been neatly combed and oiled in the Maori chieftain fashion with bird plumes sticking out of it. Red paint marked his face, and a greenstone pendant graced his neck. A taiaha and a patu were at his side. There was no evidence of his pakeha heritage except for the captain's uniform smoldering in a fire before the bier.

You've got to hand it to the Ariki; he didn't avoid fulfilling his final obligation to the man who had been both his mentor and victim. Pillow sat to the side of the platform, dutifully solemn, but her eyes could not hide a flare of surprised relief at seeing me. I was glad to see Aronui in the throng of worshippers as well as Ngati and the other young people.

The squad of heavily armed troopers patiently observed the speeches, songs, and wailings, but I didn't stay to hear them. After issuing further orders to his men, Captain Slaughter and I left the marae to join the other troopers en route to capture Daig Kildare, the Mongrel Mobsters, and the Chinese engineers.

Later, I heard that the rest of the *tangihanga* had

proceeded in the traditional manner. By all accounts, Witako had given a moving speech, wishing the Ranginui fair passage to the region where human life began and to where his ancestors would escort him to Rangiatea, the abode of Io the Parent God. Medusa, by all accounts, did a masterful job of wailing, and Pillow added a few tearful words of thanks for having had the chance to reunite with her father.

Witako's stoic performance was one thing; the reactions by Kildare and his Mongrel Mob to our arrival were quite another. To say they weren't staggered when the armed-to-the-teeth commandoes showed up on their doorstep is like saying the Irish speak well of each other.

It was Ngati who told me that Adrian Hart had fled at the first sign of our approach and was seen heading in the direction of the waterfall that fed the pool by the poppy fields. With the SAS men engaged in rounding up Kildare, the Chinese, and the rest of the Mongrels, I picked up a taiaha and headed off alone to find him.

The path to the top of the cliff from which the water tumbled was treacherously steep. On the lower reaches, I had to thrash my way through thick patches of tussock and bracken. Once there, I was surprised to see that there was an even more vertical precipice plunging hundreds of feet to the canyon below. Beyond it was a panorama of mountain ranges extending westward to the Tasman Sea.

Adrian Hart sat yoga-like on a flat slab of rock. His backpack lay next to him.

Hearing my approach, he turned his head and stared at me as if I were Lazarus. He opened his mouth, but nothing came out.

"It's over, Adrian," I said quietly. "Time to go."

"Indeed," he said, finding his voice.

He got to his feet, picked up the backpack, and, stepping to the edge of the precipice, said, "Can you guess what I have here?"

I advanced cautiously toward him. "You didn't have to kill Billy Bartow."

"I was just following the lead of Robert Anderson."

"Anderson?" The name sounded vaguely familiar, but I couldn't place it.

"Of course." Hart began to swing the pack back and forth. "Sam Gibson's erstwhile friend. It was Anderson, not the alleged wharf ruffians, who murdered his old shipmate for the third journal."

"How could you possibly know that?"

"The May 1790 edition of the *London Gazetteer*—one I somehow neglected to show you at the Turnbull Library—tells us it was Anderson who sold the last journal to the London printer." He paused for an exaggerated sigh. "My dear Bevan, you really must learn to do research."

"Set the bag down and move away from the cliff, Adrian. There's no need to end it this way."

In a flat voice, he answered, "I'm afraid there is," and flung the rucksack at me as if it were a rugby ball. I dove to catch it before it hit the ground. Then, getting back to my feet, I started to say something else. But he had disappeared by then.

The pool at the base of the cliff was shallow, most of its water splashing off to form another cataract. By the look of things, Hart had dived headfirst. When Captain Slaughter's men pulled him out that afternoon, there wasn't much of his upper body that wasn't broken.

I didn't feel good about his death. Maybe it's because I was beginning to sense there was an uncomfortable amount of him in me, something beyond the craving for books.

Adrian Hart was a knowledgeable and cunning bibliophile. Let that be his epitaph.

Chapter 37

Esme greeted us like conquering heroes when we climbed out of the NZSAS helicopter at Paradise Flat. Aside from a heartfelt handshake from Captain Slaughter, however, that was the only thanks we got in the days that followed. We'd saved the country from a radioactive nightmare, but it's not the sort of thing the government likes to mention when it was a hairbreadth away from delivering one of its premier natural wonders to ecoterrorists.

While Pillow and Tane Craddock followed her up to the lodge, I pulled out my cell phone to call home. It was nineteen hours earlier there—four thirty a.m. in KC—and after the phone rang ten or fifteen times, I heard Josie's groggy voice.

"Good morning, sunshine," I said.

"Michael! Where are you?"

"Just landed in Paradise."

"Are you okay?"

"Hundred percent. We've got it, babe."

"The journal?"

"All three of them. We're set."

"Fabulous! When will you be back?"

"In a week or two. I have some business to attend to with the feds in Wellington."

Investigators from the New Zealand Conservation Department and the national police converged on the Flat later in the day. Pillow, Tane, and I had secretly agreed not to mention the Gibson journals or Ivo Mackin's Cook ancestry claims. Besides not being relevant to the government's polonium concerns, we didn't intend to leak news of our findings until we'd figured how best to profit by them.

That was the idea, anyway.

After giving our statements, we were ordered to stay put at Esme's and not discuss our experiences with any but authorized personnel. A chopper would take us to Wellington two days later for more detailed debriefings following the mop-up of the compound at the Land of Tears.

While Pillow spent the next day in her room poring over the Gibson journals, I joined Craddock and some of the musterers to round up sheep caught in a snowstorm at the base of Mount Earnslaw. It was close to ten p.m. by the time Tane and I returned to the lodge, half frozen and covered in sheep dung, to find mother and daughter sitting in the lounge on a leather ottoman.

"Come in, boys, and take a seat," Esme said, pouring two more cups of tea from a ceramic pot. "Don't worry about your clothes. Penelope has some things she'd like to discuss."

Pillow smiled like the cat that's been in the birdcage. After I settled in the chair, she set the first two journals on the coffee table in front of me.

"I'm not going to release the last one, Michael. You can keep these."

I should have seen it coming.

Pillow may have been in on the scheme with Hart from the beginning, but I'd sensed a change in her ever since Ivo had dropped the bomb that he and she were blood kin to Captain Cook and King Kalani'opu'u. She suddenly felt she had a legacy to protect. My interests no longer counted.

I was shocked and angry at what I saw as her betrayal. She had used me to gain ownership of the journal. Now, for an entirely different reason, she was denying it to me again.

"But you can't do this!" I bleated. "Not after all we went through…"

Wasted breath, don't you know—it was like trying to reason with Salome who, after hearing the Salvation Army band, decided she was Mary Magdalene after all.

"Things have changed," she said. "I'm not who I was when this started."

"I suspect none of you are," Esme said, grasping her daughter's hand. "Penelope's decided to help me run the station."

"But what about The Book and Bell?"

"I'll find someone to buy it—there's never a lack of qualified takers in London. Mother and I thought we could bring in some of the kids from the marae and give them jobs."

The sugary gaze emanating from those Sophia Loren eyes as she blithely said she'd decided to give up that beautiful shop made me slightly nauseous.

Furthermore, the thought that Ngati, let alone Aronui, would take to herding cattle and mucking about sheep pastures seemed about as likely as LeBron James opting for a career in interior design.

"What do you think?" Pillow asked Tane Craddock. "Maybe we start our own Maori compound?"

The big man shrugged but with a highly dubious look on his face.

Pillow was sensing none of this. Nor, for that matter, was Esme. I suppose both were so happy to have found each other again that nothing could dissuade them from their dreams.

"I suppose if it's okay with Esme…"

"Good. And how about you, Michael? Will you stay on as well?"

By now, my anger had morphed from a simmering burn into incredulity.

I put on a manly "This-is-as-painful-to-me-as-it-must-be-for-you" smile. Then I gravely shook my head and said, "No thanks, love."

It was tough, but I withheld the temptation to add, "And it isn't entirely because you tried to cheat me with your partner, or that you poisoned one man and ordered the death of your husband, or that you can be an emotional three-ring circus."

"But before…" she said, looking bewildered.

"That was just a kiss."

"It was a lie."

"I'm going home, Pillow."

"To that sorry excuse of a bookstore?" She started to say something else, but her voice trailed away.

"Yes. To what's left of it, anyway. But mostly, I'm going back to the woman I love."

Well, that put a stamp on the old envelope.

Pillow's face melted into the taciturn mask I'd first noticed at Café Provence. Her fingers reached slowly up to the scars on her neck.

"Don't forget your trophies," she said in a passionless voice.

"Damn right," I said, scooping up the two journals.

Then I went outside for some fresh air.

That afternoon, the jet boat arrived with Jeb at the wheel. Pillow stayed in the lodge. Before climbing aboard, I offered to return the jade pendant Esme had given me, but to no avail. I said I'd write. Esme said, "You'd better," and kissed me on the cheek.

Tane did one better, mashing my forehead and nose with a big hangi for old time's sake.

"Take care of Pillow," I told him. "Maybe she doesn't know it yet, but you're what she needs."

"Yeah, I know. Maybe we can even make this marae thing work."

And the big fella smiled like Christmas.

I spent the next five days in Queenstown being interrogated by members of the National Defense Force and the Conservation Department.

Following that, I flew to Wellington to meet with the Deputy Prime Minister and his staff. I answered a lot of questions, had some tea and cake with the American ambassador to New Zealand. Then I was ushered into a large sitting room to meet a grim-faced representative of the People's Republic of China.

He claimed that the whole polonium-210 caper had been a rogue operation of Baotou Rare Earth Holding, Ltd., totally unsanctioned by his government. Considering that the perpetrators had hired an amateur goofus like Daig Kildare, it might have been true. I signed some kind of nondisclosure statement.

When I asked for a copy, they just looked at me funny.

That meeting lasted all of ten minutes and I was released with a polite but stern reminder to never mention China, polonium, and New Zealand in the same breath.

On the day before flying home, I got out of a cab and rushed into the Anthropology Building of Victoria University just as a torrential downpour began. The elevator still wasn't working, but I bound up the five stories without breathing hard—one of the few positive results from my highland adventure.

Cattley Middleditch greeted me with a firm handshake, but he looked uncomfortable as he slowly took his seat behind his desk, and I sat in the chair opposite him. A green-shaded desk lamp cast his long, earnest face in a pale yellow glow.

I got right to business.

"You're aware that Pillow let me have the second Gibson journal as well as my own?"

"Yes. Most generous of her."

"I'd like you to edit them."

"Ah," he said. "Gin?"

"Maybe later."

The professor, acting as if he didn't hear, opened the lower drawer and pulled out a bottle. He filled a teacup for himself and another for me in a glass that had quite recently served as a pencil holder.

"And why me?" he asked, raising the cup to his lips.

"I should think it obvious. No one knows more

about Cook than you. Of course, you would receive a percentage of the royalties."

"Hmmm. And who might you want to publish it?"

"Oxford University Press? Stanford? Perhaps the Hakluyt Society?"

"All are fine choices. But I'll have nothing to do with it. And neither should you."

"What do you mean?" I said, surprised and defensive. "Your niece gave me those journals of her own free will as consolation for her keeping the all-important third one."

"I know. Penelope told me everything."

"Even the separate note by Cook?"

"Yes. It's gratifying to know my theory of Cook's belief in his deification was correct. And the ancestry connection for Ivo and Penelope is quite fascinating. I must say, however, that I'm pleasantly surprised by her decision to not release it."

"I'm going to publish the first two, Professor. There are no startling revelations in either. Why won't you help me?"

"Once it's known the first two journals exist, there will be someone every bit as greedy and manipulative as Adrian Hart to suspect there is a third. Penelope's privacy—perhaps even her life and Esme's—would be at risk. You should know by now that, given time, there are no secrets in the high-end antiquarian business. It's inevitable someone will trace it to Paradise Flat."

"But what if she just destroys the journal?"

"No one would believe it. And she could no more do it than her father could."

I put down the glass and stood up.

"I'm sorry, Cattley. I have to consider what's best for my future."

"Then see to it, son."

He took a final pull on his cup and dismissed me with a wave of the bottle.

Late that afternoon, I dropped by the Turnbull Library to say farewell to Beryl Cowper, but was told she and her latest boyfriend were on holiday in Fiji.

I left the place, sad not to have seen her one last time.

Walking along the harbor on the way back to the Duxton Hotel—I was careful to avoid the alley between Johnston and Featherstone Streets—I stopped to buy a newspaper. The dreadlocked young man behind the counter looked familiar, and I suddenly realized with a shock that he was the vagrant who had put the injured tern out of its misery. Only now, he had lost that forlorn look. He was quite cheerful, as a matter of fact.

He told me he'd pitched in to help when the proprietor, an old gent, who used to give him food for the birds, fell ill. He said he liked selling magazines and candy to the people from City Center Square.

I gave him a dollar for the fifty-cent paper and told him to keep it.

"*Tihei mauri ora,*" he said, returning the change. "I salute the breath of life in you."

It wasn't exactly a lightning bolt that struck me— more like the nudge of a cattle prod—but there's no doubting that his generosity ignited something within my soul.

I'd traveled halfway around the world in search of a lost prize. I recovered it and a second one to boot— twice!—but acted as if I'd been cheated. It took that ragtag Maori Jesus to make me realize that I had discovered in New Zealand something far greater than a couple of old water-stained journals. And while I still believed that the best pint of Guinness was where your friends happened to be, the minimum would never again be good enough for me.

I slept easy that night and awoke refreshed and as clearheaded as I could ever remember being. After packing my suitcase and stuffing a couple of Petone Club rugby shirts in the backpack, I carefully wrapped the two journals and set them in a FedEx box that I'd picked up the night before. I slipped in a note that said, "A real bookman never breaks up a set," sealed the package and addressed it to Penelope Wilkes, Paradise Flat, Glenorchy.

Chapter 38

Five months later, Josie and I sat at the front counter of Riverrun Books, sipping Irish coffees and going over numbers. Neil Young wailed "Old Man" on my ancient CD player. We'd locked the doors an hour earlier when the last of the customers departed and turned out the lights except for the lamp on the counter.

Sales in July and August, normally a slow period, were decent enough to cover basic expenses. This was undoubtedly due to lunch and dinner traffic at the increasingly popular Café Provence, but we weren't complaining. We just accepted it as an intangible benefit of our new positive attitude.

Our customers had noticed a change in the atmosphere at Riverrun as well. Despite living a hand-to-mouth existence, we'd recaptured the enterprising spirit once I quit blaming the Internet and focused on improving our stock. We even started throwing Friday afternoon parties again.

Using the equity in my house, we took out a ten-thousand-dollar loan, paid two months' back rent with half of it, and purchased a private library from a friend of Charlie Walsh's with the rest. It meant peanut butter sandwiches, Two-Buck Chuck wine, and ramen noodles for the next year, but it was a chance to score a return of eight to ten times that amount—if we could hold out long enough. As always, a very big "if."

CSN&Y had begun singing "Ohio" when Josie got up from the counter.

"Mike," she said, pointing to a U-Haul truck that pulled up outside the shop. "I think you'd better check that out."

I looked to see a lean character wearing a baseball cap adorned with the Stars and Bars step out of the cab. He had the face of a not-very-healthy fox. Age about thirty, five feet ten, lots of tats on sinewy arms sticking out of a dirty undershirt.

"This summer I hear the drumming…"

He slunk back into the shadow of the truck when a group of customers crossed the street on their way to Café Provence. Once they had passed, he sauntered to our front door. He cupped his hands on either side of his face and peered inside.

"Four dead in Ohio…"

Lately, there had been a run of smash-and-grab robberies of storefronts a few blocks east on Oak Street. I wasn't taking chances.

"Get behind the counter and keep your head down," I said to Josie as I reached for my old hurling stick. "Be ready to call 9-1-1—and turn off the CD."

Keeping to the side wall, I edged toward the front door just as the music went dead. He spotted me when I walked into a beam from the streetlight outside.

"Got a delivery for ya!" he shouted through the pane glass.

"Sorry, pal. It's a little late for a business call, and I don't order things by the truckload."

The guy shrugged and climbed back into the driver's seat.

"What did he want?" Josie asked, stepping out from behind the counter.

"He's got the wrong address."

"That one doesn't seem to think so."

I turned to see another refugee from a Daniel Woodrell novel at the door. Unlike the other one, he didn't look nervous.

"Cletus" was the name embroidered on his gray Carhartt work shirt. He was big—wide and beefy with a twenty-inch neck, give or take an eighth. His enormous head was bare and ringed with curly brown hair. He seemed awfully tired and grumpy. His armpits were dark with sweat. Maybe he wasn't looking for trouble, but he seemed more than able to deliver it.

"Like I told your partner..." I began while making sure the door was secured.

The big man sighed. "He ain't ma pard'nuh. Best I could get at this hour."

"Buzz off before I call the police."

"You might jes' wanna put that stick thing down," Cletus said with a grunt of annoyance, "and read this h'aar lettuh."

He planted an envelope on one of the panes at eye level.

From what I could see in the dim light, the printing looked very official—three-color and in Copperplate Gothic font. I remember thinking that if these two yokels were the best the county could do for its process servers, it might consider raising the sales tax again.

Watching the big man's eyes, I opened the door with the hand that didn't hold the hurley.

"You expectin' trouble?" he said genially as he handed me the envelope.

"This time of night? Two beauties like you showing up unannounced with a truck big enough to empty everything I own? Why would I be suspicious?"

"Yeah, I suppose it seems strange. The container arrived at Inter-Model two hours ago in Lenexa. Didn't have no insurance papers with it, so they wanted it out of their warehouse pronto. My brother-in-law's the foreman. He calls me when this type of thing happens."

I opened the letter.

At the top of the fine linen paper was the embossed heading of a London solicitor's firm.

Jaynes & Naast, LLP
495 High Holborn, London WC 1V 7QR

Dear Mr. Bevan,
My client, Mrs. Penelope Wilkes-ffolkes, has instructed me to transfer, entirely free of compensation, the entire stock of The Book & Bell Antiquarian Bookstore, lately of 12 Cecil Court, London, to Riverrun Books…etc., etc., etc.
Yours most sincerely,
Alistair Jaynes, LL.B

My eyeballs shifted briefly upward, but I remained composed long enough to notice a folded slip of paper at the bottom of the envelope.

"Quid pro quo," it said, accompanied by the drawing of a floating feather.

"So you want us to bring this stuff in or not?" Cletus asked.

Chapter 39

J osie Majansik sat lotus-style among the clutter of empty cardboard boxes, Styrofoam pellets, and sheets of plastic bubble wrap. Her face was drawn, and there were dark circles under her eyes. She was dressed in the same baggy sweatpants and T-shirt from when we began unloading books eighteen hours earlier. The red bandanna tied around her head, combined with the large circular earrings, accentuated her Eastern European features. She looked like a gypsy who had just skinned a rabbit but no longer had the energy to cook it.

She stretched her arms over her head, yawned, and looked into the last of the boxes. We'd lugged them into the front of the shop that morning from the storage area where Cletus and his helper had stacked them seven weeks earlier.

Yawning again, she uncoiled her legs and walked over to where I stood on a ladder arranging books on the top shelf of Riverrun's vastly improved classic literature section.

"Time for some shut-eye, Mike. Big day tomorrow."

I looked at my wristwatch. Hard to believe it was nearly three a.m.

"When does the mayor arrive?"

"Ribbon cutting is scheduled for noon," she answered sleepily. "I imagine he'll arrive ten seconds before that. It's not like he's opening a bridge across the Missouri River."

"This proud Brooksider begs to differ," I said, feather-dusting a 1764 edition of *The Castle of Oranto* by Horace Walpole. "The new bookcases look great, don't they?"

"For thirty thousand dollars, they should."

I winced at her harsh reminder of the cost. It had taken another generous loan from Eddie Worth's bank and a month-long closure of the store to construct the thirty-two handcrafted mahogany cabinets. The museum-quality treasures Pillow had bequeathed us demanded no less.

Josie stroked the two-day stubble on my chin once I had my heels on the floor again.

"I didn't mean to be flippant, Mike. It's everything we dreamed of. I'm so proud of you."

"Thanks, babe. But the business still has a long way to go before we're farting through silk."

That brought a sigh, along with a kiss.

"You should have been a poet, my love."

"Josie."

"Yes?"

"I've been thinking about us."

"What about us?" she asked thickly.

"What say we get married?"

Josie exhaled softly. Her hand went to her mouth.

287

"For the sake of the bookstore, I suppose?" she said between her fingertips.

"That's as good an excuse as any."

"Okay," she said. "I'll buy that."

Romantic devils, ain't we?

After the kissing, I handed the keys to the Jeep to her.

"Think I'll stick around a bit longer."

"Okay, sweetie. But try not to do any more work tonight."

"Thanks. Get some sleep. I'll walk home."

Once alone, I headed downstairs to the old boiler room that I'd converted into a workshop.

The only furniture consisted of a steel filing cabinet, a cane chair, and a makeshift desk that was nothing more than a broad piece of plywood resting on stacked concrete blocks. Rolls of brown wrapping paper and boxes of Styrofoam lay helter-skelter on the bare cement floor. The canvas backpack that once belonged to Adrian Hart dangled on a hook affixed to a hot water pipe.

I cleared a space on the table, then walked over to the filing cabinet and unlocked the door. My body felt loose and relaxed from the hard day's work in the way it used to get after a grueling but immensely satisfying rugby match.

The drama that had begun twenty years earlier in Newport with my discovery of Samuel Gibson's first journal had not yet ended. As I removed the linen bag from the bottom drawer, I wondered if it ever would. Something within me had changed, something born of having touched the void and survived unscathed when everything seemed lost.

It was one of those epiphanies in which all the

contradictions of life converge to resolve themselves. I felt the pure old things I used to operate on when I was twenty-four and immortal.

I needed to know if it was real. After placing the bag on the desk, I settled onto my chair and gently removed the cloth. Then I proceeded to have a nice long chat with the captain.

It's amazing what you can still get through customs these days.

A Look At Book Three:
THE WIDOW'S SON

Age-old retributions and blood atonements bring our unlikely hero back to solve one last spiritually-steeped mystery.

Michael Bevan is finally content with his used bookstore. When he's offered a valuable first-edition Book of Mormon that bears a strange inscription alluding to blood atonement, it disappears—with two people lying dead in its wake.

After extensive research, he discovers that the book's disappearance might have something to do with the murder of Joseph Smith—a Mormon prophet. After Joseph's death in 1844, his zealots swore to avenge his death by not only killing the men responsible, but by also eliminating the murderers' future generations.

When Michael's friend is kidnapped, he fears the worst and journeys to a clandestine camp of vengeful men hellbent on ritual sacrifice. To save a life, he must summon every ounce of courage, brawn, and wit imaginable. But to defeat the fanatics consumed by an unholy vision and steal the Book of Mormon back, a little divine intervention couldn't hurt.

Can Michael save an innocent life from being sacrificed and obtain the Book of Mormon…without risking his bookstore in the process?

AVAILABLE MAY 2023

About the Author

Thomas Shawver served four years as a judge advocate in the U.S. Marine Corps. His civilian career began as an investigator for the National Collegiate Athletic Association. He then practiced law with career breaks as publisher of *The San Jose Business Journal* and *Kansas City Magazine*. From 1995 to 2012, he owned Bloomsday Books, an antiquarian bookshop in Kansas City. He now writes full time.

A graduate of the University of Kansas, his interests are rugby, collecting rare books and international travel. He is married to a journalist.